Six Seconds

E.R. Mason

E.R. Mason

Editor

Sam Thornton, PE PhD
https://www.facebook.com/SamThorntonP
E
SamThorntonPE@outlook.com

ISBN: 978-1-7328697-2-1

Chapter 1

"I don't think we should do it."

"May I remind you, Director Bernard Porre himself asked as a favor. Of course, it's not as though you need to make any points with anyone, being in such high repute as you are with the space agency and all."

"So funny I forgot to laugh."

"Wow, I haven't heard that line since fifth grade. Man, the PAV traffic above us is packed in tonight."

"Yeah, somebody's vehicle died up there and it won't lower down. They're waiting to be towed."

"Kind of ironic. All those fancy flying cars up there and Adrian Tarn's black, antique 1995 Corvette is down here passing by them all."

"Yep, and when we get into the city we'll be almost as fast as a kid on a hoverboard."

"The fallacy of modern technology. The more complex it becomes, the less progress is made."

"Damn, now I've set you off. Mr. R.J. Smith, technology's scourge. I better change the subject fast. How come you're back from Enuro without Elachia?"

"Putting aside my dissertation on the ironic contradiction of technological evolution for the moment, her duties as ambassador to the Antares System required last minute attention. She'll be along soon."

"You were gone a month. Did you have fun stormin' the castle?"

"Gentlemen do not discuss such matters, Adrian. Besides, you have your own firsthand knowledge of intimacy with her unique genetic design type. And by the way, Fantasia *was* there."

"That was the tow vehicle that just went by overhead."

"Ah-ha! Changed the subject. Touched a nerve there, didn't I?"

"Did she ask about me?"

"In fact, she did. As I recall, her exact words were: how is the tall, ornery man with the piercing blue-gray or was it just gray eyes doing?"

"Well which is it? Gray or blue-gray?"

"I think it depends on whether or not the moon is full."

"Ornery? She said I was ornery? What'd she mean by that?"

"I believe in your case the term was intended to infer unpredictability, discordance, or just botheration."

"Everyone's entitled their opinion. You know they make an antigrav kit for this car now? It's for highway use only. Gets the wheels just off the ground. Ion emission takes over. You have to be going at least 50 to engage it."

"She also asked why you didn't accept the Captain's chair on the Electra mission this time. The Palacia System is not that far from Enuro."

"She didn't think I turned it down because of her, did she?"

"I explained that spending a year mapping fields of new rock fragments was not a part of your... vision."

"I wouldn't have minded seeing those two bodies collide though. I'll tell you that. Solar demolition derby."

"Curious. Fantasia expressed a similar sentiment. Makes me wonder which two bodies the two of you were actually referring to."

"Good grief...."

"You know, every time I mention her your right leg twitches and we speed up. A few more times and we may jump to light."

"There you go with the back seat driving."

"That's a red traffic STOP barrier up ahead. It's just a hologram, of course. You could speed through it, but the crossing traffic might cause unscheduled instantaneous disassembly as you rock-jocks like to say...."

"Do I back seat drive when you're driving?"

"Personally, I believe we should have stayed with the old traffic lights hanging by wires like they had in the old days."

"Oh yeah sure, and I suppose you also want the high-tension wires that ran along the sides of the road. Thirty-two thousand volts on the ground every time somebody crashed into one of the wooden poles holding them up."

"I'm no longer sure if that's a standard blue flight suit you're wearing or a driver's fire suit. Where is the pace car?"

"If we're critiquing men's wear, I would call attention to the flaming red 'Neanderthals Unite' T-shirt you have on."

"We will rise up and rescue humankind from technology."

"R.J., your T-shirt, jeans, and tennis shoes were all made by robots. You're a walking billboard for technology."

"Would you prefer I was sitting here naked?"

"Man, now there's an image I don't want burned into my brain."

"In any case, I think we should do it."

"Do you think I'm ornery?"

"Knowing you as well as I do, no. That's not the term I would use."

"You'd use a term? What term would you use?"

"Oh brother. Knight to Queen's three, check."

"That's okay. I'll discuss this with her myself, the next time I see her."

"Please, let me be there."

"What were we saying?"

"I think we should do it. It's entirely a civilian mission, financed by a university and private individuals. No higher authority... your favorite!"

"Speaking of Elachia, aren't we supposed to take the Griffin to Enuro to pick her up?"

"There's no set time on that. We can go when we're ready. Next excuse?"

"Well let's review, shall we? Here's the part I don't like; the agency wants to attach an expendable lander, shaped like an arrowhead, piggyback on *my* spacecraft...."

"It's a triangle-based pyramid construct, using small, reinforced hexagon panels which can safely deflect ring rain and ice."

"Right, sure. We fly 750 million miles to Saturn's A-ring and once on orbit three of us EVA transfer to the lander using terrain-style hardsuits because there's not enough room in the lander for regular EVA suits. Then we descend and land on a small moon inside the ring...."

"It's Daphnis, and it's not exactly inside the A-ring. It's slightly above it, and there's an open channel where it orbits."

"Right, sure. We land on Daffy...."

"Daphnis. This is not a Looney Tunes mission."

"Are you sure? We disembark the lander and search this mini-moon with rocks and ice flying all around us...."

"Daphne's five miles wide. It's got a mass of like 5 times ten to the thirtieth. It has enough gravity to affect the Keeler Gap."

"As I was saying, we help some eccentric doctorate person search this mini-moon that's probably covered with ice, just to look for pretty rocks, then get back in the lander, return to the Griffin, all without getting wacked by a snowball the size of a bus. Then do another near-naked EVA in our recharged hard suits to get back into Griffin."

"You just described the entire mission."

"That's the part I don't like."

"Are you sure? We'd be just like Neil and Buzz. Nobody's ever done it."

"Nobody's done it?"

"Especially in ring rain."

"That's another thing."

"Yes. Just imagine; the suits will be statically charged to oppose the charged rain. We probably will be standing in the pouring rain and not a drop will get on our suits or visors."

"But I did mention there can be ice chucks the size of elephants, right?"

"They're getting bigger each time you mention them. Most of that stuff is locked in Saturn's gravity well. That's why they call it a ring, oh lamenting crier of the very obvious."

"We'd be part of a giant Slurpee."

"Can you imagine the view?"

7

"You're still psychically linked to Elachia, right? Is she hearing all this?"

"Why are you asking questions you already know the answer to? Yes, she and I are always psychically linked, but she only hears what I choose to telepathically send her."

"What is she doing right now?"

"She's sitting at a conference table discussing trade imbalances. Again, why are you asking things you already know? What is this about? Are we back thinking about Fantasia, one of the two most extraordinary women in the universe, the treasure that you dumped?"

"You're attached at the hip to a woman who was designed by a crazy genetic scientist who wanted to create the ultimate companion for a man, gave her a telepathic link so she could anticipate your needs before you could ask, and she'll probably remain young and beautiful while you grow old and gray."

"Incorrect misinformed-breath. Nice to see you're actually going to stop at this intersection. Elachia will remain beautiful and gracefully age along with me, and even in very old age she will still be beautiful. Why don't you admit it? You're regretting breaking the link with Fantasia, aren't you? That's what this is all about, isn't it? You're thinking you may have made a huge mistake. Only two of them were ever created, Elachia and Fantasia. No others like them anywhere in the universe, and now you're second guessing yourself, aren't you?"

"So, do *you* think I made a mistake?"

"Duh!"

"Now that I think about it, maybe we *should* do it."

"Right, because something that dangerous is the only thing that will take your mind off of Fantasia."

"If we have to go see Bernard Porre, you go and make an excuse for me, okay?"

"Oh, I don't know. He so looks forward to your company."

"He keeps accusing me of having secretly fathered his oldest daughter."

"Ah yes. The girl voted most likely to crash one of everything. An honorary member of the Urban Air Mobility Police. Now how could he have made that connection?"

"Very funny. But here we are at your forty story condo on the top floor with a wall removed to expand it to double the size. All for a man who is opposed to technology."

"It was Elachia's request. I generally use only one of the nineteen rooms."

"Tell me, will you evacuate if the weather service loses control of one of the big bastard hurricanes that come through?"

"As a matter of fact, this sector's dome emitters are on top of this building's roof, so we're directly under the dome if it's used to shield this area."

"Yeah, but how about one of those real mothers that are too big to manage?"

"Now, now, hurricanes are a necessary product of nature. Let us not be disrespectful. They are check valves for the atmosphere. If there's a problem, flying buses would be brought in to evacuate us."

"So you'll tell Bernard Porre that we'll do it?"

"Yes, but I'm not vouching for you about his daughter."

Chapter 2

We sat at a long, worn, plain wood-grained conference table, on the top floor of the Headquarters Building at KSC. My chair creaked when tilted back. It couldn't be trusted. There were faded photos framed on the walls, depicting events familiar to just about anyone. The only ultramodern architecture gifted to the room were the large display screens mounted on the walls at various locations Overhead, old dingy-white ceiling tiles needed to be cleaned or replaced.

R.J. surprised me. He wore a corduroy sports jacket, possibly obtained from a thrift shop somewhere, a style made popular at some point during the 1960's. He wore a white collared shirt beneath it, and brown slacks with desert boots. It was the most formal wear I'd ever seen him offer to any official meeting. It made me wonder if Elachia was having some sort of domesticating effect on him. It also made me concerned that my wash and wear blue flight coveralls were not enough. R.J. studied a tablet full of Saturnian legends, lies, and lifeworks. I creak-swiveled back and forth and tapped my fingers on the table hoping someone on some camera somewhere would get the message that time was a-wasting.

Door to the left finally opened. In charged Dr. Andrea DeSortes, stiff-backed, arms clutching tablets, notebooks, and loose papers, all trying to slide.

Standard situation where you try to appraise someone without looking directly at them. In these situations it is very important to give an impression of disinterest. It is the high ground in first contact.

She was dangerously attractive. Dangerous like that allure a black widow might impose upon a viral male. How many male spiders have thought to themselves; maybe she's okay? The Doctor possessed that odd presentation of mouth made famous by stone face drill sergeants, a curious contradiction where the curve of the lips gives the false impression of a smile, a deception familiar to any new recruit who happens to be in the line of fire of the vile wordy appraisals emitted from that contemptuous grin.

She had dark eyebrows so upturned it made me wonder if there were Spock ears hidden beneath the shiny bundle of dark hair captured behind the head. I tried to catch her eye just for sport but in the few microseconds of alignment there was not the slightest touch of contact from those dark-brown iris windows. She had very light unblemished skin tone as though too many hours had been spent under white LED light in laboratories or classrooms.

Behind her, a Squire of sorts followed attentively. He was somewhere between young and middle aged. Wet black hair short enough to be proper, long enough to appeal to the opposite sex. He wore a dark suit cut to look as modern as a conservative position might allow. Beneath the open jacket was a deep blue turtleneck, completely inappropriate for Florida. It ended in a narrow black belt and chrome belt buckle so polished that it could have been used for signaling. Black loafers with the little tassels.

"Captain Tarn, Commander Smith...." DeSortes leaned across the table and offered a hand. We all shared practiced smiles with the exception of R.J. who has that irritating habit of always treating everyone as though they are old friends.

"This is Brock Mullar, Doctor of Philosophy in Archaeology. He will be joining us on this mission."

Once again we exchanged handshakes with cautious reservation.

DeSortes sat and spoke as she arranged her tablet and documentation. "I'm sure you've both read the mission statement, just as I'm sure you both have questions. If the mission seems ambitious to you, I'd be forced to agree with that. To be honest there's quite a bit more to this than is contained in the official outline. This is not...."

DeSortes' cell rang. She stood and turned away to take the call.

R.J. leaned over and in a lowered voice declared, "Told you she was beautiful."

"Like a hungry spotted leopard."

He wrinkled his brow. "What? What's all these negative vibes? How did Fantasia describe it? Ornery? You're ornery!"

Brock Mullar took notice of our private discussion. We both straightened up and assumed stolid nonchalant expressions.

DeSortes returned to the table still talking on her cell. We picked up the last line before she tapped off.

"Yes, have them come right in."

To my dismay, a few moments later, the door on the right side of the conference room opened. A line of men and women in military Space Corps uniforms, along with white lab-coated associates entered the room and took seats around us, seeming to ignore our presence completely.

DeSortes remained standing and smiled at the entourage and spoke, "Admiral, Captain Tarn and Commander Smith."

I leaned over to R.J. "Oh, my, God."

R.J. returned a look of apprehensive confusion.

The Admiral stood by his chair. "It's a pleasure Captain, Commander. Let's all sit and get started."

"I've only just referenced the mission statement so far, Admiral," said DeSortes as she sat. "Gentlemen, Admiral Lansing."

"Captain Tarn, Commander Smith, I apologize for the clandestine nature of this mission."

I could not help but offer a pronounced worried look. The Admiral took notice.

"Let's close it up and bring up the imagery please," said the Admiral.

The conference room windows turned opaque then black, the room lights dimmed, and the wall display screens came alive with a color video of a portion of Saturn's rings. As always, even just a fragment of the Saturnian system was breathtaking. Centered within the image was a clear view of the Keeler Gap and the tiny moon Daphnis moving within it.

The Admiral motioned to DeSortes to take over.

DeSortes paused as though to contain her excitement. "Not much attention has been given to Daphnis since it was discovered by Cassini in 2005. It was just a four-kilometer rock causing interesting waves in the ring edges along the Keeler Gap. It was too small to create much curiosity. That all changed after the scanning probe SP43Y was launched to search for any bodies containing precious metals that might be orbiting Saturn. On its very first flyby, that probe sent an alert that Daphnis was of artificial construction, and not a captured mini moon at all."

R.J. sat up straight and leaned forward with great interest. I sat back tried to console my feelings of apprehension.

"Obviously a second probe was redirected to photograph Daphnis through the entire spectrum. Please bring up that first image.... As you can see, the base geometry has been modified by ice picked up from the rings, but beneath that outer layer there does appear to be an artificial structure, most likely that of a spacecraft. And with that, I should turn the floor over to Dr. Mullar."

DeSortes turned to Mullar who stood and spoke, "I do not believe there's any other explanation for what we are seeing. Please step through the other photographic spectrums as I explain what little we know. So yes, a spacecraft. A very, very old spacecraft probably in the order of ten thousand years or more based solely on the ring evolution calculations. We believe there was no Keeler Gap in the A-ring when this craft first arrived. Only after centuries of Daphnis gravitational influence did the Keeler Gap form. Our mission will be to land on Daphnis, confirm these findings, and gain access to this craft if possible."

Mullar glanced around and slowly took his seat.

DeSortes said, "At this point I believe we're ready for questions."

R.J. did not wait. "Do you have any indication why this spacecraft came to be there, if it really is a spacecraft?"

Surprisingly, Admiral Lansing took the question. "Please bring up the first image and zoom in to full magnification."

Daphnis came into close view with imagery enhancement added. More surface detail could be seen.

The Admiral continued, "If you look closely forward, you will see a large indentation at the nose of the structure. At first it was thought to be an impact crater. We now believe that is actually blast damage, most likely the blast that destroyed this vehicle and left it stranded in the A-ring. We theorize that Daphnis entered the Saturnian ring system to hide from attackers but was discovered and destroyed there. That will be a part of the hypothesis we hope to confirm during this mission."

DeSortes spoke, "Captain Tarn, Commander Smith, everyone else already has been involved in this discovery. Do you have additional questions, or should I ask your impressions of our proposal?"

I tried not to sound disgusted. "This is a completely different mission than was brought to us."

"Not really, Captain. Assume orbit around Saturn. Land on Daphnis and investigate. Return home," answered DeSortes.

"Why do you want the Griffin for this? Why not take a large salvage vessel and just tow the thing home?"

Admiral Lansing replied, "If you think this through, Adrian. You will understand why that is not an option. Every so often we encounter archeology in the solar system that rewrites history. It has been agreed that we will not allow shock effect discoveries to affect our society. History will be updated slowly and carefully over time so that society can adapt. We do not intend to publicly announce that a ten-thousand-year-old ship involved in some kind of intersystem battle has been located orbiting Saturn. This mission has been publicized as a civilian exploration mission financed publicly by two universities. Any attempt to send the big guys in to extract Daphnis or set up a long-term exploration of it would set off the conspiracy people to no end. Were we to affect Daphnis in any visible way we'd be accused of damaging the natural order of Saturn's rings and system. I hope you'll agree this must be done in a way as to not attract unnecessary interest in Daphnis. When we're done, we will announce that Daphnis is a simple, common composite moon that does not deserve further study. We'll find a way to make it off limits to everyone. Don't you agree?"

R.J. piped up, "I do."

DeSortes looked at me.

"Can I have some time to think this over?" I asked.

The Admiral answered, "We are already marshaling stores in the refrigeration rooms near the VAB and the XGP 236 Lander arrived yesterday and is in the Vehicle Processing Center being prepped as we speak. Preparations for this mission began three months ago. It's been highly classified in hopes of avoiding the rumor mill but things like this always have a way of leaking out. We need to get there before anyone else."

"How will the Lander be attached to my spacecraft?"

"Four end-effector units converted to be docking attachments will be installed on the Griffin. They will be removed after the mission. You will not be able to tell they were ever there."

DeSortes tried to sound persuasive, "You can see why you and Commander Smith are the perfect individuals for this mission, can't you?"

I rested an elbow on the table and rubbed my forehead.

The Admiral jumped in. "You can take a little time to think about it, Adrian. We'll continue preparations until you tell us to stop."

"No, no, that's alright. We'll do it."

I felt R.J.'s jubilation.

Admiral Lansing added, "You'll need an extra pilot to stay aboard Griffin during the EVA, Adrian. We have an excellent list for you to choose from."

"Thanks, but I already have someone in mind."

The Admiral sounded appreciative, possibly the only time I have ever sensed that from a high ranker. He continued, "We held our breath when they offered you the Electra mission this last time, Adrian. It was a great relief when you turned it down. So that's it everyone. Let's finish up getting ready to explore a ten thousand-year-old spacecraft."

Chapter 3

I stood in the highbay watching the big yellow gantry crane lower the XGP 236 Lander Body onto my beloved Griffin spacecraft. Although I probably did not deserve ownership of such a Class A medium displacement spaceship like the Griffin, complete with artificial gravity, image-projecting inside wall paneling, antigrav vertical takeoff and landing, and deployable wings that allowed for conventional atmospheric runway landings if needed. She was mine, nevertheless. I had done a deep, long distance favor for a very advanced race called the Nasebiens once. The Griffin had been gifted to me by them, much to the envy and disdain of a few Earthly military and political types.

Like a nervous mother, I annoyed the crane operator to no end as she used the snail button on the gantry crane control much more than she would have liked. I was almost disappointed when the modified end effectors snapped into place on the bottom side of the XGP 236. A big dart with no windows and a black body surface that looked like it had been borrowed from a military submarine was now attached atop my treasured Griffin. A vehicle obviously and forebodingly designed to deflect impacts.

As I tried to resolve my inner discomfort with the safe mating, Danica Donoro walked up beside me.

"You think I'm always just doing nothing and ready to hightail it over here whenever you call, right?"

I smiled at her, overcame the urge to pick her up in a hug, and replied, "Well I just figured who would want you in the left seat anyway?"

She slapped my right shoulder a good one and laughed. "I've kept up with my martial arts, have you?"

"Perhaps I misspoke. I meant to say, anyone would want you in the left seat."

She hugged me and we both laughed in each other's face.

"Really, you are a sight for sore eyes."

"It'll be so good to be up front with you again, Adrian."

"It will be a scenic trip, I can promise you that."

I stepped back to look at her. The green eyes dared me to comment. Her dark brown hair was still kept short, curling under the left ear. The pert, upturned nose always seemed like a dare. The cherry red lips made her look as though she was secretly smiling. Baggy cargo pants with black lace up boots. Gray collared cargo shirt with the sleeves rolled up. She was a strikingly attractive woman, but our history kept me back a bit. Once long ago I had crashed a simulator approach only to have Danica climb in and fly the same approach to touch down. She'd made it only by the skin on her teeth, but it still took points off my man-card. Competition aside, she was still the only other person I would trust the Griffin to.

"What's the pointy thing up there? How'd they get you to allow that?"

"XGP 236 Lander. Four of us will go down in it, while you watch over the Griffin."

"Four? You can get four suits in there?"

"Special suits."

"There can't be room for an airlock in there."

"External access only."

"In special suits."

"How's it fly?"

"Solid State thrusters, standard panel, joystick. Nav screen that's touch and click. It'll land itself. Nothing new."

"So where are we going, anyway?"

"Saturn?"

"You're kidding? Aren't there plenty of people out there already?"

"Not where we're going."

"Saturn, wow! Our own backyard. I've been wanting to park there for a long time. What departure?"

"I called ahead. It'll be direct waypoint EARTH 1 then straight up and out. No orbits."

"When do we leave?"

"Stores and baggage are loaded. We're just waiting for the paying customers and R.J."

"You've done the walk-arounds?"

"Just waiting for the tug."

"Mind if I do one anyway?"

"I'd expect no less. Where's your gear?"

"The duffel bag over where the hangar door's open a crack. Thanks."

As I headed for her stuff, R.J. came strolling in with his own plaid antique suitcase. He wore farmer's blue jean coveralls with a T-shirt underneath. He gave a chin-up smile, wiped his free hand down on his trimmed pale red beard, spotted Danica, and asked, "Is that...?"

"R.J.!" came the echoing cry across the hangar. The two friends ran to greet each other and upon meeting began a disjointed dance that ended with R.J. being twirled around followed by a big feminine dip with Danica planting a wet kiss on his mouth. Hysterical laughter ensued.

I shook my head and resumed my job as mission porter.

The ground team showed up a short time later, opened the big bay doors and hooked onto Griffin using a beaten up, quite old tug. We paraded out to the tarmac in time to meet the elevator on wheels being brought in and set up at the front airlock position. Danica insisted on being in the lift for the quick test run up, much to the dismay of the operator who was no match for her womanly wiles. She opened the airlock door and disappeared into Griffin before the elevator car had even finished being positioned. The operator gave me a terse look that made me feel like I should tip him, but that just isn't done.

I handed R.J. Danica's duffel bag. "Want to make yourself useful and usher the customers up when they get here? I better get up on the flight deck before she takes off without us."

Danica was already in the left seat with the main displays powered up when I climbed in.

"Do you mind?" she asked.

"Be my guest."

"Is this the one?" She pointed to the Nav screen. It had a departure map on it labeled GFNKSC2029.

"That's it."

"How's the jump set up?"

"Saturn happens to be close by. A thirty-minute trip. One dare not break the Terran System speed limits. We'll drop out well short of the satellite system, then recalibrate for insertion above the rings. Those people better get here. Our flight plan's only good for another forty-five minutes."

"I'll run through the ship's EICAS displays while we wait. So, you still single?"

"You know the saying; sky pilots make bad soul-mates."

"Wasn't there that one from Enuro? A duchess or princess or something?"

"Did R.J. tell you to mention her?"

"No. I was just wondering about your status."

"Well how about you? Got any permanent infusions?"

"Sky pilots make bad soul-mates, remember?"

"So see?"

"I hear the elevator." Danica twisted around in time to see passengers being ushered aboard by R.J.

I said, "Thank God. If I had to resubmit that flight plan I would've choked one of them or something."

"R.J. said you were in a cranky mood..., no ornery he said. He said you were being ornery."

"Oh brother." I leaned around to call to R.J. "I show sealed all around already. Nice job. Are you guys buckled in?"

"You may proceed, Captain."

"KSC Ground, Griffin."

The radio crackled to life. "Go ahead Griffin."

"Griffin is on the tarmac on the northeast side of the VAB. Ready for departure."

"Standby Griffin."

Danica wiggled herself into position for takeoff.

"Griffin, KSC, climb to thirty feet, heading three-five-zero degrees, and hover. Expect clearance in a minute or two."

"Thirty feet, three-five-zero, and hover, Griffin."

"You sure you remember how to do it?"

"Very funny, Boss." Danica twisted the correct autopilot knobs and Griffin rose slightly, stabilized, and ascended to thirty feet. As we climbed, the nose swung around to north. Before us was a busy land of launch complexes and service buildings. Cars and trucks dotted the roadways.

I nodded. "Gear up. All green. Wells pressurized."

Danica spoke as she continued to check displays. "I'll cut in the autopilot flight code as soon as we reach the waypoint. Do you agree?"

"Sounds good to me."

"Griffin, KSC, climb and maintain two-thousand-five hundred you are cleared direct to waypoint EARTH 1, then initiate departure. Contact Orlando Traffic on four-eighty-one point four-two-five. Have a safe trip."

"Griffin climb and maintain twenty-five hundred, to EARTH 1, cleared for departure. Orlando four-eighty-one point four-two-five. Thank you, sir."

As we coasted over the space center landscape I made the call. "OSTC, Griffin with you."

"Griffin, cleared for departure at waypoint EARTH 1."

"Understand Griffin is cleared."

Danica manually followed the green line on her navigation display toward waypoint EARTH1. The little green EARTH 1 dot on the display turned to flashing yellow as we approached. I had a few seconds to look around and sync myself up with reality. Griffin's display screens were alive with moving information. Colored lights everywhere in the cockpit assured us that systems were behaving as desired. Each time Danica glanced down I could see the nav screen lines reflected on her face. It was an almost Christmas tree environment that reminded me this was where I belonged. No matter how diabolical life events could become, they were all meaningless here. An obedient ship alive and speaking in its machine voice. Outside the viewports, the landscape scrolled by. To my right I could see Flatpad 39A, the place where very brave men first launched and landed on the moon. Later it became a jumping off point for a company called Space X, a company that repeatedly did things everyone had thought impossible. A company that literally changed the world. It had been a wakeup call to a people who had forgotten they were born to be explorers. With the advent of antigrav, the pads were more underground now than above. But the history was engraved in our memory. Forever.

A tone from the nav system sounded as the EARTH 1 checkpoint turned to flashing red. Danica nosed Griffin up twenty degrees and switched in the autopilot. We were thrusted back in our seats as the ground fell away. It is always an awe-inspiring ride as the sky view turns to a dull gray for just a moment followed by inky blackness and stars. It's at that point for some reason I always feel a wave of freedom come over me.

Danica spoke matter-of–factly, "Outside the exosphere. We're slowing."

"As you know, it'll be about five or ten minutes for the nav system to recalibrate and check the flight path. You want to go back and reassure our guests, Captain Donoro?"

"I've always liked watching the edge detection video perform its mapping of the stuff near our path. Think I'll sit right here, if you don't mind. After we make the jump I'll go back there and try to be gracious."

I smothered a laugh. "Okay, I'll go reassure them they're still alive."

"Like R.J. said, you do sound a little ornery. I see the artificial gravity is at ninety-seven percent. Shouldn't be any puking going on."

I unstrapped, tested the artificial gravity, pulled back past the engineering stations and into the living area. They were all still strapped in their seats. Dr. DeSortes was staring intently out the nearest portal. Brock Mullar was flipping through pages on a tablet trying to look like space travel was nothing to him. That façade never works. It's like riding a horse. They'll tell you they were a rodeo champion of years gone by but in the first five seconds after mounting the horse, you can tell their feet have never been in stirrups before. With space travel, it's the little things. Dr. Brock Mullar's nonchalant expression was betrayed by the deepened lines around the eyes and mouth. He was staring down at the tablet too long without a glance around for a check out the window. For new spacemen, the window is especially something to be avoided. It is irrefutable proof that everything you're familiar with is far, far below you.

"Everyone comfortable?" I asked. I leaned against the entrance to the flight deck with my hands in my pockets, body language that usually suggests to a passenger's subconscious that everything is just hunky-dory.

DeSortes turned and almost smiled. "On that middle monitor there, the Earth has stopped moving away. Why are we stopped, Captain?"

"Not stopped really. Coasting. The navigation system needs to check that the flight path is clear. We'll jump to light in a few minutes."

"This is a very luxurious living compartment you have, Captain."

"Thank you. The walls are white now, but R.J. can show you how to set them to any color or image you like."

"I am impressed. How are the sleeping quarters?"

"R.J. will give you a tour as soon as we jump to light."

"It will still be only a thirty-minute flight there?"

I could tell her idle conversation was actually a subliminal search for any discordance in my voice. "Yes. Then another stop to set up for the more complex orbital insertion."

Her relaxed body language indicated she'd decided everything was okay. "I can't wait to see it," she said half to herself, and she turned back to the window.

R.J. was seated on the opposite side of the compartment watching and listening. He was buckled in, but his feet were up on a nearby seat. He had an old, printed book, closed in his lap. He looked up with smirk and asked, "When does the refreshment cart come through?"

"You just wait right here and I'll check."

As I headed back to the flight deck he called out, "Where would I go?"

I took my place in the right seat and strapped back in. "How's it looking?"

Danica spoke while still staring down at the nav screen. "It's mapped about ten dozen objects, all already in the database. We should get green across the board any second."

Just as she finished speaking a pleasant bing sounded on the instrument panel, and the navigation display switched back to our flight path.

Danica gave a big smile and rested one hand next to the auto pilot. "Engage?"

I nodded, "Engage."

This time there was only a slight push back in the seats as the inertia dampeners kicked in. The view out the front window blurred for a second, then became a tunnel-like vision of stars. As Griffin settled into her cruise, the tunnel of distant stars slowly widened into an almost normal view.

"We look very, very good across the board, Captain," said Danica with a notable tone of satisfaction and pleasure.

"We forgot to warn the passengers."

"Hopefully their souls have caught up to their bodies by now."

"As I recall you promised to go back and be gracious."

With a fake sneer she unbuckled and climbed out of the pilot's seat then ducked back to the living compartment. I could not make out what the voices were saying, but the tone was one of satisfaction and excitement. She returned a few minutes later with two steaming cups of coffee, a gesture that warmed my heart.

"The natives have been appeased, sir. They keep looking for Saturn out the side windows even though it's not in our present flight path. Also, they seemed bemused by the toilet," she said as she slipped back into the control seat.

"Knowledge-wise, our Doctors seem perfect for this mission, but they don't strike me as EVA types and this one ought to be a doozy."

"I take it they've been in the training pool?" she asked.

"Yes, but I don't have any info on that. They're certified to do this job, but we'll practically be walking on the rings of Saturn."

"Yeah but who can prepare for that?"

"Point taken. You will have remote control of their suit life support systems. Be ready to add CO_2 if one of them starts hyperventilating."

"You'll have R.J. along, too."

"That's the only good thing about it. He could talk a horse across a glass bridge if he needed to."

"So what's the big secret about this chunk of rock?"

"You know the old joke; I'd tell you but then I'd have to kill you. But, I'll tell you all about it when the time's right. We're coming up on the deceleration point, Ma'am."

Danica leaned around toward aft. "Time to buckle up kiddies. We're almost there already."

There was small tug forward against our bodies. Danica glanced at the engine display. "Both reversed nicely."

I carefully balanced my coffee, sipped, and watched the view out the windows as the blur sharpened into normal space. A few minutes passed and we went from coasting to station keeping. Cries of jubilation began to be heard in the back. I leaned over to look behind us through the side portal.

Earth's solar system is a Disney World of delight, seldom visited despite easy access to space these days. Everyone is going somewhere. My humble abode on Earth is just a few minutes from Jetty Park in Cocoa Beach, but except for an occasional bout of surf fishing I rarely make it to the ocean. The Terran Solar System is the same way. Even with all the jumps we make to destinations beyond, we are never in a position to catch a glimpse of Sol's satellites. So today, as a portion of that giant multicolored Saturnian ball and its glowing rings came into view, I became as awestruck as everyone else. It's one of those times when your soul asks you, why haven't you come here before?

There is a Godlike stillness about Saturn, its rings, and its moons. Through the portal the entire view looks like an unreal snapshot in time, which it is. The layers of colors that circle the planet contain massive storm formations, most not nearly as large as Jupiter's, but huge visible storms nonetheless. But you can't see them churning. And though the ice rings are turning, it does not look that way. Probably every ice fragment and body within those rings are moving independently within the gravitational current, but you don't see it. And the many shiny diamonds that hover around Saturn seem locked in place as well. You have to sit and watch for quite a while to realize it is all moving and turning on a scale too grand to fathom. Ice from the rings is being constantly sucked into Saturn in a magnetized rain that will eventually drain the rings completely. The diamonds around Saturn will close in more and more, all in a timeline seen by God's eye only. I wondered how it would be when we dropped down to become one with the A-ring. Suddenly, I was looking forward to it.

"We're station keeping right in synch with the T2 Navigation Marker Beacon. Let me thrust around to face the planet."

With a light touch any gamer would envy, Danica tapped her side joystick and brought the nose around so that Saturn filled our forward view. There were moans of complaint from behind us, followed by a crowd at the flight deck entrance and as they took in the view, a chorus of new, "Wows!" broke out.

"Okay, I make the Keeler Gap at 103 degrees mark 098. The nav system has begun its mapping. My God, it's so beautiful! If you focus you can see the changing colors!" said Danica

"The moons still look like stars," said R.J.

"Believe it or not sixty-two of them have been documented," said Brock Mullar.

"You can clearly see the north pole hexagon," said R.J.

"Caused by a six-sided jet stream," offered DeSortes.

"All of this in a giant rotation, it's amazing," said Danica.

"A Saturn day is about ten and a half hours," replied DeSortes.

"How far out are we?" asked R.J.

"In simple terms, about eighteen million miles," replied Danica.

"I can't wait to get down there," said DeSortes to herself.

I twisted around to look at DeSortes. "Doctor, maybe this would be a good time for you to go over the insertion software your people preloaded for us."

The Doctor recovered her gaze and returned to her matter-of-fact tone, "Well, you should all have read the amplified mission description by now, but in this phase, the navigation system radars will scan for and lock onto Daphnis and then calculate a trajectory and speed that will put us above and behind it. As we follow Daphnis around the A ring, radar will continue to scan three hundred and sixty degrees for ice and will automatically use thrusters to evade any conflicts. As I mentioned, approximately every ten-point-five hours we will pass behind and through Saturn's shadow for approximately 1.1 hours. If the Keeler Gap environment is deemed to be acceptable, and I have no doubt it will be, we will access the Lander prior to a shadow period, and upon emerging from the shadow zone, we will undock and descend for a landing on Daphnis. That will give us a full nine hours in daylight to complete our mission and return."

Danica leaned over to me and whispered, "Wow, that was a mouthful."

"Did you say something, Ms. Donoro?" asked DeSortes tersely.

"Oh, sorry. I was about to say, our comm system has just now locked onto the Albiorix moon mining facility's tracking antenna. We should text them a greeting."

"I'll leave that in your capable hands," replied DeSortes. "Does anyone have any questions about our rendezvous?"

As the hum of the Griffin computers continued, and the massive colors and rings of the planet filled our view screens, an apprehensive silence fell over the spacecraft.

R.J. felt the need to interrupt. "I have this terrible urge to suggest we bring a picnic lunch, but perhaps in this instance I should forego such satirical humor," said R.J.

DeSortes made a, "Tsk," sound and pulled away to head back to her sleep chamber. Mullar continued to stare at the colorful ringed ball suspended in nothingness, surrounded high and low by sparkling diamonds. But, the worry lines in his face had deepened noticeably.

Chapter 4

Griffin ran its scans and analysis and seemed busier than I had ever seen her. Displays came on and off, data scrolled, and lamp indicators created moving patterns in the light of the flight deck. The navigation system had automatically taken control of no less than eight display monitors, presenting various angles, compass maps, and positional data it felt we should pay close attention to. We had displays of planetary and moon aspects on our main panel and above our heads, moving updates and flashing items, all considered significant to the preservation of human life. Whichever university had authored this software for DeSortes, they were masters of their craft.

When the procession of intense radar and scanning had run its course, and the three nav computers were satisfied with the outcome, the panel made a loud beep that I'd never heard before, one that sounded like an old microwave oven signaling food ready.

"Wow!" said Danica.

"I do believe we're approved for the approach."

We stared down at the primary flight management computer. The screen prompt read,

"To initiate orbital insertion during the next rendezvous event window please select; Y, N."

"You know they've kind of taken all the fun out of this," said a bemused Danica.

"I'll bet if it all goes south, it'll hand responsibility back to us real fast," I replied.

"Should I warn the VIPs?"

"Please do."

"Ladies and Gentlemen, please take your assigned seats and strap in. We'll be ready to descend in a few minutes."

There was a sudden solemn silence from the passenger compartment, followed by low voices and the sound of people tensely seating themselves.

"I guess you want me to type the Y so that it'll all be my fault, right?" asked Danica with a smirk.

I smiled and gestured approval. Danica made the entry.

In a classic example of anticlimax, nothing happened. The prompt on the FMC disappeared, replaced by, "System engaged, standby for entry window."

It felt like we were sitting on the world's biggest roller coaster, hovering at the peak, waiting for that first steep drop off.

Danica smiled once more and clicked on the intercom. "The system is now engaged. We're waiting for Daphnis to come around into position. Standby."

Our primary navigation displays had become images of Saturn, its rings and its moons. Numbers on the top right-hand side of the screen were racing ahead showing location, speed, and closure time. The representation for Saturn was a small dot in the center of the screen. I found myself looking down at the tiny dot, and then up at Saturn. It may have been the greatest example of gain I had ever seen. The display moons and rings were inching precisely along their pathways. A flashing red dot on the left side of the screen within the A-ring was Daphnis. It followed a thin dotted red line around the planet. As it closed in on our left, it became flashing yellow.

Danica called out, "Get ready."

The navigation marker turned to a rapidly flashing green; all the main engines displays jumped to life. We were kicked back in our seats a little more than usual as the view out the window became a moving orange giant and its highway of rings. It began to fill the view in front of us almost as though we would crash into it, but as our approach steadied down it was clear we were on an entrance ramp to A-ring road. The overall beauty of it was overwhelming. It made me glad this approach and descent was being done by autopilot. The sight could have entranced any pilot. A glance at Danica revealed her own awe was more than she could conceal.

We became a property of Saturn, simply another of its many satellite holdings. As we continued to descend, the rings began to look like the biggest, widest, rock runway I had ever seen. The size of the planet beside us was so immense I felt as though I could somehow hear a rumble from it.

The Keeler Gap became much more visible, its twenty-six-mile width still barely noticeable compared to the scales being set around it. Each second of approach brought more new perceptions. The rings were no longer flat. They were at first a scattering of tiny moving particles, but as we lowered down, they became boulders of ice, millions of them. Gorillas in the mist. The ring surface was no longer well defined. Ring rain fog blended the collage. Many objects moved along at various distances above the main flow, large and small chunks that seemed out of place. The cool cabin air seemed to fit our position well.

It took me that long to spot Daphnis. As the Keeler Gap grew more and more respectable, the hull-shaped form of Daphnis could be seen near the center of the Gap. It was slightly off to the outer side, but still above and well clear of the A-ring edge.

We settled into a position above and behind Daphnis. Our display screen switched to heavy duty radar and rapid scanning. Dozens of objects nearby were being identified, categorized, and tracked. Coordinates were scrolling down some of the screens. Our main nav display had become an overhead animation view of us and our relationship to Daphnis. Other displays were monitoring object movement and spacing. The monitor beside our primary display looked like weather radar, but it was depicting waves of rain-sized particles. Our thrusters were firing periodically in tiny bursts. The environment was just far too much for any pilot to handle.

As we sat watching all this with some emotional misgiving, DeSortes showed up and leaned in next to Danica, a tablet in her right hand. "You'll need to read and sign-off on both of these document icons. It was necessary to withhold this information from you in case we didn't get this far, but since we have, you will be monitoring our suit coms so you will be hearing highly classified information which is explained in these documents. The first icon is simply an oath that you will never discuss anything found here during this mission. The second icon is the amplified description of the mission. I need you to complete these lawful requirements before we can proceed. Any questions?"

"I guess it would be a real bitch if I refused now, wouldn't it?" replied Danica sarcastically.

"We would be forced to restrain you back in the main compartment and strap earphone silencers to your head. One member of the team would have to remain behind to do your job."

"You're shitting me, right?"

"Ms. Donoro, just sign the damn oath, will you?"

Danica opened the first icon, speed read the material, and signed the tablet with an odd-looking pen DeSortes handed her. The document disappeared from her screen.

"When you're finished reading that amplified mission briefing be sure you sign off with only that pen. You'll find any others won't work."

With that, DeSortes headed back to change.

Danica looked at me. I tried to appear innocent.

"What the hell?" she asked.

"It's not a moon. It's supposed to be a ship."

Her anger changed to intense curiosity. "Whose ship?"

"Ten thousand years old or older. Maybe much older."

It took a moment for her to process the possibilities. "So... why all the secrecy?"

"They don't want to rewrite Earth history overnight."

She nodded, still in a daze. "What do they expect to find down there?"

"No idea."

"Can they get in?"

"You better read that doc. I need to get my suit undergarment on and make sure the newbies are dressed correctly. Wouldn't want them freezing their tootsies."

They were all fussing around in the aft airlock. R.J. was trying to assist both of them at once. DeSortes was trying to remain in authority despite having one foot stuck in the sleeve of her inner garment.

Nervously out of breath she said, "Captain Tarn, could you please hurry and get in your suit. If we can make the transfer to the lander in the next forty-five minutes we'll beat the next shadow period, otherwise we'll have to wait for the next time around."

I smiled and went to my suit locker. The custom suits that had been provided were actually quite attractive. They were hard shell two-tone brown and black, so much smaller than the full white standard EVA suits. They had flat pack back packs that were only about seven inches thick, quite a small area for temperature fluid controllers and oxygen. Somehow the designers had compressed ten hours of oxygen into them which sounded like a bomb waiting to happen, to me. In addition, they had powerful magnetic shoes with some kind of special rotating magnetic field that guaranteed the correct amount of contact and release. Even more impressive was the promise that the suit would generate its own variable magnetic field intended to act as a shield against electrically charged ice particles. R.J. and I had both already tried the suits on, surprised by the ease of movement in the joints. The only bothersome thing was that the suit model number was SX2001EXP. We both knew that EXP stood for; Experimental.

I know all the tricks to getting an undergarment on and aligned. I had the legs and torso in place in about two minutes. I glanced over to see how DeSortes was doing and had to catch myself staring. Her human side was showing. She was in panties and braless. She finally had the undergarment pulled almost up to her crotch with the torso hanging behind, but she was struggling to get the interwoven tubes lined up correctly. Her bare skin seemed to be resisting the tube material. From my angle she was suddenly a very desirable woman. I fastened up my front, went to her and knelt to help facilitate a little more dignity. There was a moment of eye contact which was quickly diverted.

Mullar was a little bit comical which was also a bit disconcerting. He was doing everything correctly but was so jittery it was taking far too long. R.J. had intercepted him for rescue.

The outer suits were easier. Once in them, the power button on the left sleeve instantly brought all the helmet indictors to life. There was a tiny bit of hum and a bit more vibration from behind than usual. With visors up, we stared at each other, waiting for the suit heaters to circulate.

DeSortes looked up from her sleeve display. "We have time to make it," she said as the suit environment green lights began to switch on. She sounded slightly out of breath.

I tried to sound reassuring, "Visors down. Suit compression on. Call out when you're good to go."

After a short pause, one by one they all acknowledged. As his visor snapped down in place, Mullar looked around wide-eyed.

"Okay, I'll go first with Commander Smith bringing up the rear. Everyone okay with that?" I asked.

"I'll follow you," replied DeSortes.

"Danica how do you read us?"

"Loud and clear, Adrian. I have all four suit readouts."

"We're sealed and ready for decompress of the airlock."

"I see that. All suits are decompressing and air mixtures are correct. Airlock decompression armed and... engaged."

The red lights began to rotate. We could faintly hear the warning horn. Readout displays above the airlock door came alive and began running numbers. I eased between the hard-shell suits of the others to the outer door. The bar lamp on the hatch switched from red to green. There was a familiar big clunk from the locking mechanism. Pulled up on the big lever and the door slid smoothly aside.

It has been said that no mortal man can gaze upon the face of God and live. The view outside the airlock was about as close as you could come. It was a stormy sea of floating ice that led to a planet so huge it filled the horizon and sky. Although the carpet of rocklike ice chunks were well below us, they were alive with movement, many bumping each other and slowly turning away. There is nothing like first-hand vision. No remote lander camera can match it. Saturn's storms were slowly swirling in a hypnotic collage of dull color and design.

A few moments were required to believe it was real. The mind needed time to process, absorb, and just accept it. I had to force myself to look away to retrieve the safety line clip, unlock the feed, and snap it onto a suit ring. Stepping out of Griffin's artificial gravity to begin the hand-over-hand climb, forced me back into focus. It would have been possible to use the mag shoes to walk up the side of Griffin, but hand-over-hand was much faster, and much safer for newbies.

Halfway up the frosty shell of Griffin, I checked back to see DeSortes already cautiously following close behind. For a newbie she was doing everything quite expertly. Mullar was half in and half out the hatch, leaning back to look up as though deciding whether or not to decline the transfer. R.J. was right behind him, patting him reassuringly on the hard shoulder like a good jump master.

Atop Griffin, the mag shoes took over. The heel to toe breakaway was surprisingly comfortable. To the left on Griffin's topside, back-dropped by the lively A-ring and silver moons glinting in the blackness, the pointed Lander waited, its coarse, tar-colored surface well frosted. Half a dozen magnetic steps brought me to the rear access door. Within a small alcove, a simple double-hinged pull handle made the hatch pop open slightly. It took a tug to pull it open fully. No room for motorized hatch doors on this spacecraft. Just inside the door was a locking ring. With my left hand I held some slack in the safety line, unclipped it from my suit and snapped it in place.

DeSortes had fallen behind a bit. She was just floating up over the side, her feet headed for Saturn, her eyes locked on me, a death grip on the line. She finally managed to pull herself upright and stood, staring down at her mag shoes as if she was surprised they worked. She turned awkwardly and looked over the side. Having dispelled her own immediate fears she decided to harass Mullar about his. "Dr. Mullar, please stop lagging!"

R.J. came to his defense. "We're fine. It took a moment to feed more line from the reel. We're on our way."

Lights came on inside the Lander. Four tightly spaced seats shape-formed to accommodate hard suits. Blank panels on the front walls confirmed the no-windows design, added protection against ice impacts. I've never met a pilot who didn't want real windows. I've always been one of them. Cameras are just fine, but if there's a main power failure and the screens go dark, sitting blind inside a box waiting to die has a special excruciation to it. We land aircraft and spacecraft on instruments all the time, but we can see the weather's white-out through the windshield, and the hard ground just before we touch it.

Mullar and R.J. clomped up beside us a moment later. I unclipped the safety line and tossed it out toward Saturn. "Danica, take in the line and seal the airlock."

"Safety line retracting," was the response. A minute later, "Door closing."

We continued to stand as a group for a moment, taking in the giant swirling sphere, it's shelves of rings, and a few glittering moons in the distance.

"We'll be in shadow in thirty minutes, everyone. Let's get in and take our seats," said DeSortes as she too scanned the spectacle around us.

I took a last long look, shook my head from the sheer disbelief of it and stepped up into the Lander. Inside, an awkward step over the reclined rear seats brought me to the left front. There was a feeling of vacuum-packing as I lowered down into it. The seat motored forward automatically. Lights came on across the instrument panels.

According to the manual this vehicle had an nuclear power source, so my first instinct was to do away with our blindness. I switched on external cameras and was pleasantly surprised when a wide, wraparound view screen came alive where real windows normally would have been. There was a complete one-hundred-and-eighty-degree view with a touch of three dimensions added. I had to admit the visibility was even better than a window would have been. I'd still have preferred a window. Simulator time in this vehicle would have been nice too, but there was no simulator for this vehicle.

R.J. climbed in beside me and twisted around to look. "Better than expected," he said.

"Now if it just flies nice," I suggested.

"Now if *you* just fly nice," mocked DeSortes as she sealed the hatch.

Mullar was already in his seat behind me. He appeared to be hurriedly looking for seat belts.

"Relax, Dr. Mullar," added DeSortes. "We have a ten-minute wait until shadow, and then another hour or so until we emerge from it. Commander Smith, would you pressurize us so we can raise these visors."

R.J. obliged and diverted from his assigned checklist. He activated the compartment's atmosphere control system. We watched a readout on the main display showing cabin pressure as it rose to twelve PSI and stabilized. My suit indicator agreed. The hard suits were able to use a much higher internal pressure than soft suits while still providing good mobility. I canceled suit air, opened my visor, and tested the air. It was freezing. One by one the others followed, as cabin temperature quickly rose.

R.J.'s good humor kicked in, "Ladies and Gentlemen, get ready for a pleasurable, slow cruise around Saturn. A one-hour ride you can't get at Disney Land."

We stared at the wrap around display showing the alien world around us. We were like four captivated people in a tiny movie theater. We soon entered Saturn's shadow; an experience even more mystical than that in the light. There were still darkened views of the ring-world around us, but the shadow gave the place a creepy Godlike aura. Time seemed to have stopped. We waited in silence, using the time to reconsider the wisdom of our life-choices.

Chapter 5

We emerged into Sol's light slightly more than an hour later. Daphnis remained ahead and below us, an easy target. This was the leg of the journey where DeSortes' people had found themselves unable to program the autopilot. There was just no way to anticipate all possible obstacles. That meant I would take the Lander in using manual thrusters only. Thank-you, Lord.

We decoupled smoothly and moved three meters straight up for clearance, then a gentle bank to the left and a steady jet forward. Our wrap- around fake window continued to do a great job with the panorama, adding notation to anything close by, flashing a green circled icon to denote Daphnis. There was also a faint approach line, the recommended path, if possible. Captain's prerogative.

The Keeler Gap looked like a twenty-six-mile-wide, black landing strip, thirty feet deep with no bottom. It was a strange contradiction to the mind's eye. Were it not for the boat-shaped outline of Daphnis, it could have been a channel to an alternate dimension. As we closed in, the A-ring became much more active and diverse. The chemistry of the ring became a field of stone-ice, all fragments moving generally along the same path, but bumping, rolling, and rotating into new positions. Saturn engulfed the backdrop. Daphnis began to have greater detail. The crater near the front of the bow shape was clearly visible and no longer looked like a typical impact area. There were ripples in its surface, like twisted metal.

The pointy-nosed Lander handled like a dream. As Daphnis began to get real big on our screen, DeSortes could not contain herself.

"Remember it has to be a zero-impact touchdown, Captain. The magnetic lock will not pull you in. It has to see zero separate on all three locks to activate," she said nervously. "Isn't it time you turned one-eighty to face the ring motion?" she asked.

A dozen smart remarks came to mind. I could see R.J. smirking as I turned us around to face the oncoming ring ice, a position that would allow use of the Lander's pointed nose as a deflector. The landing would be made backwards to our direction of travel. DeSortes became silent, intently watching for touchdown, ready to back seat drive at any moment if called for.

The Daphnis icon on the main screen was flashing rapid red now. As we lowered down, Daphnis' surface rose up on both sides of us. Ground radar put us six feet above the landing coordinates. Daphnis five-mile width finally looked expansive. Slight down-thrusters were required to settle. As the separation readout neared zero, I could feel DeSortes holding back a scream of, "Stop!" At the last minute I tapped the *up* thrusters and we stopped without feeling contact. Suddenly a strong vibration jittered our seats as the Lander's magnetics locked us down.

I could tell that for a moment DeSortes thought to compliment me on the docking. But, she just couldn't bring herself to do it.

On the wide-screen view we were now an upper part of the Keeler Gap. It was another striking view that no one had ever seen from these coordinates. What's more, we could now leave the spacecraft and walk out there, a first-person commune with Saturn's family. Even DeSortes was still too stunned to start giving orders.

But the break didn't last long. DeSortes stood in her seat. "Dr. Mullar, unpack the EVA case. Captain, let's seal suits and depressurize. Let's make this happen before any problems crop up."

"Tarn to Griffin. Have you got us, Danica?"

"Loud and clear, Adrian."

"We are preparing to exit."

"Very good. I see each of your body cams, and have you on the tracking display. Nice docking. Vitals and suit systems green across."

Suit depress was faster than usual again. I was reminded once more that hard suit joints are easier to move so the suits can utilize a higher operating pressure. We were all quickly suit-ready and fully motivated to step outside. Mullar had brought out some type of black, shielded case the size of a medium, fat suitcase. It was polished and ribbed for strength. We bumped into each other moving to the hatch and when R.J. finally hit the open-main switch, we sort of oozed out the back.

The first interesting discovery was that our magnetic shoes worked perfectly against Daphnis icy surface, but that wasn't such an unexpected event. Probe data had suggested ferromagnetic content in Daphnis' surface material. But, the reality of it kept alive the theory that we were standing on an ancient spacecraft.

"There is an opening back at the vertical section of the tail," said DeSortes, as the rest of us turned in awkward circles to take in the view. Each step brought a new, "Wow!" Even DeSortes lingered before again urging us on.

"Let's go, Dr. Mullar. Captain Tarn, Commander Smith, you can remain here if you'd prefer. We'll keep in touch on the com."

"Not on your life," answered R.J.

"Very well. It's up to you," replied DeSortes, but there seemed to be a touch of annoyance in her voice.

We had set down roughly five-thousand feet from the tail section. I made a quick inspection of the Lander's three magnetic locking points and wondered how much of an ice boulder impact they could resist. Danica could take remote control of the Lander in an emergency so barring extreme damage, the Lander should remain available to us even if knocked off those landing locks. I had to hurry to catch up to the group. It was a long, slow march aft, but the visual reward was so compelling no one cared. We were walking the A-ring Trail.

Something began to bother me. I couldn't put my finger on it. There had been something in the tone of DeSortes' voice, something about the large shiny case the ever-silent Dr. Mullar was tugging along beside him. He seemed more concerned than awestruck. I shook off the misgivings. They were probably a part of my so-called orneriness.

As we reached the vertical section of tail, a large opening came into view, previously hidden in the tail's shadow. And, within that opening, the question of Daphnis natural or artificial origin was answered absolutely. There was no longer any doubt. It was a rectangular hatch opening. Ladder rungs leading down made us all believers. DeSortes switched on her headlamp and leaned in to stare down into the hole.

R.J. couldn't stand it. "What do you see?"

"Machinery," replied DeSortes and she straightened up and turned to face us. "Perhaps at this point, Dr. Mullar and I should proceed and you two should remain behind in case we get into trouble."

"We wouldn't be any help to you up here," replied R.J.

"If anything happened, you two would be able to report back," said DeSortes. The suggestion was her first glaring mistake.

"Everything is being recorded!?" answered R.J. "Danica's monitoring everything we do!"

DeSortes quickly realized her error. "Perhaps you're right," she said. "But if the two of you remain back a small distance, that might put you in a better position if there's a problem."

"Lead on," said R.J. and through his visor I could see him winking at me as though something was going on.

DeSortes went down first. Mullar followed, barely fitting the big case down the shaft. At the bottom of the cold, steel pit, we found ourselves in a long narrow aisle bordered by frozen, dust-covered alien machinery that resembled the engine room of a military submarine. There were tubes, pipes, circular storage tanks, cable harnesses, shafts, racks, vertical tubes, all so wracked by age that they almost blended together. Underneath the dust and frost everything seemed to be a fading gray as though the centuries had dulled any color. There was no understanding any of it. It was all alien technology. When I checked, DeSortes was already gone, somewhere farther ahead in the aisle. Muller was also well ahead of us in obedient pursuit.

R.J. eyed me through his visor again. Without speaking he made it clear more was going on here than was being said. He peered ahead and cautiously pushed after them. I followed closely.

It was quite a long, winding machine passageway with turnoffs to other equipment sections. We held to our course forward. After a half mile or more of tight squeezes and multiple intersections, the landscape finally began to change. I had the feeling we were emerging into some type of power section. The interior opened up to large, more dingy multicolored rooms with low ceilings, wide vertical tubes, odd looking consoles, and dust/frost-covered control stations. The place was too big to search. We could have maneuvered around and gone in almost any direction, on and on through miles of ancient spacecraft. We tried to wind our way ahead hoping to keep tracking forward. R.J. began using a scanner to map our progress by marking electronic breadcrumbs along the way, a homemade GPS to help us find our way out.

What seemed like a mile more of walking brought yet a new kind of interior. Banks of barrel shaped containers were stacked on rack after rack. There were long aisles of these racks that looked like they went on forever. As we made our way further, R.J. spotted a shelf section that had collapsed, releasing its barrels in a scattered chaos. R.J. stopped to inspect, then toured the area of damage. He looked back at me and pointed and waved me to join him. He was standing beside a fractured barrel container that had cracked open. His scanner flashed a rapid green light. A flow of liquid had frozen while rushing out. R.J. looked up at me. "It's water, Adrian. Very pure water. This ship was transporting water."

"I wonder why?"

"A precious commodity for some worlds. Easy to believe."

I motioned toward my sleeve control and gave the hand signal for private channel. He switched and looked at me.

I glanced around to be sure we were alone. "I get the feeling this isn't what our associates are interested in."

"You have that impression also?"

"Have you even spotted them lately?"

"Nowhere to be seen. Almost as if they lost us intentionally. I'd like to know what's in that case Mullar is carrying. But, maybe we're just suspicious individuals, you know?"

"We're definitely suspicious individuals. I don't think they're communicating on the public channels anymore but we'd better switch back to public and see if we can catch up to them for their own good. Keep scanning for them, will you?"

At some point ahead, a second bulkhead forced us aside to another partially opened hatchway. From there, the more forward we traveled, the more to port we were being diverted. I suspected some huge power core was taking up the ship's center space and we were being maneuvered around it. It was colder here. The suit heater core was being taxed. After long zig-zags around closet-sized cabinets, flat table spaces, and vertical tubes that looked like elevators, we reached a new kind of bulkhead that was packed with sensors and multiple closed doors. A thousand or so feet toward starboard one set of doors was partially opened. We squeezed through and stopped to look.

R.J. held up one gloved hand. His voice sounded tense but very controlled, "The crew is still here, Adrian."

There were aliens at various points around this new section, frozen in time, frost covered and gray like the rest of the ship. They were humanoid but not human. Some were slumped over consoles, some sprawled on the floor, their moment of death captured in icy detail. Others had remained in control seats. They were tall, probably seven feet or more. Big pronounced ridges lined the center of the face. They were hulky and powerful looking. They wore hard shell frozen black suits, most with no helmets. A few individuals on the floor had managed to pull theirs on but not in time. The ship controls were beyond anything I had seen. Large, once transparent screens were mounted around this area. The consoles were big arc-shaped tables. The interior design went on for a very long expanse, but far ahead we could see another change.

R.J. and I exchanged a stare. "Wow," he said. That covered it.

It had become obvious that DeSortes and Mullar were not communicating on a public channel. They had switched to private. As we continued forward, I began stepping through comm channels in search of them. R.J. noticed and began the same search.

As we moved forward there began to be signs of damage. Twisted consoles, broken conduit, equipment piled up in corners. Soon the damage became structural. Bent bulkheads, twisted partitions, panels wedged high into ceiling concaves. The frozen dead continued to be stationed around the debris.

R.J. grabbed my arm and pointed to the comm. We switched back to private.

"I've got them," he said. "Step down through the channel six subchannels. They're four steps below it. They went a long way to lose us."

It was fortunately that our ranks allowed us both to access all private channels. DeSortes had probably not realized that. I typed in the channel.

"We need a lever. Find something!" It was DeSortes speaking to Mullar. "There's got to be something around this mess."

R.J. and I continued forward as we listened.

The ship's headroom began to diminish. We could see starboard and port bulkheads coming into view but they were partially crushed. There were empty, high-back seats with no control consoles in front of them, probably for observers. This horseshoe-shaped chamber contained even more display screens and operator consoles. More and more of them held victims still in their seats. Center and not far ahead, among the carnage on the deck, was what appeared to be the back of one very large seat. We approached it on either side.

Still seated, the Captain had held his position. His head was bent downward. He was perhaps more than seven feet tall and very powerful looking even in his frozen state. His face was not visible. He wore a helmet with the visor up. A partial mask and hose attached to his nose and mouth ran down between his legs like an elephant's trunk. His feet were in stirrups that appeared to be part of the ship's steering system. His fingers were splayed into grooves in the seats arm rests.

DeSortes' voice cut in on the com. "It's just frozen in place, damn it. Stand here, we'll lift together."

As we listened, we turned and looked forward. A short distance ahead, the ceiling suddenly sloped down sharply. Everything beneath it had been crushed. It was clear that quite a bit more manned flight deck area lay ahead, but all of it had been flattened and destroyed.

R.J. motioned to the comm control. We switched back to private. He pointed to the damaged front end. "That's the area forward we saw on our way in, the area that was impacted by something. It crushed this entire section of ship. I think the compression killed everyone here and the explosive wave went all the way aft and blew out that tail hatch we used to get in."

"It's a good bet. We'd better get going and reign in the other two. I don't like the sound of the discussion going on back there."

"They sound like mischievous children. I don't get it, if they were going to be doing this clandestine stuff why did they bring us along?"

"Part of their story was true. They wanted this to look like a civilian exploration, a mission not that important."

"Oh, yeah. And if anything blew up in their face, they'd have you along to blame, the one person most famous for getting in and out of trouble."

"Set your comm to monitor their channel and let's switch back to public so they don't get suspicious."

We started back and passed through the first main bulkhead. I tried a call on the public channel. "Tarn to DeSortes. We've located the flight deck. The crew is here, frozen for all time."

No answer.

Finally, a reluctant reply came. "We are documenting the power section, Captain. We'll join you shortly."

R.J. shook his head and gave me a knowing look. We continued to search for them.

We followed R.J.'s scanner map back through the ship using a different path, keeping to starboard this time. After a few hundred feet of winding through equipment and vertical tubes, we picked up boot prints in the frost. The trail led us toward Daphnis' power section until a faint glow of silver light caught our eyes.

They were inside the largest vertical tube yet seen. It was nearly as wide as a water tower, rising from floor to ceiling. A large pressure door had been pried open. Inside, there was an inner containment barrier. DeSortes was leaning in and out its garage-sized door that had been rolled open.

R.J. and I approached and stood outside peering in. Beyond DeSortes, Mullar was deep inside attempting to remove a clear cylinder the size of a fireplace log. It was flooded with a blinding silver light. The control-laden pedestal that held the thing somehow seemed to be resisting letting go of it.

Within that brilliant tube was something I had never experienced, a dancing silver light that emanated ultra-thin laser-like beams of silver, billions of them, and when a beam touched your eye directly you wanted nothing more than to keep staring into it to try to understand, even though the sensation seemed hurtful and forced you to look away.

That was the reason DeSortes kept backing out. I pulled R.J. away by the shoulder but he looked at me and nodded that he understood.

DeSortes became excited. "That's it! You've got it! Here! The case is open and ready!" On the floor near Mullar's struggle, she had positioned the case for him. It was then I noticed a formed compartment in the case that seemed to match the silver light cylinder perfectly.

Mullar staggered away from the core lugging the heavy cylinder. Bent over, he nearly fell into the case atop of his precious trophy. With a last grunt of effort, he adjusted it into its spot and pushed the case closed. He fell against the sealed case, exhausted from the effort. DeSortes stepped in beside him and checked the latches on the case.

"Here, I'll help you up," she finally said. She gripped Mullar under one arm and pulled him up. He looked dazed.

"Dr. DeSortes, what is this thing you plan to bring aboard my ship?" I asked.

DeSortes paused to measure her response. "It's been referred to us as Diamond Light, Captain. Once again, I should mention to you and Commander Smith, this is all highly classified. Nothing here can ever be discussed with anyone."

"Just how dangerous is it?" asked R.J.

"Not at all. The case is made of dialedium. No known photonic or radioactive energy can penetrate the shell. It's a new power source we've found here. It may help mankind in many ways. Let's just get back to the Lander. Dr. Mullar, are you okay? Can you make it?"

Mullar did not look good. He was teetering. At the compartment's hatchway R.J. had to steady him. We started back with R.J. supporting Mullar. Reluctantly I accepted the case. Although the case was almost weightless, it took a good amount of balance and steering. DeSortes followed closely to keep an eye on her treasure, Mullar now of much less concern.

The walk back seemed much longer than the walk in. To fit through the passageways, R.J. had to keep making adjustments to Mullar support.

Danica's voice cut in, "How are you doing down there? Dr. Mullar's vitals are all screwed up. They're not making sense and Dr. DeSortes' BP is way up. Is everything okay?"

I answered, "On our way back, Danica. Dr. Mullar is a little off. Standby."

At the ladder we had to stop to plan the extraction of Mullar and the treasure case. Even in Daphnis' low gravity Mullar was a challenge. With R.J. up top, Mullar was just conscious enough to pull himself up, hand over hand. His legs did not seem to be working. With me pushing on his butt, climbing as I went, R.J. was able to get a good enough hold to pull him out. I looked down to see DeSortes holding the precious case above her head for me to take. At least she had allowed Mullar to go first.

Topside, the Lander waited. For the first time it looked comforting. Once again, the distance seemed longer. DeSortes passed by the struggling Mullar and R.J., and arrived first to open up. Mullar's condition was worsening enough that he could no longer unlock his magnetic shoes from the deck. With case in my right hand, I had to help R.J. support him with my left. R.J. finally paused and tapped at Mullar's sleeve controls to turn off the shoes. The rest of the way was an awkward drag of a barely conscious man and a bulky case. Around us, the overwhelming panorama of Saturn's rings somehow seemed to become accusive.

Inside the vehicle, there was suddenly new cause for alarm. We were to keep the suits pressurized in anticipation of translation to Griffin, but a look into Mullar's visor showed a face brilliantly sunburned. His eyes had become milky. There was a small spot of drool near the corner of the mouth.

I took him from R.J. and tested him, "Dr. Mullar?"

No response.

"Dr. Mullar, can you hear me?"

No answer.

"Danica, how do Mullar's vitals look now?"

"They're still screwed up. They're jumping all over the place. I can't read them. What's the deal?"

DeSortes cut in, "Let's just hurry back so we can get him out of the suit, okay?"

R.J.'s voice became terse, "What is wrong with him, Dr. DeSortes? He looks burned."

We sat Mullar down. I stepped forward and powered up the Lander.

"Whatever it is we can't treat him here. We need to get him back to the Griffin and get his suit off," replied DeSortes irately.

"So you've determined his condition is not contagious or harmful to anyone else, then?" asked R.J. sarcastically.

"What choice do we have, Commander Smith? If you have one, I'm willing to listen."

I interrupted. "Strap in, and make sure he's secure."

Quiet discord marked the seating process. I detached the mag locks and the Lander began to drift slightly. The nav screen was already showing vectors back to Griffin. The ascent and rendezvous were easy and took less than an hour. The coupling to Griffin's modified end effectors went smoothly.

When the hatch was opened it was my job to retrieve the safety line from Griffin's airlock. Danica already had Griffin's outer airlock door open and the brakes on the feed reel released. The big black suspicious case would remain in its Lander compartment which seemed like a very good idea at that point. I was tempted to skip the mag shoes altogether and push straight across to the first handhold on the side of Griffin, but for once caution overcame valor. At the airlock entrance, the safety line fed out obediently from its reel. Back atop Griffin, this time I did skip the shoes and launched myself to the back of the Lander, then clipped the line to the welded hold beside the open hatch. By necessity, Mullar had to be first. Hooked securely to the line, I carefully towed the inanimate spacesuit victim followed by R.J. steering the legs. DeSortes closed up the Lander and made her way down.

When Griffin's outer door had closed and pressure filled the chamber, we ditched our helmets and gathered around Mullar. R.J. popped open Mullar's visor for a quick close look, as he continued to uncouple his own suit.

The man was a bright red sunburn and was looking much older than his years.

I shook my head in concern. "Let's finish getting the suit off him and we'll put him in a lower sleeping compartment and set him up with a Med Reader."

"He's going to need a topical ointment on those burns right away, and we should lower the temp in his compartment as low as it will go," said R.J.

"Perhaps we should call for a rescue craft to meet us," suggested DeSortes.

"It's less than an hour back to Earth, Doctor. We'll request a MedEvac call sign. They'll give us a straight in and direct descent. Waiting for a MedEvac ship would take longer, even if there is one available."

As quickly as possible we tucked Mullar in. His condition made us all want to look away. With a vital signs display attached to his compartment, we watched vital stats so erratic it made the monitor system seem broken. We took our seats on the flight deck. After an ominous exchange of looks with Danica, we engaged the departure program.

R.J. looked back toward the sleeper compartments as he spoke, "Maybe we shouldn't have done this."

I nodded. "I believe that was my line."

Chapter 6

A crowded, peculiar assortment of individuals greeted us when we hurriedly touched down at KSC. There were a few military men not in uniform. KSC security was in attendance investigating the use of a Medvac call sign. A team of stolid doctors not wearing scrubs or white coats quickly became bossy. Some technicians in plain work coveralls looked confused. An unexpected, off-white, heavy-lift transport aircraft without a marking on it was parked with ramps and ladders ready. The Lander was detached and loaded directly into its open rear cargo door, precious case still stored inside. Mullar was also taken aboard that aircraft after being placed in a sealed life support tube. DeSortes followed along talking excitedly to men in dark suits.

None of them paid us any mind. A few words here and there as necessary. Their tone was completely noncommittal, practically disinterested. R.J. described it as, *"quite brusque."* Except for a couple of quick medical scans using a handheld, no other exams of us were deemed necessary. For some reason, that flagrant disregard made me a little sick to my stomach. I think their hasty indifference had to do with the cargo.

R.J. wanted to leave Earth immediately, something about a very bad taste in his mouth. I had agreed to take him to Enuro to pick up Elachia but the mating adapter end effectors were still being removed from Griffin. I filed the flight plan and we lifted off as soon as the ship was ready and clearance given.

That turned out to be a good idea. When you are left with the unshakeable feeling that you have been royally molested, you need something to keep you busy. A week-long trip at Griffin's maximum light speed is a wonderful distraction. It was an empyreal way for each of us to dispel our lingering displeasure about everything that had happened. R.J. took to hard cover books in between vicious chess matches between the two of us. Danica invested much of her time writing software code for something she would not tell us about. I spent a good deal of time sipping coffee in the pilot's seat with my feet up on the instrument panel, watching stars that we'd never reach.

When we finally landed in the vehicle receiving area behind Elachia's castle estate, I remembered that the majestic towers of the equally grand castle on the opposite side of Lake Menoir belonged to Fantasia. I stood outside the ship on the expansive green grass lawn and stared across the lake. My gaze felt involuntary.

It is possible to run away from yourself. Some people spend a lifetime doing it. Brides left at the altar. Grooms left at the altar. Happily married spouse, great job, nice home, children, gets up to go to work and never returns. Siblings, supposed to start college like father planned, run off to nowhere.

In many cases, rather than run away, we use one or more types of adverse chemistry to avoid ourselves. Smoke, tablets, or syringe.

Millionaires, movie stars, stockbrokers, drop outs, or just the disillusioned. The list is endless. Contrary to popular belief they are all equal, after all. Hurry and take any life-passage that escapes the prescribed conventional life because, if you can stay far enough away from friends and relatives, you also can avoid seeing reflections of yourself in them.

But abandoning yourself that way invariably turns out to be a strange wayward path to a dead end. Usually it is caused by the mind disagreeing with the heart and until the two can be reconciled there will be two opposing forces controlling an erratic rudder through society's ocean of emotion. Often the prospective dropoutee will show no outward appearance of internal conflict, at least until they end up in the proverbial alley with the paper bag that holds the bottle. Everything in their life appears perfectly logical, even to them. Their physical avatar is acting exactly the way society expects. All behavior fits right into social norms. But inside the cranium the battle wages on in an endless loop. *You should have done this. You should have done that. Maybe you could do this, or maybe you should do that.* Right and wrong can become such a confusing contradiction to good and bad. Why so often is the thing you'd prefer not to do, the right thing to do, and vice-versa? A wise man once said, if you need to understand why you're here, think about what you knew when you were thirteen or fourteen. That's the age when most of us used to believe we finally knew everything, although it could take a year or two to teach it to our parents. Compare what you knew back then, to what you know now. The difference between the two, is *why* you're here.

When we knowingly make a bad choice, eventually reality makes it clear why it was a bad decision. Mistakes are also a reminder that free will is the only way a soul can learn difficult lessons. Don't touch the candle flame, junior. It will hurt you. Yeah Mom, sure. Later in life, after testing the candle repeatedly, we learn that love is the true flame. The pain from the candle was nothing compared to it.

I realized I'd been standing and staring across the lake at Fantasia's castle for too long, then wondered why I was mentally debating these things. The last time I had seen Fantasia was on a cruise to hell. It was supposed to be a diplomatic envoy. We were just hitching a ride at the time. Terrorism turned the trip into a nightmare and eventually left me staring up at Fantasia's angelic smile from a medical recovery incubator.

R.J. and I had met Fantasia and Elachia on that same fateful cruise. They were sisters, sort of. The mysterious Dr. Lana Flint, said to be an insane experimental geneticist, pursued a lifelong dream of creating the perfect mate. He was noted for using a biologically sterile incubation process. No actual parents were connected to the embryo's development. All DNA mapping had been designed and authored by him. He had run trillions of combinations, using supercomputers to monitor his designs. Fantasia and Elachia were his last two attempts. Early in their life they were assigned to an advanced foster training facility. During that period Flint was found sitting in a laboratory desk chair deceased, a look of concentration still locked into his face.

Had Flint lived, he may have found that he finally had achieved his life-long quest. The Flint sisters were found to have very high IQs. They were reserved, gracious, and attentive. Both seemed to know what others were feeling, thinking, and even what they were about to say.

A transcript left behind by Flint for his two creations explained his design concept. It was kind of a user's manual for the genetically engineered. One trait in particular was controversial. Flint somehow had arranged that when mating occurred, a subconscious link between his creation and her chosen companion was established. From that time on, the daughter would know the companion's every mood, whim, and desire. She would be able to please her mate in ways even he hadn't considered. The link could never be broken with one exception. Flint had left behind a formula for a bio-fluid which when taken internally would sever the link. His reason for the antidote was to provide assurance to both individuals that the link between them was by choice.

Much to my great concern, R.J. had been the first to take the relationship plunge. It surprised the hell out of me. R.J. has always been the wary one, avoiding even secure short-term relationships. When he confided in me his willingness to take a chance on Elachia, I'd thought he was kidding. They were such an unlikely couple. It was like a world-class beauty queen hooking up with Einstein; no disrespect toward R.J. intended. And, as unlikely as it seemed, Elachia had initiated the overtures. R.J., looking like a stunned wildebeest in the headlights, had not run away.

My own connection with Fantasia was equally odd and even more unlikely. I was sworn to bachelorhood, one-night specialist able to leap out of bed in a single bound. For me, Fantasia had been a trick play, a one-night stand. I had wondered how to let her down easy. But, somehow the one-night never ended. Even after she had explained the threat of the link to me and I knew we were psychically tethered, that one-night persisted. It seemed impossible that the two most relationship-immune men could have both allowed such a bonding to take place. Each time I tried to secretly study Fantasia from a distance she would glance over at me, narrow her stare, and smile a Mona Lisa smile. I would then find myself standing helpless once again like that wildlife in the headlights.

Our high Space Systems ranks made it possible the girls were some kind of espionage incursion. If that was the case, it had worked. I wasn't willing to bail, and neither was R.J. In fact, R.J., the worst skeptic of the two of us, was entirely comfortable in his dubious relationship. As for me, I finally settled on the time-tested idiotic plan that I could quit it anytime I wanted but for now I'd let this go on a while longer and see what happened.

At the close of that cruise from hell we all had obligations to attend to. We would rendezvous later at Fantasia's castle on the planet Enuro and explore the future. Even thousands of light years apart, the link still worked. There is a very old Earth song called, "All I Have to Do Is Dream." One line is; *"whenever I want you all I have to do is dream."* That was the way it was with the link. Still together, with someone who was a million light years away. And, there was not a single thing unpleasant about it.

Sitting in the Captain's chair of a large starship, having just returned from war, old fear had surged back in. A nice home, two vehicles in the garage, a white picket fence, two-point-five children, picnics on Sunday, volunteer work at the community center.

I took the potion and broke the link.

Then never stopped arguing with myself about it.

You can run away from yourself. The only problem seems to be that the other you pisses you off eternally.

There in the distance, across the beautiful reflecting lake, clustered in Sherwood-Forest-like surroundings, rose the five towers of Fantasia's castle home. A kaleidoscope of emotions swirled through me. I barely noticed the very short, very properly adorned uniformed Enuronian attendants arrive, sliding up on a floating cart to declare themselves assigned to Ms. Danica Donoro to see for her every need. They busied themselves collecting her duffle bag then carried her away in their chariot to her personal quarters to freshen up and rest.

I stood staring at the castle across the way.

"Yep. That's it," said R.J., suddenly standing beside me.

We stared across the lake in silence. It became uncomfortable.

I said, "I don't see your better half around here anywhere."

"She'll be along. Big supper in the main dining room. Two artificial meat turkeys, everything else imaginable to go with it. Private waiters for each of us. All the Culatta Blue you can drink."

"I think you just made my night."

"Aren't you going to ask if *she'll* be there?"

Silence.

R.J. continued, "Of course she won't be there. You know how the sisters are. They know what you want before you do. She's already figured out you need some settle in time. She's the one that sent the Culatta Blue."

"Do you guys have horses?"

"A stable full."

"There are trails?"

"More than you can ride in a week. You can also ride on the neighbor properties, but they are all separated by ravine jumps. You need to be sure of your seat if you chance it."

"I think I'll take a long healthy run on those trails tomorrow morning. Maybe get something out of my system. This place is so beautiful. A person could live here forever."

"Did you really just say that?"

"Oh, I didn't mean it that way. I was thinking it's kind of fairy tale here, you know? That's all I was saying."

"Right."

"No, really."

"Here comes our host."

A polished black carriage trimmed in gold, pulled by an equally sleek high-stepping black Friesian-styled breed approached us across the lawn. Elachia pulled up on the reigns, leapt from the carriage, and locked her arms around me, head on my chest, laughing and laughing.

"Finally! I was beginning to think you'd never visit! It's about time. Consider yourself trapped. We will have fun, then we will have more fun, and then we'll have more fun after that."

She stepped back to look me over. Her thick golden hair was a styled collection of big curls. It was in a swirl above her head but fell well past the shoulders and onto her chest. Her DNA artist had given her fine features and super fine skin tone. One corner of her mouth was permanently raised in a kind of knowing, sexual smile. The rest of her was equally well sculpted. She wore high black boots and riding apparel.

She hung onto me with one hand and managed to hook her other arm through R.J.'s. We were summarily dragged to the carriage, R.J. in the back while I sat up front.

"Adrian, I'm learning to play the Earth game Golf. Do you play?"

"It's hard to tell."

"We had a course installed out back to see if we like it. I seem to have a knack for it."

"You built a golf course just to see if you like the game?"

"I believe I do," she added. "You must play with us. The putting is easy enough but sometimes I'm off a little with the long clubs."

"Oh boy."

Our trusty steed brought us to castle gates. A small uniformed guard in Enuro blue opened the arched door and we clitter-clacked through a shadowy cobblestone tunnel to a large courtyard, complete with fountains, flowers, and statues. Elachia rambled on about this and that in her soothing, melodic voice.

We were kindly sent to our rooms to change and rest. We were to explore the castle as much as we liked. There were no restricted areas. Enuro staff were at work in various shops. Dinner would be served promptly at six.

My room was a tennis-court-sized chamber, sky high ceiling with fresco and a dozen red curtains from ceiling to floor. Windowed doors on the southern side opened to a long ivory balcony overlooking the main courtyard. An attractive little blue Enuronian woman in a colorful garment that looked like a kimono asked me if I'd like assistance washing. I thanked her and declined. She short-stepped out the main door. Apparel easily suitable for several different solar systems hung in the large, long, sliding doors closet. There was a soft brown dinner jacket I decided I could bear but I pulled my jeans and a white T-shirt from my bag to complete the ensemble.

Danica did not show for dinner. When asked, Elachia giggled and tried to be evasive. Something about Danica being sighted on horseback riding with a gentleman of the

Enuronian Royal Guard, a man in black wearing a sheathed sword, a friend of hers.

R.J. leaned over next to me. "My God that was fast," he whispered. It made me laugh.

Elachia spooned her soup and gave me a provocative stare. "By the way, Adrian, Fantasia said to say *hi*. She's swamped in diplomatic work right now, but she said perhaps the two of you could get together for tea someday before you leave."

My heart skipped a beat, completely without any authority to do so. Then I remembered just how astute Elachia was at reading people, so as a diversion I opened my mouth to say something but nothing came out.

Elachia to the rescue, of course. "She's so busy these days. She took on too much, you know. Everyone wants her for negotiations. She always knows what will satisfy the two parties. But I think she needs to take some time off. The volunteer work she does is enough by itself. Did you know she was responsible for moving the Beline Tigers off Yumarna before the sun nova'd? If it wasn't for her horses she'd never have any fun."

I tried again and this time words came out. "Speaking of that, Elachia. Do you have a horse I could take for a run in the morning maybe?"

"Oh, you'll love it. The trails go on forever. I'll have them saddle Emperor. What style do you prefer?"

"On Earth it's called old fashion western? Is that okay?"

"Ah, you want a horn thing. Just fine. By the way, I understand your mission to Sol's Saturn had some controversy?"

"Questions were left unanswered," I replied.

"Do you suspect there was something underhanded going on?"

R.J. intervened, "Ela, you know we can't talk about that. Just as your diplomatic missions are also confidential." R.J. had already transmitted the sentiment psychically. The words were just a formality for my sake.

"I have great misgivings from what I sense in both of you. Rowland. Would you pour me coffee, please, dear?"

The conversation was guided into Enuro politics, then the Griffin's refitting that had been done on Enuro, and other matters of local interest. When we had consumed all the decaf possible and exhausted ourselves with an Enuronian-whipped desert, R.J. begged off. I watched as Elachia clutched his right arm, leaning hard against him as they walked off. She spoke to him in a low, very personal tone, talking endlessly to him because he was the most important person in the cosmos.

In the morning, I found that while I'd slept, someone had brought out a deep purple silk shirt, black riding pants, and high black boots. A breakfast tray stood alongside. Downstairs, eventually I found my way outside and the smell of fine horse led me to the stables. In the distance a herd of well-groomed horses looked up from grazing. In the mile-long stable, Emperor was waiting, saddled and ready to go. He snorted and shook his head impatiently. He appraised me. I tightened up a bit. He was jet black with a long mane and a full tail that had been trimmed to just touch the ground. Two uniformed staff brought him out to a portable step. I dutifully led him away from it, hopped my left foot into the stirrup and swung up and over. My Enuro support crew bowed slightly as a reward for the effort. It was a full western-styled saddle, padded seat, large horn. Emperor was a dream ride. He had the flattest of trots, the one where your hips sway from side to side, not up and down. He could be guided simply by the level you kept the reins at. No verbal queue or even heel signals were required at all. I became certain I could steer him with only leg pressure if desired. He also seemed to have a preference for particular trails. I gave him his head and he took me on a tour. Obstacles here and there on the trail required small jumps. I was notified each was coming up by a switch to a sideward trot then into a broken canter.

The colorful scenery and wildlife were awe inspiring. Trees with trunks as wide as a bus, tangled with fat limbs. At one point there was a corridor of them, some brown, others a bluish hue within the green. The trail was golden sand bordered by lush vegetation. Quick little rainbow birds seem to follow us along the way. Every so often we would ford a small running stream lined with loose shale rock, or come up against a fallen tree trunk. About an hour into the ride we came to a very long straight stretch of trail sheltered by overhanging limbs covered in cherry blossoms. Emperor stopped and began to prance in place, tossing his head, nostrils flaring. I gave him his rein and off we went. It was the smoothest wide-open gallop I had ever held to, one of those experiences you wish would last forever.

When Emperor finally broke gate and skidded in the sand to stop, we were overlooking a deep trench, probably thirty feet down to a rock streambed. The gap was at least ten feet wide. The trail continued on the opposite side. I suddenly realized from the tower in the far distance that this was the trail that led to Fantasia's. Had I taken this route subconsciously hoping to run into her? The thought caused a pang of fear. The drop off was a tempting challenge, but if you fell short on the other side the results would be catastrophic. I suddenly realized Emperor could have made the crossing easily but had stopped out of concern for me. I turned his head away and started back.

For the next two weeks of blissful vacation, Emperor and I ran the trails each morning. We got to know each other well. On one particular day when the forest was glistening with dew against the rising sun, Emperor bucked when we reached the deep trench so that I had to collect him and re-gather my seat. I looked up from my dancing horse and there across the gap sat Fantasia on a snow-white steed, smiling back at me.

Chapter 7

She was seated on a long mane, long tail Lipizzaner, the horse's head curled down against its chest. She was riding bareback, dressed in wisps of blue veil, and barefoot, her long, light-blond hair gathered around to one side. With the sun behind her, colors were glowing in an aura surrounding her. Her horse danced in place.

"Well aren't you a sight for injured eyes," she called across.

"I think you mean a sight for sore eyes."

"Oh right. I've been learning Earth idioms. You look quite fresh and rested, Adrian."

"I think it's the horse therapy."

"Here on Enuro they say there's something about the outside of a horse that's good for the inside of a man."

"Stolen from Winston Churchill, all the way from Earth."

"What?"

"Nothing. You look quite well yourself, Fan. It's been too long."

"Whose fault is that?"

"Can we ride together a ways?"

Fantasia smiled. "I don't know. There seems to be a large gulf between us."

"I'm willing to chance it."

"Are you sure?"

"You're worried the horse might get hurt?"

"No, I'm certain the horse will make it. I'm just not sure you'll still be atop him."

I did the only thing any man could do. I brought Emperor back away from the drop off, turned him sideways to it, then charged at it with poorly veiled doubt.

Emperor had no such misgivings. He presented his most noble and powerful demeanor, given that Fantasia's Lipizzaner mare was watching intently. Horses are a prideful group.

At the edge, Emperor pushed off with the back legs and went up and into a wide stretch, front feet together, ready to catch a piece of the other side. Halfway over I had to grab the horn with one hand, embarrassed to do so but not willing to gamble my neck on vanity. We thumped down on solid ground with Emperor dancing to dress up his big finish.

Fantasia's Lipizzaner was even more beautiful close up. She was an unusual silver white. The silver white mane hung way down to the shoulder and seemed to have tinsel in it somehow. Each movement brought reflections from the light. The proud tail had the same characteristic and was so long it touched the ground.

Fantasia smiled at me and laughed. She continued to sit with one leg hooked over so that it gave the appearance of side-saddle. A soft breeze kept picking up parts of her sheer blur veil revealing the soft curves beneath and rearranging the material into a completely different outfit.

Fantasia was still drop dead, world-class beautiful. Perfect features that seemed younger than her actual age, as though her beauty would be preserved throughout the passage of time. Maybe it would. Her naturally pink lips had a slight upturn to them like a kiss waiting to happen. A darkness around the blue-gray eyes felt like a gravity well pulling you in. I understood why I had broken the relationship off, but now wondered how any man could have. I suddenly realized I was staring. She was smiling and staring back. Emperor moved under me and broke the spell.

"Come on, I'll give you the tour," she said.

I suddenly realized there was not even a bridle or halter on her ride. "How are you...?"

She laughed again. "Docolena is touch-taught. Hand and foot signals."

"But can you...?"

"Come on. You'll see."

We held them back to a slow trot. Fantasia kept a large handful of mane. Fantasia's trails were as beautiful as the others. There seemed to be more small streams with waterfalls. As we went, I struggled inside trying to come up with some small talk to ease the silence. Each time I thought I had something, I discarded it and searched further.

She sensed my disquiet. "Perhaps we should canter?"

I nodded and immediately Docolena went into a slow rocking horse canter. Emperor insisted on keeping up. He was willing to stay behind but only as a guardian for the beautiful mare.

We loped our way along the winding trail of color and life and sound. There was no longer a need to break the silence. In fact, of the thousands of things that could have been said between us, silence seemed the only adequate converse.

"Your horse wants to open up. There's a straight section just around this next curve."

"Are you sure? You have nothing but horse under you."

"Silly man."

"Lead on. I will follow, My Lady."

"Wow! A sprightly moment of from you, Fine Sir. Let's see if you can keep up."

And she was gone. My only view was of her horse's tail straight out, trailing in the distance. Emperor charged ahead with warning, nearly tipping me over backwards. The forest sped by as I regained my seat and leaned into the wind. Emperor's ears were flat down in determination.

We ran and ran and ran. Occasionally I would catch up and pull up alongside her only to see her smile anew and shift to a faster gear then pull away.

We ran until there was white sweat on the chests of the horses. She finally slowed as we approached a slope that was a series of loop back trails going down. It was like riding down into a forest-covered valley. Near the bottom, she followed a stream and stopped for a moment to let our rides drink.

"You'll love this next part," she said, and she led on to a massively large cave entrance that narrowed as we entered. The trail into the cavern was well worn. The air became cool. There were small tunnels of light coming from above. The light diffracted into unearthly colors on the wet, irregular walls. We followed an underground stream deep into a place where stalactites sometimes forced us to maneuver around. As I began to wonder how deep we would go, a horseshoe-shaped light appeared in the distance. We exited the cave into an open area with a wildflower garden.

There was a tan stone gazebo within it, with marble seats and a statue that looked like the Goddess Athena.

"I brought my lunch. I think they're cooled down enough. They would like some time alone together. Let's get down and I'll share it with you, Adrian."

"Should I pull off my saddle and bridle?"

"Just the bridle would be good and loosen the cinch. They'll graze."

So we let the horse wander free and sat beside the goddess Athena. We ate some sort of fish sandwich and drank ice tea from a thermos too cold to hold.

I finally got up the nerve to ask, "Fan, are you linked to anyone?"

"That's a bit right-to-the-point, isn't it? Funny you should put it that way, Adrian. I do not link with just anyone. It has to be a particular someone."

"You know what I'm asking."

"Yes, and as I said, a bit indelicate. I go out quite regularly when my schedule allows. But, link with someone? No. Not yet. But my social life is very satisfying. By the way, the Starship Star Seven has returned to service. I was asked to be an ambassador on an upcoming diplomatic junket. I turned them down this time."

"No, serious relationship? Yet, probably every man anywhere would give his right arm to be with you."

"Not *every* man, Adrian."

Before I could try to recover from my repeated stumbles, a communicator somewhere on her person bleeped. She smiled and took the call. I could not hear the conversation, only her answer.

"Very well. I'll be right there."

She clicked off and gave a frown. "They say it is an emergency. I don't know what. Probably some negotiation that is disintegrating. Anyway, they think it is life or death. I'll have to hurry Docolena back to the stable. Can you find your way back?"

"I'm sure Emperor can."

We stood and gathered up our things.

Fantasia packed away her items, came to me and gave a kiss on the cheek. I watched her slim figure vault up on that big horse, cast a last long look, and turn away into a gallop. I felt part of myself pulling away with her.

Emperor and I found our way back to Elachia's without a problem. The jump over the ravine was a little less confident, but just as successful. In the stable, I waved off the staff and unsaddled Emperor, and gave him a good brush down as he cashed in on fresh hay. In my room a set of clothes had already been put out. I showered and dressed in dark slacks and white silk shirt and made it downstairs just in time for the early dinner.

R.J. eyed me with a smirk. Elachia tried to appear disinterested. Danica was again absent. We ate and traded comments on everything possible, topics that were of no importance at all. Everyone was tired from the events of the day. We retreated to our rooms. I spent the night twisting and turning in half sleep. I dared not dream.

The new morning was misty, so much so it could have qualified as rain. The staff had saddled Emperor and given him hay in his stall in case I still wanted to go. They had also left a long coat and wide-brimmed western-styled hat. The weather was of no concern to Emperor. Fog or not the ride was too inviting to skip. Emperor volunteered to trot down the first length of trail. Half an hour into the ride we stopped to look over a wet, glistening cliff side. My cell went off. It was Fantasia.

"Adrian, meet me at the drop off right away."

"Now? You're riding in this weather?"

"Yes, to find you! This is important."

I held it to a canter. My soul wanted to go faster. At the trench she was already waiting.

She had on soaking wet formal business-styled clothes. Her hair was drenched. She looked like a fairy princess in a drizzle of rain, but her expression was one of concern.

She called out as I moved up to the edge. "Adrian, you've got to get back to Earth right away! I've already told them to prepare Griffin for departure."

"Are you kidding? Why?"

"Something's wrong. Something serious."

"What?"

"They don't know. Communications were cutoff a couple days ago. There were some maydays from ships. Then a Nasebien emissary appeared in the Enuro council chamber and specifically requested you get back there."

"That's unbelievable! Me? The emissary requested me? You're kidding?"

"You know there's a long communication lag between here and Earth. Whatever is going on there we're finding out very late. This is very high-level stuff, Adrian. I've already called Elachia. The staff should be bringing Griffin out when you arrive."

"You could have just called me."

She paused and her expression softened. "I wanted to see you again before you left."

"Oh, yeah, me too."

"You better get going."

She reined Docolena around, looked back, and cantered away, disappearing into the mist.

Chapter 8

No one had any answers. There was an Enurian High Council Diplomatic Request delivered by courier directing us to hurry and get back to Earth. That was the new mission. We were in space at light, less than four hours later, still wondering why. Originally our trip had been to pick up Elachia, so there was no leaving her behind, but she mumbled during launch about too many misadventures. Danica had to be taken directly to her sleeping compartment, still only semiconscious from too many nights of partying. I wasn't sure she even knew we were leaving Enuro.

Once we were set up and on course with auto pilot engaged, the three of us began working the comm systems, looking for any signals of Earth origin or even traffic-comm from those coming and going. All we needed was a single packet communication from Earth to reassure us that things there were at least somewhat normal, but all the Earth-comm streams seemed to have gone silent.

Four hours into our channel searching we were left confounded. R.J. and Elachia leaned into the flight deck and stared at me with confused looks.

R.J. tried to sound unconvinced that there really was a major problem. "Well, it's not as though there aren't any communications coming out of there. There are a few seconds of carrier occasionally. It's just that it's fragmented garbage. That may mean sunspot interference or some other natural phenomena."

"There are occasional bits of voice communication that seem almost coherent," added Elachia.

"Yeah, I've picked up pieces of those too," I replied. "Doesn't sound like sunspots to me."

"It's got to be subspace distortion. Stuff has to still be working on Earth," said R.J.

"But the bits of voice transmission are unintelligible. They're like gibberish," added Elachia.

"See! That's got to mean some form of communication interference," said R.J. "But it's funny, voice and data streams from the outer planets are normal. They're having the same trouble contacting Earth as everyone else. So the problem must be isolated to Earth."

Elachia said, "We must face the fact that after four hours of collecting comm fragments, we have not been able to string together even one understandable line of communication from Earth. That indicates a fundamental planetary problem of some kind."

I looked up at them. "In a few days we'll be close enough to communicate real time with the Musk City Station on Mars, and some of the other outposts. Until then, let's monitor spacecraft channels, see if we can find anyone outgoing who knows anything."

And that was what we did. For days we sifted through a pile of garbage that was data and audio communications originating from the Terran System. Except for constant attempts by the outer planets to contact Earth, there was nothing but small fragments of Earth comm streams. R.J. graphed the collection of findings which seemed to suggest momentary Earth transmissions on a periodic basis. Elachia attempted to analyze the subspace carrier structure but found nothing wrong with it. By the time we were approaching Sol's heliopause, we had talked ourselves into believing nothing was wrong with Earth except an unusually disruptive burst from a solar flare or a new nearby pulsar that no one had yet identified. As soon as we were in real-time range, R.J. donned an engineering headset and worked excitedly to contact Mars Station.

"Utopia Planitia, this is Starship Griffin."

"Utopia Planitia, this is Starship Griffin."

I switched the comm to external speaker. It took them a full five minutes to respond. They seemed surprised that anyone was contacting them. "Griffin, UP Control here. Please state your location and destination."

R.J. wrinkled his brow. It was an unusual way to make contact. "UPC, Griffin, approaching Mars perihelion, inbound for Kennedy Space Center."

"Griffin, have you made contact with KSC OTC?"

"Negative UPC. There seems to be communications interference."

"Griffin, be advised, we have not been able to establish contact with Earth for several weeks."

Danica looked at me and rolled her eyes.

"Griffin, we strongly advise that you abort your approach to Earth."

Danica jerked her head forward in disbelief.

R.J. looked forward at us and gave an incredulous stare. "Did they really just say that?"

"Griffin, we repeat, we recommend you abort your approach to Earth."

Danica became sarcastic, "And do what, live happily ever after here?"

I readjusted my mike and clicked in. "UPC, please standby."

"Dan, how long before we pass by Mars?"

"We'll intersect Mars' Earth orbit in nine minutes."

"Let's drop out of light now and take a few minutes for a little chat, shall we?"

Danica went to work. "Gladly."

We strapped in and waited for Griffin to back pedal us to normal space. At station keeping I looked back from the copilot seat to be sure Elachia was paying attention. It was unnecessary.

"UPC this Captain Adrian Tarn. Would you please identify yourself?"

"UPC Resident Director Ethan Grayson, Captain. It's good to speak with someone arriving to help."

"Can you tell us the nature of this emergency? This is not just some sort of communications glitch?"

"Captain, we have not received any support shipments or staff members from Earth for several weeks. Two security shuttles were dispatched to KSC to find out why there have been no communications and no resupply. We lost contact with both when they were approximately 400 kilometers from Earth orbital insertion. We recommend you abort your flight plan until this situation is understood."

"UPC, what about contact with Lunar Station One?"

"Captain, negative contact with Lunar Station One."

Danica shook her head and whispered. "You've got to be kidding."

"UPC, what about contact with Saturn Three?"

"Saturn Three is in the same situation that we are; negative resupply, negative comm or data.

Apparently, the loss of signal is confined to the Earth and Moon only."

"UPC, haven't you registered any ships departing Earth?"

"No radar or marker beacon contacts with any vessels departing Earth have been registered for weeks."

"Director Grayson, have you issued requests for assistance?" asked R.J.

"We have, but our manifest records show the nearest command level ship to be the Electra and it is several weeks out."

I asked, "So are you or any other installation in danger because of no resupply, Director?"

"Not at this time, Captain. As I'm sure you know, we are all required to maintain a twelve-month supply of all critical materials."

To my surprise, Elachia spoke into R.J.'s headset, "Director, do you have any visuals of Earth that show anything?"

"Unfortunately, with all the satellite networks in that region down, the only sightings we can do are by direct optics. We haven't been in a position to get much from that, just low-resolution images that we're trying to clean up. They don't show anything useful."

"Director, standby," I said.

"Captain, perhaps you should consider putting in here so we can discuss this in greater detail. Possibly more information will come in."

I looked around at my concerned group. "Suggestions anyone?"

Danica spoke first, "We need to get closer."

"Never to be heard from again?" mused R.J.

"Somebody's got to go," countered Danica.

I looked back at Elachia. "Anything more from the engineering consoles?"

"Rowland and I have monitored Sol during this entire trip. There has been nothing unusual in the signature of the solar wind and no abnormal sunspot activity. We've seen no cosmic influence that would interfere with Earth communications."

R.J. spoke hesitantly, "We haven't considered that Earth might be under attack of some kind."

"There would've been activity everywhere and comm channels full of enemy exchanges," replied Danica.

"It depends," answered R.J. "Remember the Salantian Spiders? They show up without warning through stargates."

"I don't like that idea at all, R.J.," said Danica.

I interrupted. "So it sounds as though we are all in agreement we need to get closer?"

R.J. nodded, "Cautiously."

I clicked on my mike. "Director, we're going to try for a closer look."

"Griffin, recommend you stay well back from the Moon's apogee."

"No, we got that, Director Grayson. We'll keep a data channel open to you at all times, and we'll report in as soon as we know anything."

"Very much appreciated, Captain. I don't have to tell you how important Griffin is to us right now."

"Tarn out. So, R.J., Elachia please strap in the engineering stations and run wide scans from here on in. Anything at all out of the ordinary and we stop and back off a ways. Danica, plot us to just outside four hundred thousand miles and take us there slowly say, set power to make it a two-hour trip. That should be slow enough to spot anything out of the ordinary."

R.J. spoke as he buckled up. "I've got to tell you, Adrian. I'm suddenly really worried about this. Invasion is the only thing I can come up with that would explain this."

Danica added, "In a real invasion they wouldn't have broadcast it, either. They would've stayed off the air."

"So, anyone want to disembark at Utopia Planitia before we go?" I asked.

"Dumb question, Adrian. That's a really dumb question," answered Danica.

"Very well. Engage."

Thirty minutes into our slow approach there was still nothing to indicate a problem with Earth, and the familiar blue star was now easily visible. At the one hour mark I began to have doubts again that maybe this was all a big misunderstanding, a simple interruption of departures and communications due to some unexpected cosmic event.

As we left the halfway mark behind us, Elachia finally called out, "Something on radar."

R.J. added, "I see it too. 090 mark 14. Whatever it is, it's only just beyond the moon's orbit, Adrian. Two hundred and sixty thousand miles out. That's a bit closer than we'd like."

Elachia said, "It's either traveling very slowly or it's drifting."

"Got an ID on it?" I asked.

"Negative. No transponder being broadcast," replied Elachia.

I started to ask for rendezvous time but was interrupted.

"Oh, oh! There's another one, Adrian," said Elachia. "315 mark 19. This one seems to be station keeping. It's just two hundred and five thousand out. Well inside Lunar orbit perigee."

I looked over at Danica. "Would you set up a fast escape panic code? Something that will allow the autopilot to take us immediately out of here at the push of a button in case these are hostiles?"

"Sure thing, Adrian."

"We should also transfer some power to bring up shields, and would you wake up both cannons, charge them, and have them ready to fire?"

"Wow! I'm on it."

"R.J. is there anything at all to tell whether these guys are hostiles or not?"

"Not yet," he replied.

"Well, you guys stay strapped in and be ready for a sudden exit then. We'll alter course to drop us out of light within visual range of the object that's closest. The one on our starboard. R.J. concentrate your scans on both contacts. Elachia, would you focus yours on Earth. We'll keep moving in slowly and drop out in about twenty minutes."

"We've got Earth on camera four," said Elachia a few minutes later. "Nothing to see yet. Still just a blue star."

"We also have a pencil dot on monitor three. It's that first outbound radar contact," added R.J. "Still no confirmed bad guys on the wide scan radar."

As we closed in, R.J. added, "It is definitely a ship and it isn't under power. It's drifting."

"R.J., you still have no transponder info?" I asked.

"Just pulses of completely garbled data. No ID."

Danica added, "We're coming up on drop out, Adrian. I have the panic button programmed, shields are now up, guns charged."

"Standby for decel in one minute everyone," I called out.

Our view out the windows blurred. We were pulled gently forward in our seats. The sun and stars returned to space normal appearance.

Danica quickly nudged Griffin slightly to starboard to center us on the target ship. "All stopped and station keeping," she said.

Before I could ask, R.J. began stepping the camera through magnifications to zoom in on the vessel in question.

"Looks all normal so far. Weird," remarked R.J.

"You got engine emissions?" I asked.

"Dead," he replied.

We all took a moment to study the magnified image on overhead monitor number three. It was a small cargo vessel with a wide, orange, forward flight deck probably with living and crew quarters directly behind it. A long superstructure with a dozen gray cargo modules attached to each side, modules shaped like half a pentagonal prism intended also to fit into the cargo hold of an orbiting cargo descent vehicle, or the land-craft trailer that would receive them. At the tail end of the ship, two plasma drives nacelles that should have been glowing blue were dark. In fact, there was not a portal on the ship illuminated.

"What do you guys think?" I asked.

"Closer," was Danica's immediate reply.

"With due caution," added R.J.

"Let's do a single orbit of it as you move closer, Danica."

"My thoughts exactly."

We cut our distance in half. The port side of the ship looked normal. The tail section showed worn, dark engine emitters.

But as we came around from behind to starboard, R.J. was the first to notice something. "What's that blurry cloud just behind the flight deck section? Is that a debris field?"

"Scans are showing a hole there. A pretty big hole," said Elachia.

"You guys still are watching the wide scans, right? There's nothing out there headed our way, right?"

"It's clear in every direction, Adrian," replied Elachia.

"It doesn't look like weapons damage, Adrian," said R.J. "It looks like from the inside out."

"Okay Danica. Half again please."

"Continue to circle?" she asked.

"No. Let's get a better look at the damage."

We crept in like a mouse sneaking up on a piece of cheese in a mousetrap. We stopped with the ship and its debris field full in our flight deck windows. The ragged hole in the side of the ship was the size of a cargo door.

"Is that somebody's shoe wedged in the side of that hole?" asked R.J.

There was no mistaking it. An athletic shoe, its lace wrapped around a twisted piece of superstructure floated just outside the torn opening. No one answered. We sat in silence trying to understand.

"I have to ask, still no comm contact?" But I already knew the answer.

Again no one replied, an affirmation that this ship was probably a floating grave site. It was very slowly passing by us, still coasting along its previous heading.

"What do you think, Danica? Can we dock with it?"

Chapter 9

"There's a hatchway directly over the flight deck section. It looks flat enough for a docking but we'd need to use our docking ring. When's the last time you used it?" she asked.

"Oh brother. I can't remember."

"Has it been included in the annual inspections?"

"Yes."

"No problem. We extend it and if we get a good seal, we're in. If not, we retract it back into its compartment and do something else."

"Okay, let's do it."

"So we're going inside this thing?" asked R.J.

"Anyone have any better ideas?"

Silence.

"You know I'm the one going with you, right?" said R.J.

"It would be a waste of breath trying to talk you out of it," I replied.

Danica brought Griffin around, thrusted over to the target vehicle's front end, then rolled us on our side to match our front airlock outer door with the hatch atop the other ship. She called up the mating program on her nav display along with an extra starboard camera, and with very quick, tiny jets of thrust moved us over the top of the cargo ship, deftly aligning the hatches for docking without affecting the other ship's attitude, no small achievement. When she was within limits, she brought in docking position station-keeping, gave me a quick sign of fingers crossed, and tapped the deploy-docking-ring control icon. We watched as access doors slid open and the accordion tunnel slowly ballooned out to embrace the other ship's hatch. We turned together to study the docking nav screen. To my surprise, the red pressurization icon turned to green.

"Piece of cake," said Danica.

"I am impressed, as always, Ma'am."

"So this means we could all go over," commented Elachia.

"Actually Danica's got to stay to watch the dock, and you need to be here to explain how we were lost, Elachia."

"I do not consider that to be funny, Adrian."

"I'm sorry. We need you here to keep scanning for approaching unfriendlies."

"You guys realize that entire ship is probably depressurized anyway. You're probably not going anywhere," said Danica.

"You want to take a hand scanner and check that R.J.? I'd like to watch over the docking stability for a few more minutes."

"You stay ready to get out of that docking tunnel, R.J.," added Elachia. "If a cylinder or something bursts over there, Griffin's reaction control might not be able to adjust quickly enough."

"Okay, but I hate womanly intuition."

I waited in the pilot's seat while R.J. worked in the airlock, sealing off our flight deck and the aft area of the ship for safety. I watched the panel closely as he opened the outer airlock door. We waited as he floated free and pushed over to the other ship's sealed hatch. After a long five minutes, R.J. announced, "Their flight deck is still pressurized but their hatch is jammed."

I nodded to Danica and climbed out of my seat. Presumably it was safe to open the flight deck to the forward airlock but Danica watched closely as I opened the pressure hatch. In the airlock I pushed into the transfer tube to meet R.J. a few feet away. I tried the other ship's hatch. The emergency release panel door slid open smoothly. The release lever pulled down easily. The door should have hissed and unsealed, but there was nothing.

"It's definitely jammed," said R.J. He put a foot against the superstructure and pulled on it with both hands.

Nothing.

I joined in but even together we could not open that door.

I shook my head. "It's either warped or something's overriding the release mechanism."

R.J. gave me a perplexed look. "It would take an explosive to open this thing. We know there's structural damage. I'll bet this hatch is just wedged tight."

"Why does it always have to be the hard way?" I answered.

"We're not getting in this way. That's for sure, and I already know what you have in mind."

"Yeah, let's go see if that hole is big enough for an EVA suit."

So we closed up and waited as Griffin re-stowed the mating ring. Once again to my pleasant surprise the seldom-used accordion adapter compressed into its compartment and the compartment doors slid closed.

"So I'm guessing you guys will want to go out the aft airlock and in through that hole now?" said Danica.

"How come everyone here knows what I want to do before I say anything?"

"Backing away and reorientating," added Danica.

I gestured to R.J. "Join me in the suit area, sir?"

"Why thank-you. I believe I shall," he replied.

Danica set us up with the rear airlock hatch roughly aligned with the debris field and big hole in the side of the other ship. She had to jet thrusters from a good bit of distance and then wait for us to drift in closer to avoid disrupting the debris. She could not use station keeping for fear of thrusting too close. A very skilled manual control was needed to avoid stirring things up.

R.J. and I quietly suited up.

"Of course I'll be careful," he finally said, matter-of-factly.

"I know that," I replied.

"No, I was talking to Elachia. She's up front with Danica. She's not too crazy about this idea."

"Having a conversation with someone who's not here still bewilders me. You've got a strap hanging out the back of your suit pants."

"You've had those little silent talks yourself."

"What?"

"Carried on conversations with Fantasia before you broke the link."

"Can you hand me my gloves over there?"

"Still changing the subject when Fantasia's name comes up, aren't we? I *promise* to be watching for sharp edges, honey. Don't worry."

"I know that. Don't call me Honey. It's not funny."

"Witty rhyme Tarn but no, I was talking to Elachia again."

"This is too weird. It's like there's three of us here. You need help with the torso?"

"Nope, us short guys get under and up easy. Better than you tall ornery guys."

"She didn't really say I was ornery. I met her on horseback. She was nice to me."

"Yeah, so?"

"You ready for helmet?"

"Channel one?"

"Channel one."

As a common gesture of courtesy I grabbed R.J.'s helmet, gave him a big smile, and put the fish bowl over his head. It twisted smoothly into lock.

"Okay you got me?" he asked on the comm.

"Loud and clear. Your pressure is coming up already. Let me just snap my hat and I'll join you, Bubble Head."

"So that's the way it's going to be, Ornery? What are we going to do if we actually get in there?"

"Try to figure out what the hell happened to them and what the hell is going on."

"You going to open the inside doors to the flight deck if you can?"

"We'll try knocking first."

"There could still be unconscious people alive in there."

"If we get that far we'll try the knocking then decide."

"I'm up to pressure, the gas mixture is correct, and it's started the depress adjustment program."

Danica cut in over the com, "Gentlemen, I have your vitals. You are all green here, if not professional."

R.J. started to rock his way toward the outer door.

"I need another minute or two, Balloon Boy," I said.

"Man, this is the most ornery I've ever seen you! We're probably on our way over to a giant casket, you know? Shouldn't you be somber or something?"

"She never said I was ornery."

"It's okay. I'll be somber enough for both of us. This sort of thing gives me the creeps."

"Okay let's open up."

"Inner door good seal."

Danica squelched in, "Confirming good seal."

"Unlocking outer. Waiting for airlock depress."

When the door's display screen turned green, we turned down the latch to let the door pop inward then slide to one side. Beyond the door was a discomforting view of a spacecraft parts-cloud and beyond it a gaping black hole in the side of a large gray vehicle that should not have been there. There were tools, pieces of cargo tarps, fragments of metal, a spacesuit helmet, nuts and bolts, globs of leak seal, a cargo strap, rolls of wire, and a few larger pieces of space craft panels. It was a truly alarming, macabre view. Below us was an endless star fall. To one side, departure point Earth, to the other and above, a similar star beauty. But directly ahead, forefront of all that beauty, an ominous scene of destruction and probable death.

"So over the ball of crap, not through, right?" asked R.J.

"Right."

We pushed out of Griffin's gravity and jetted up above the carnage. From above we could look out over the long body of the spacecraft, its gray cargo segments locked together like ribs. There were yellow rectangles on the top of each and I finally noticed the name Orconian spread out over the center frame.

"See what you have on the name Orconian, Elachia."

"Standby."

The tail section continued to look completely intact, the top of the forward crew section also undamaged despite its jammed hatchway.

"R.J. let's see what we can see through the flight deck windows."

We thrusted along the top of the Orconian to the nose section. We turned in place to face the forward windows. They were frozen over enough that our vision of the interior was a blur. Using the suit's snail-mode, we moved in until we could touch the windows. I wiped away a clear spot and tapped my upper jets to get my helmet almost to the window's surface.

They were in there, staring out at me in frozen death. Both pilots were still strapped in their seats, looks of surprise horror on their chalky faces. Two rear flight deck control panels were still illuminated. The front panels appeared to be dark.

I gently pushed myself away. "We've got to go in to see what we can see."

"I agree," replied R.J.

R.J. followed as I maneuvered along the top of Orconian once more. We descended feet first to the hole, brushing aside small bits of floating debris. The hole was large enough to enter, but had ragged edges curled outward as though the explosion had happened from within. The interior was so dark our helmet lights brightened before we'd even entered.

"No gravity," remarked R.J.

"And this thing did have it," I added.

We moved inward, very conscious of the jagged edges as Elachia had warned. I pulled myself inside rather than use suit jets. The place was tomblike. More debris floated in place. Blankets, clothing, personal items. This had been the sleeping compartment area, the last place you'd expect an explosion to happen. Some bunk compartments were closed off by accordion doors. Others were partially open and empty. There were no lost souls floating in this cold vacuum.

I could hear R.J. checking his breathing as he searched. Slowly he returned to EVA normal respiration.

The compartment walls were a Navy green. There was one closed hatch in the forward bulkhead that led toward the flight deck. It had a live flashing indicator panel next to it, suggesting there was atmosphere on the other side.

"We'll never get past it," said R.J. as I took a closer look.

"Good chance I can bypass it," I replied and I drew my suit tool kit from my left pant leg pouch.

"Sure you want to?" he asked.

"We've got to get to the bottom of this, R.J. I have a feeling our situation is worse than we think."

"There could be a closed compartment between us and the flight deck. There could be somebody unconscious but alive in there," he added fearfully.

"Yeah, use your hand scanner on the hatch while I try to open this keypad panel."

R.J. held his scanner against the door. He gave it a full sixty seconds. "Nope. Nothing. But it could be so cold in there we don't get life signs."

"After what we've seen, I'm going to take the chance," I replied.

The cover on the hatch control finally came loose just by twisting it around. It floated by wires. As I expected, it was a simple switching mechanism. Jumping a hot wire to the correct door control line would unlock the hatch. I twisted and wiggled off the fattest wire of the bunch, the wire I thought was the hot lead, then

Six Seconds

began poking the other wire connections one by
one. On the third attempt, there was a big
"click," from the door. I looked at R.J. and we
exchanged grim expressions.

"You hang on that side, I'll take this side. I'll
swing the handle. Ready?" I said.

"For what, exactly?" he replied. "Yeah, go
ahead."

The handle snapped down easily. The heavy
hatch burst open to a rush of escaping air. Debris
around the room whirlpooled from it. We both
had to keep wiping stuff away and holding on. As
we struggled, a man's body came floating out like
a chalk-white superman. He wore a light-green
flight suit. His name was embroidered above the
left pocket; *Roy*. His hands were clasped in front
of him. He had a wide-eyed stare, glassy eyes,
frozen black hair. To my relief and dread it was
clear he had been dead for some time.

R.J. was checking his breathing again.

As the storm of garbage settled down in the
steady flow of escaping air, I managed to look
around into the next compartment. Something
didn't make sense.

"I'm going to tie this guy down," said R.J. "I'd
prefer he not pop out the side. You go ahead. I'll
be right behind you."

I pulled myself into the next compartment
and tried to get my bearings, but the place was a
mess. There was no up or down. This was the
common living area and kitchen. Usually they are
set up with a standard floor and ceiling
represented, but this area had no set layout. The
bodies of two more crewmen made the sight
even more arcane. One body was upside down in
a corner, feet together, hands holding his head.
The other was captured underneath a dining
table, but the table was positioned against one
wall and had been welded to it. Welded furniture

was a normal arrangement in any environment that could become weightless but locating a table on a wall was absurd. Two chairs which would have complemented the table were welded to what should have been the floor. A kitchenette and counter were embedded in the opposite wall but strangely were only two feet high. The size discrepancy caused me to stare as my mind tried to resolve the disproportion. On the wall opposite me the hatch to the flight deck waited. It was at an odd forty-five-degree angle but its lock light was green.

It took a kick off the nearest wall to send me forward across the room, wiping more debris out of the way as I went. The opening of the oddly orientated hatch would cause another rush of air, so taking cover alongside was again necessary. I clanked down the handle and braced. The door inched open. Surprisingly, no atmosphere escaped.

A careful tug on the door opened it the rest of the way. Another wary look beyond showed it was indeed the flight deck, sealed in a vacuum long before we 'd arrived. The two pilots were still in their seats. It was a good guess they had died from rapid depressurization.

I suddenly realized we hadn't kept our promise to communicate with Griffin and they'd been hearing R.J.'s interrupted breathing and watching our helmet cams.

"Griffin, there's no one left alive over here."

"Understand no survivors, Adrian," answered Danica.

In the heavy silence that followed, I pushed forward off a bulkhead and held myself between the two grossly deformed spacemen. Then there was something else even more unreal. The legs of the man in the right seat were embedded up to the knee in the control panel. It was such an incomprehensible sight I had to maneuver over to one side to be sure it wasn't an optical illusion.

There was no damage to the control panel. There was no blood stain from the first officer's legs. They looked as though they had become a part of the panel. There was no choice but to push against one leg to see if it still might be an optical illusion but the leg was tightly embedded in the metal and surrounding gages. A floating tablet bumped my helmet and startled me. I backed away and turned to find R.J. staring from behind.

"What the hell, Adrian?"

"Good choice of words," I replied.

"How did they die?"

"Rapid decompression. The pressure doors were all unsealed when the explosion happened. They couldn't close up in time. It killed them and the computer finished closing up the compartments. Something went wrong here on the flight deck. It never pressurized."

"And what's with the first officer sticking out of the instrument panel and this mangled interior?"

"No idea."

"I understand less now than when we entered."

"Maybe we can pull a memory module from somewhere and take it back with us."

"It's a standard layout. They use gel tubes. They'll be in one of these rear compartments here. Let me check."

While he searched for computer memory modules, I took a closer look at the Captain. His face was less distorted. Bald head with ripples running down the brow to the nose. Sideward slits for breathing. Round eyes bulging. Wide lips that looked like lizard skin. Four fingers on each hand. Left hand still grasping the side joystick control, two fingers embedded right through it just like the copilot's legs. As best I could tell both pilots had looks of disbelief on the faces.

"I've got them. A good dozen. Let me tuck them in and let's get the hell out of here before we end up like these guys."

"Are you sure those are the right ones?"

"Absolutely. They must be the flight deck recorder memory. There are no others I can find."

"We need to seal the ship back up for future posterity," I said. "Did you fasten Roy down good?"

"He won't be going anywhere. Let's get out of here."

Finally, a call came from Griffin. "Adrian, R.J., do you know what caused the explosion?" asked Elachia.

"Man, I hadn't even thought about that," said R.J. as we moved back into the distorted living area. "You know, I haven't seen any sign of burning or explosive residue anywhere. It's like a big hole from nowhere."

"We'll take another look. I don't see any damage to these bodies and this middle chamber was still at one atmosphere."

We pushed back to the sleeping section and closed the hatch behind us but made no attempt to lock it.

"See! No burn marks. No powder residue. Even antimatter would have melted some of this."

"Elachia, we can find no explanations for anything over here," I said.

Elachia answered, "We've seen the structural damage on your helmet cams. Perhaps you should bring a victim back with you for autopsy," she answered.

I held to the bulkhead and looked at R.J. "She can do that? I mean... Elachia, you can do that?"

"You have a good med lab here. Yes, I can operate a medical scanner."

"Oh man, I don't know," complained R.J. "Do we really need to do that?"

I replied, "We need to decide right now. We'll have to put the body back when she's done."

"So one of us has to bring Roy along," said R.J. with great distaste.

"Okay, I'll do it. You head back. Roy and I will be right behind you."

Back in the sleeping section I unhooked frozen-man from the bulkhead and turned him so that he was pointing toward the hole.

There is no dignified way to drag a body along while you are crossing weightlessly through space. Unfortunately, I had done it before. You can grab onto a frozen arm but that takes up one hand used for suit joystick control. There is a suit leash of course, with a nice clip but it has to capture the top of the shirt so that the cadaver follows in a reasonably straight line as opposed to plowing along behind you. Roy's flight suit had a zipper. I had to use a pocket tool to make a hole in the top of his suit to latch into. Roy stared at me in silent disapproval.

So there went the three of us. A sad parade, up and over the debris field and down to the aft airlock entrance. The med lab is just behind the aft airlock so it was a relief that we would not have to carry Roy through the living area gravity in Griffin. There were some awkward moments positioning him in the airlock. We dragged Roy indignantly across the floor, then had to step back and forth over him to close up which wasn't easy in space suits. The three of us waited in silence for the pressure to come up to one atmosphere while our suits followed in recompression stages to match it. When that had been accomplished, and our mixtures readout showed standard, we popped our helmets off and hurried to unsuit, because Roy was slowly thawing out.

"Oh I'm not sure this was such a good idea," said R.J.

"And we were worried about everyone seeing a body," I added.

"Can you see if my suit torso is hooked into the stand?"

"Excuse me, Roy." I stepped over and adjusted R.J.'s docking latch.

R.J.'s head disappeared down into the suit.

As we continued to get down to our suit liners, the forward inner airlock door slowly opened and Elachia peered in. She stared down at Roy and seemed completely uninterested in us in our suit underwear.

"No sign of trauma at all?" she asked.

"Not a mark on him that we've noticed," I answered.

"We've got some telephoto images of Earth, but they're not good enough."

"What do you see?" asked R.J.

"Signs of destruction in some areas, but nothing makes sense. I'll set up the examination table in the med lab. We'll need to remove everything he's wearing."

"Just what kind of medical training do you have, Elachia?" I asked.

"I have a small degree in general medicine."

"A small degree?"

"A small degree, oh wait, you call it a minor degree."

"So does that mean you're actually a doctor?"

"It depends what planet you are on."

She pushed past us and over Roy. I finished stowing my suit and dropped my liner down to my waist.

"I'll wait in the med lab," said Elachia and she disappeared through the hatch.

R.J. was already pulling on his coveralls.

"Did you know she was a doctor?" I asked.

"She acquired that degree when she was a teenager. I don't think she's actually a doctor like we think of a doctor, but she's got that perfectly engineered mind, so who knows what she is."

"So you don't even know who your significant other really is?"

"You'd be in the same boat if you weren't so ornery."

"Oh boy."

"You want the head or the feet?"

We rocked and struggled Roy into the med lab and hoisted him onto the silver table using too little finesse. Elachia narrowed her stare at us then began cutting away Roy's flight suit.

"If you don't need me for anything, I'll leave you three alone," I said.

"Actually, both you gentlemen can be excused," she replied.

As we stepped out of the lab R.J. straighten his hair back into the usual Einstein mess and asked, "Are you thinking what I'm thinking?"

"Everybody over there is dead, fresh body on the slab? It's Miller time. Or, a large bourbon on the rocks?"

"So indeed you are. Of course, we are technically on duty."

"It should be considered medicinal. When will we not be on duty?"

"Point taken. I'll get the ice."

"Let's take a look at those Earth stills and figure out a toast."

"We'll meet at engineering station two then."

"If she calls for help cutting and sawing back there, that'll be you," I said.

"Make mine a double."

Chapter 10

R.J. already had cups with ice and two tablets with imagery at the conference table when I arrived with the bottle. Danica had set the ship's station keeping to automatic with audible alarms. She took a seat beside R.J. I stood leaning over between them. After one quick toast to us, followed by a healthy burn of bourbon we began stepping through the Earth pictures.

"Still not close enough," said R.J.

"There's almost two hours of telephoto here," said Danica. "We're looking at China in these first few. You can see there's some really weird stuff down there."

"I see three separate large smoke trails," said R.J. "Some places are burning."

"And even in the unpopulated forest areas there seems to be some form of impact destruction in some places," added Danica.

"Starting to look like Earth was attacked," said R.J.

"You got a good one of a large city somewhere?" I asked.

Danica stepped through the pictures to find one in particular. "This is Japan. Want to see something really crazy?"

"I can just make out big clogs of traffic," said R.J.

Danica pointed. "But look closely right here. We're still not close enough, but this little area right here looks like a major bridge collapse, but if you stare at it, it looks like this section of bridge has bent ninety degrees to the south without breaking, or am I just imagining it?"

"We've got to get closer," said R.J.

"We may already be too close," I replied.

"I've set up a probe. We can send it to a synchronous orbit, but it will still take almost two days to get there. We'll get hi-res close-ups then," said Danica.

"Launch it, Dan," I replied.

We stood silently sipping and staring at the images as Danica went forward to launch our probe. I dared to refill my cup. R.J. held out his. Before we could find something to say, Elachia appeared in a white lab smock, removing her surgical gloves. She looked around for a disposal compartment. R.J. pointed her in the right direction.

"Well, that didn't take long," she said, and she eyed our cups.

"You want one?" I asked.

"Are you kidding?" she replied.

I started to say, "No?" but R.J. waved me off and went to get another cup. He returned with ice brimming from it and poured. Elachia took it, sipped and sighed.

"You were correct. There wasn't a mark on the body," she said.

"So it was rapid decompression, right?"

"Royland Ducartes Bellimunia. Communications Officer for the Orconian. He had a security badge in his clothes. The scanner recognized their language immediately."

R.J. asked, "So Adrian is correct, right? Rapid decompression?"

"I don't know exactly what killed him, dear. Every cell in his body has been disrupted. Brain, heart, internal organs. He never had a chance."

"It *wasn't* decompression?" persisted R.J.

"No, Darling. I know what *didn't* kill him. I just don't know what *did* kill him. His entire cell structure was disrupted. It was not a disruptor weapon, either. They leave damage in a localized area, not uniformly over the entire body."

"Some sort of large disruptor field?" I asked.

"Yes, a field perhaps, and it passed through him from the front to the back. There is slightly heavier distortion on the front side of the body."

"Have you ever seen anything like this or read anything that might be related?" asked R.J.

"No. This is new as far as I can tell. There will be no medical books to consult on this I would guess."

"At least we've learned something. A disruptor wave of some kind."

"We need to return the body to the Orconian, Gentlemen, so it can be recovered at some point in the future. I've wrapped it and taped it up. It's ready to go."

R.J. looked at me with a raised eyebrow.

"I'll do it, R.J. Take a break."

"Are you sure? That's two you've had."

"It's not enough I know, but I'll do it."

"Okay, but I'll owe you one."

The re-internment took another two hours. My suit began having trouble holding temperature. I kept having cold spells on my way to the Orconian. It seemed like an appropriate problem for the task at hand. With Roy finally securely fastened inside again, I hurried back to the airlock and fidgeted impatiently in the suit, waiting for recompression and the suit air mix to return to real life. R.J. entered the airlock and began helping me.

"We got some more good shots off your helmet cam of deformed superstructure over there," he said.

"Yeah what the hell is that about anyway?"

"It reminds me of an old Earth movie about the military experimenting trying to make a ship invisible. That ended up with guys embedded in the deck."

"That's just Sci Fi, R.J. This is reality. At least I think it is."

"It does add a nasty element to our already difficult situation."

I lowered down and out of the suit torso and pushed down on the suit legs. "Which of us has the best physics background?"

"That would have to be Elachia," he replied.

I stopped and looked at him to see if he was kidding. "Elachia? Elachia has done post graduate studies in physics?"

"Actually it began in her elementary years. It was considered necessary for her to understand the limitations of her environment."

I stepped out of the suit legs and leaned over to ask, "Is she smarter than us about everything?"

"She's not good at bowling. Something about the spin direction of the ball throws her off. I've beaten her several times."

"Has she said anything about the mangled frame over there?"

"No, but I can tell she's been thinking about it."

"Well, let's go quiz Dr. Elachia."

In the Griffin living area, the bottle had been stowed and replaced by eggs over easy, hash, fried potatoes and toast. The smell was overpowering. My three compatriots sat at the table eating and talking in surreptitious tones. A plate had been set out for me. The scene made me realize I was starved and no thoughts of having transported a dead body were going to interfere with that Neanderthal instinct for food.

"Elachia, were you watching the suit cams while we were over there?" I asked between forkfulls of hash.

"Of course, Adrian."

"Then you noticed the table attached to the wall and the pilot embedded into the control panel, and the other stuff?"

"We weren't sure we were interpreting the video correctly," she replied. "You're saying those things were actually as they seemed?"

"Yes."

R.J. returned from the kitchenette with four cups and a hot coffee pot. He poured black for all of us then set out condiments.

"I've never seen anything like that," continued Elachia.

"It all has to be related, right?"

"A single wave that deforms inanimate objects and disrupts living cells? And we are still only theorizing it as a wave based on how the effect passed through that crewman's body. I know of no type of energy that could do that."

R.J. blew on his coffee before testing it. "How about something related to time itself? A temporal wave?"

"A reasonable hypothesis my dear, but deformation of solid objects seems more like an element of dimensional shift than a warp in time," answered Elachia.

"Do any of us still think we should move in closer to Earth?" asked R.J.

I sipped my steaming coffee and thought about it. "Let's just wait and see how it goes with the probe. I keep thinking of the proverbial snake and mouse. There's that species of snake that coils, camouflages, and waits for its prey to come in striking distance. Know what I mean?"

Danica asked, "We should break off station keeping lock with the Orconian, Adrian. Put some distance between us and it."

"Thanks for reminding me. Please reset the auto pilot to hold us at these coordinates. Let that ship drift away. Are we still sending out hails on all Earth channels?"

"We are. There'll be an audible alert if we get any answers."

"You don't think people on Earth have died like the Orconian crew, do you Elachia?" asked Danica.

"We have not seen anything that suggested mass casualties in the photos so far. We cannot even say Earth was exposed to the same catastrophe as that ship."

"Let's keep going with the telephoto and monitor the probe cameras during its approach. If we lose the probe, we'll know the snake is out there waiting to strike," I said.

"Too bad we're not in position to photograph Aldrin Lunar Base. We'd get pretty good close-ups of it," mentioned R.J. "All we can get when it comes around is a bad angle. And, there's all those other alien outposts on the moon but they're mostly underground. I do not recall if we have anything going on anywhere on the dark side. The One World Space Station will probably be our first hi-res object. But, there's been no trans-data from it, either."

"Let's get everything we can just in case there's anything helpful. We'll start getting good imagery from the probe by this time tomorrow," I said.

"There is one other ship out there dead in space, Adrian," said Danica.

"I have a feeling we'd only find more of the same," I replied.

"There could be survivors," mused R.J.

"That other ship is too close in. There's been no distress calls." I replied.

"I agree with Adrian in this case," said Elachia. "If the probe survives, we might consider moving in closer, but for now we should wait."

"It's going to be an eerie twenty-four hours," said R.J.

"Why do you say that?" asked Danica.

"Haven't you noticed?" replied R.J. "In all the time we've been here, neither the radar nor the comm system has picked up a single thing. Not a single ship visiting Earth or leaving for any reason. The word must be out. Don't come here."

With Griffin set to hold its distance, we took turns sleeping and studying imagery. As the probe passed through its halfway mark, higher res photos began to come in. From that closer viewpoint, we began to see damage across the planet's entire surface. At noon the four of us grouped at the table, ate sandwiches, and passed tablets around with enhanced photos, calling out specific areas of chaos. There were destroyed regions that looked like an earthquake had occurred. Other areas looked like a bomb had been dropped. Some sections of forest looked like meteor impact; all the trees knocked down in a westward direction. Large fires were burning, leaving long smoke trails.

But it was the cities that made the least sense. R.J. squirmed in his chair, set his tablet down on the table, and wiped thoughtfully at his beard. "Well, at least we know there are people alive down there. A lot of them."

"It's mass confusion," added Danica. "Some groups seem to be running away, others just linger. There are huge crowds at what I believe are hospitals, and some sections of cities seem to be completely deserted."

Elachia said, "No machinery is operating down there. No lights anywhere. No cars seem to be moving. No activity at airports."

"Our probe passed through the moon's orbit sixteen hours ago and it's still working," said Danica. "Maybe that means we can get closer. Maybe what happened down there is over and it's safe now."

They looked at me. I stopped biting down on my sandwich for a second. They stared. I swallowed and said, "Let's just wait a little more, shall we?"

"It bothers me that you're still afraid of the proverbial snake," said R.J.

"I hate snakes."

"How long should we wait, just hanging here in the middle of nowhere?" asked Danica.

Before I could answer, a loud beeping from an engineering station interrupted.

R.J. and Danica scrambled over to the console.

"Oh my God! There's a ship coming in," cried Danica.

I stood up, sandwich in hand. "Hail them, quick!"

"Yes, on all frequencies," said Danica to R.J.

"Starship Griffin calling the spacecraft approaching Earth. Please respond. This is an emergency!" said R.J., holding a headphone and mike near his face. He looked up at us. "There, that's set to repeat until we get a reply."

I put down the remnants of my sandwich, wiped my hand on my pants leg, and went to the station. "Let me have the headset," I said.

"You're still on all channels," replied Danica.

"This is Captain Tarn of the Starship Griffin. Spacecraft approaching Earth, break off your approach. You may be in danger. Break off your approach. Do not make Earth orbit. Do you read?"

"Okay that's repeating now," said Danica.

R.J. switched the radar screen to the main overhead monitor. We stepped back and watched breathlessly. The ship continued its approach. There was no answer.

"Can we get them on the probe?" I asked.

R.J. answered, "Yeah, it can track them. Let me use station A. We'll tell the probe to scan for them, then we'll get the probe's main camera to lock on. It'll only take a minute or two."

As R.J. worked, there was still no response to our hails. It pissed me off. I went back to my sandwich but never took my eyes off the radar image on the overhead. The damn fool came all the way in on warp and didn't drop out until he was deep inside the solar system limits. It was like a punk kid speeding up somebody's driveway and skidding to a stop. Too rude.

"I don't believe it," said R.J.

"What now?" asked Elachia.

"The guy's got no transponder. No ship ID being transmitted."

"He's inserting onto orbit. Maybe synchronous," said Danica.

R.J. straightened up. "Okay, the probe has him. Switching to camera lock." R.J. transferred the probe data to the side overhead monitors and again stepped back to look up at them.

On the right overhead, we now had a picture looking down at the distant outline of a ship on orbit passing behind Earth.

"Do we go after them?" asked Danica?

I shook my head. "Patience. They'll be coming around soon enough. We're set up pretty good. Let's see how their ride goes now that they're in so close."

"It's a small ship. Bet we can get markings from the probe cam when they come around," said R.J.

"We're over the North American continent right now. What happens if they go in on the other side?" asked Danica. "They could drop in and we'd never find them."

I answered. "The orbit was too high. They were looking for a specific place. It'll probably take them at least twenty minutes to navigate down through the levels since no OTC controllers are helping them. Trust me, we'll see them come around."

So we studied the newest confusing surface imagery while waiting. Our consternation grew as more and more destruction became apparent. And sure enough, thirty minutes later the radar unit began squawking again as the probe turned its camera and zoomed in on the unfriendly visitors. As the ship moved closer, we finally had a good magnified image. It was an ugly dirty gray superstructure, shaped like half a centipede with tentacles dragging along behind. From our vantage point there wasn't a single marking on it.

"Are you sure our hail is still going out?" I asked.

"Yes. Still no answer," said Elachia. "Not even an empty signal carrier."

"No transponder, no markings, and no replies. Who are these guys?" asked Danica.

"I believe I know," answered Elachia.

"You do?" asked R.J. in surprise.

"Pirates," replied Elachia. "Looters."

We all looked at each other in silence, wondering if the suggestion could be true.

"They're dropping down," said Danica. "They've entered the atmosphere. Looks like the east coast, probably New England."

"They seem to be in control. No problems with the descent," said R.J.

"Starting to look like some part of New York," added Danica.

R.J. nodded, "Definitely New York. I think it's around Manhattan. Good God, a business district? Is Elachia right about this?"

We watched and waited. The probe magnification was enough to see them descend on the southeastern side of the Island not far from the Brooklyn Bridge.

"That's it. They're down. I lost them in the high rises," said R.J.

"Adrian, you're not going to let them just fly off, are you?" asked Danica.

"Dan, we have no idea what they're doing here. You want to chase after them and shoot them down when we catch up?"

"But...."

"And, what if it turned out they had permission to be there, like if they were sent in as part of a recon team? We need to hang in here, and figure out what the hell is going on, pirates or looters or not."

"I guess you're right."

We quietly bided our time and watched. It was a one hour wait. Then Danica called out, "Oh brother, here they come," as the radar alert squawked. "It's an eastward departure."

"And the hails are still repeating?" I asked.

"Aren't you getting tired of asking?" said R.J.

"They're leaving the atmosphere," said Danica.

"Wait! Something is happening on the surface," said Elachia. "It came from the west. It's like a fog moving across the surface, a storm line, incredibly fast. It's approaching the Atlantic."

"Look at them!" interrupted Danica. "I think they're in trouble. They've stopped gaining altitude. They're holding position just above the atmosphere."

"She's right," said R.J. "That ship is in trouble. If they lose control, it will be a very long fall."

"I don't understand this. Earth's surface has completely changed," said Elachia, almost to herself.

"Wow! What the heck was that bright flash of light on the east side of the display. It's still fading! Was that our display screen?" said Danica.

"Oh no! That ship is in real trouble. They've lost it! There they go," said R.J. "They're starting to spin. I would not want to be in that spacecraft."

We watched as the tiny image of the ship became a pinwheel headed for the ocean. The mood in the cabin became funereal as the ship picked up speed downward. As it neared the surface there was a moment where we could no longer make out the craft, but the explosion of water that followed was plain enough to see.

As we stared aghast, as the image from the probe flashed brightly and became snow.

"Wow!" said R.J. after a moment of silence had passed.

"We've lost all data from the probe," said Elachia.

Chapter 11

"Would someone recap for me, what just happened?" I asked.

There was an uneasy silence.

"So the proverbial snake really *is* out there waiting," said R.J. finally.

"I don't believe that just happened," said Danica. "They fell from nearly suborbital all the way down and couldn't get it back."

Elachia spoke in a concerned voice, "That's not all that happened. That ship wasn't the only thing affected. We've definitely lost the probe."

We turned and looked at her for further explanation.

She shook her head in disbelief. "Look at this. It's a replay from just before they lost control." She replayed the video from the probe's wide-angle camera. It showed most of the North American continent. Suddenly the image became foggy. A line of disturbance sped across the display from left to right, disrupting all the surface and air detail. Cloud formations swirled angrily at its passing. Details on the surface became distorted. It was like the leading edge of a planet-wide tsunami of disarray. The line passed over the New York area just about the time the pirate ship lifted off. We stared at the wave front as it disappeared off the right side of the screen, after which there was a strange stillness of sorts. An eerie state of normalcy seemed to have returned. Then, just a few seconds later, there was a bright flash and a new frontal line of distortion abruptly burst into view, this time coming from the right side of our monitor and sweeping left. The camera view shuddered as though our probe was being pushed around by a space storm even though that should have been impossible. An instant later, before the image could stabilize, the probe stopped transmitting.

Elachia stared at us in earnest. "It has to be some kind of massive heliacal wave. These waves must be what killed the Orconian crew and damaged their ship."

"Would you run that again please, Elachia?" I asked.

We watched the scene over and over. A strange wave sweeping over the Earth from the west, then a few seconds later, a second wave somehow different from the first, racing over the Earth from the east.

We began studying the imagery frame by frame, using the probes camera recordings with enhancement.

R.J. finally sat forward in his chair and opened his hands in a gesture of disbelief. "You guys do see what's happening here, right? It's not just me?"

We looked at him and waited for explanation.

He continued, "I know this sounds crazy but it looks like Earth's surface changes back to a normal state after the first wave passes by, as though there is no damage at all, but then everything goes back to destroyed a few seconds later after the second wave, right? Aren't you all seeing that?"

"Just one more time in slow please, Elachia," I begged.

We watched it three more times.

"It's an optical illusion," said Danica.

"Okay, okay, just watch this. Let's use a close-up of New York," said R.J. "Focus on that piece of bridge that's half fallen into the river. Just watch it right after the first wave comes in from the west. Step through it slowly, Ela."

We all stared intently at the broken bridge, and as the first wave passed over it, Elachia quickly paused the image. Once again, we fell silent.

"Okay, see? I'm not crazy. That bridge is now back in place, and undamaged. It's good as new. It's like that first wave that came from the west somehow repaired or restored that bridge. I know this is insane but we're all in agreement on this, aren't we?" asked R.J.

"We need to compare more points," suggested Elachia.

An hour later we again sat together, silent and bewildered.

R.J. resumed, "Since I'm the only one here willing to sound crazy, just listen. We see massive damage all over the surface of the Earth. Then some kind of wave front comes in from the west and as it passes over the surface, it fixes everything. The world goes back to normal! A few seconds later there's a bright flash from the left and another wave comes out of the east and as it sweeps across the planet it destroys everything in its path, the same kind of damage that we originally started with. That's what we're seeing here, right? Anybody disagree?"

"Danica, do we still have a camera tracking the Orconian?"

"Yep."

"Can you put that up on a screen and run the same time index where the two waves swept over Earth? Give us a good magnification. It should still be close enough," I asked

Danica pushed up and went to engineering station A.

I turned to R.J. "That pirate ship didn't go down until *after* the first wave had passed by. That ship and the probe were okay up until the second wave swept over them."

"Okay, replaying the video of the Orconian, Adrian. It's on your left side monitor," called Danica.

We looked up to see the Orconian still drifting away. It had shifted into a nose down attitude relative to us. The cloud of debris was still clearly visible. We watched a replay of the waves passing over Earth's surface, while keeping an eye on the Orconian in the same time period.

"Well, the first wave may have restored the Earth but it sure didn't repair the Orconian, did it?" I said.

"If only we hadn't lost the probe. We'd have extreme close-ups now," said Elachia.

"Still nothing in your particle physics training that reminds you of any of this stuff, Elachia?" I asked.

Elachia shook her head and stared in thought.

R.J. said, "We need to send out another probe."

"How long did the last probe work before it was knocked out?" I asked.

R.J. replied, "Twenty-three hours forty-five minutes."

"Dan, switch off the North America lock and set us back at station keeping so we can get video on Earth's entire surface as it rotates. And, yes send out a second probe even though we'll probably lose it too."

"How many probes in your inventory?" asked Elachia.

"Four, this will bring us down to two remaining. Having no probes on board is a very bad thing."

"How can something pass over Earth and repair damage that has been done to it?" asked Danica. "It's impossible."

"There are several possibilities," answered Elachia. "But none would be considered plausible."

"Really?" I asked. "You can see some possible answers to this mess?"

"Danica only asked about reconstruction of a destroyed land mass."

"Okay, reconstruction then. Name one possibility."

"Temporal loop back. A temporal wave resets an area back to a previous point in time," said Elachia. "But that doesn't make sense because only Earth's surface is being affected. The planet isn't being reset back to its original position in space, that is; its original place in orbit."

"So if this *is* a jump back in time, it's affecting only the planet's oceans, land masses, and atmosphere," said R.J., "but not the planet's core."

"And it extends into space to some degree," added Elachia. "The second wave took down that ship while it was outside Earth's atmosphere."

"Elachia, you said *several possibilities*. Name another," I asked.

"Interdimensional shifting. After the restoration wave, the destroyed area somehow interlopes with an identical alternate dimension that is undamaged."

I looked at R.J. "Get that?"

"Let's not do the math," replied R.J.

"Okay, Elachia, of these cosmic possibilities floating around in that beautiful mind of yours, is there one that you favor above the others?" I asked.

"Those two actually. That's why I mentioned them first. I prefer them over the other possibilities since the others mandate that we are all no longer in our own universe, *or* we are not even here at all, as though this is all happening in a shared lucid dream."

"Okay, but you did say that in your examination of the Orconian crewman it looked like he had been hit by some kind of wave, which is what we're seeing in the videos, right?"

"Correct."

"So do you have any idea what might cause such a massive global wave?"

"I do not. Waves exist in many different states of particle physics. But, waves are only behavioral aspects. They are not fundamental subatomic components. There would first need to be a collection of source objects which under the right circumstances emit in the form of a wave, or there could be a very unique particle stream that responds to a certain stimulus in the form of a wave."

I rolled my eyes. "Well now that we've got that straight."

R.J. laughed.

Danica interrupted, "The second probe is away Adrian, and we are back at station keeping with cameras recording."

"Thanks. Elachia, these waves we're talking about can't be one-time events. They must repeat, right?"

"There is no way to be certain until we know the source. If the wave originated outside our solar system one possibility is that any subsequent events would have long intervals."

"How long?" asked R.J.

"You are asking for wild guesses, dear."

R.J. nodded. "But didn't the scans you did on the crewman's body give any other data at all on this kind of wave?"

"There was cellular disruption but no subatomic signatures that the scanners could detect."

Danica interrupted, "Adrian, look at this live image from before the camera view passes out over the Atlantic. That's eastern New York again. Remember the pictures we enhanced of the damaged bridge that was repaired? I know it's hard to see from this distance, but that's the same bridge we studied earlier. It's been destroyed again just like it had been. You can see that, right?"

We stared up at the main overhead monitor. We strained our eyes at the tiny rectangular buildings bordering the river. There did seem to be the same gap in the bridge's span.

"Are you sure this isn't a previous time code?" I asked.

"This was probe real-time optics super enhanced," answered Danica.

I rubbed my eyes and shook my head. "We all did see video of that bridge fully restored just a few minutes ago, just before the probe died. Does everyone agree?"

Silence.

"Griffin's cameras were still recording when that happened, Adrian. We have it stored in memory," said Danica. "We can super enhance those also during that whole timeline."

So we went back to the Griffin long distance video played it over and over and used computer enhancement to get better, though still fuzzy magnification. An hour of sharing each other's findings and suppositions brought us back to the table in even greater bewilderment.

"Elachia, would you again please sum up everything we think happened," I said.

Elachia nodded. "On the videos we see wide areas of unexplained damage and destruction on Earth's surface. There is a suggestion of casualties, but also evidence of survivors. Activity on the Earth does not seem to make sense given the terrible circumstances there. As we watch the video, a wave front of unknown origin appears, traveling west to east. Somehow, as it passes over each area it seems to repair or restore all the surface damage. After that first wave disappears to the east, a few seconds of restored normalcy exists, but then we see a second wave front appearing from the east, traveling to the west and *it* destroys everything once again. This second wave front looks almost like a storm front carrying debris along with it as it moves. After this second wave, no other wave fronts appear. Earth's surface remains destroyed. Did I leave anything out?"

Danica interrupted, "Adrian, the One World Space Station is coming around again. Too far to get a good look, but it doesn't seem to be in the correct orbit."

"Record it, Dan. Okay, anyone got any theories based on Elachia's summery?" I asked.

"I think we should get back to studying the rest of the planet's surface, Adrian. We've only looked at the North American continent," said R.J.

I nodded in agreement. "Something just occurred to me, Guys. Those few seconds that everything on earth seemed to have been reset to normal, did we pick up anything on comm in that period?"

R.J. hurried to engineering station B, plunked down in the seat and called up the comm units archive. He tapped keys to find the right time period and switched the system to overhead speakers. Static from the comm abruptly changed to a crowded chorus from heavily used frequencies.

"R.J., give us just Orbital Traffic Control, KSC departure," I suggested.

R.J. fiddle with the comm controls. "There is something, Adrian. It's weak and it just got here. We're really too far out for that stuff."

"Play it."

Transcon 325, hold short, expect clearance for takeoff in just a minute.

After an odd moment of silence, static burst back over the speaker.

"That's so weird. It's like normal traffic control in that few seconds, Adrian," said R.J.

"Try Security Dispatch," I suggested.

"Yep, there is a small packet."

Unit Five, please contact the visitor's center on one-three-five point seven-six. Expect to escort two....

The transmission also ended in static.

We listened to several more bits all with the same ending.

"So in that brief period of restoration, the world did not seem to know the trouble it was in," I said.

"That's incredible," said R.J.

"And there's something else," I added. "Something we left out of your summery, Elachia. That pirate ship was nearly suborbital when it fell out of the sky. Our probe was still in space when it died. And, none of Earth's geosynchronous or any other orbital satellites are functioning. Elachia, would a wave from outside the solar system circle just one planet like that?"

Elachia stared into the distance as she answered, "It does not make sense. There are no tunnel shaped waves that we know of. Waves behave like ripples in a pond, not like weapons fire."

"Weapons fire?" replied Danica. "Are you saying this might be something to do with a giant disruptor weapon?"

"That wouldn't explain the first wave that reset everything," said R.J.

"Okay, I think we need to step back and take some time to think about all this and go back to long distance images while we wait for probe number two to get closer," I said.

"Earth is rotating around to Europe, Adrian. But, it's shrouded in cloud cover," said Danica.

"R.J. would you update the Mars colony via subspace? Have them pass on to all the other outposts what we've found so far. Ask them if anybody has ever seen anything like this," I said.

"Do you think they'll believe me?" he replied.

Chapter 12

Another Griffin-day of hanging in empty space. Everyone mulling around with tablets, searching blurry magnified images of Earth's surface for more clues. Elachia made a buffet styled breakfast and spread it out on the table. Except for small talk there did not seem to be any brilliant revelations from the past evening's discussions. The atmosphere in Griffin was one of tired frustration. At one point we all happened to be standing around the living area table. The silence became uncomfortable.

"Probe is still operating," said R.J. to no one in particular. "We're coming up on the U.S. west coast. California looks just as messed up as it has been."

"Maybe we can never figure this out, Adrian. What about the more advanced races? Won't they want to fix this?" asked Danica.

I sipped my coffee. "According to Fantasia and the Enuro Council, the Nasebiens are aware of this situation and they requested we look into it. Don't ask me to explain that."

"Probe 2 has been operating for almost twenty-four hours, and it's well passed the moon's apogee," said Danica. "Maybe it's all over. Maybe there won't be any more waves."

"R.J., we should have put out a continuous general hail message on all comm frequencies to any other ships entering the system. Warn them not to approach Earth. Want to set that up?" I asked.

"Why didn't I think of that? I'm on it," he answered.

"How long can we hold here, Adrian?" Asked Elachia. "I'm in no hurry to leave. I'm just wondering about provisions."

"It's a good question. How long we can stay would depend on how far away we need to go to get resupplied. I'll need to sit down and do the math on that but we left Enuro with ninety days worth of stores for four people. So we should have plenty of time."

R.J. suddenly called out, "Hey, we got a reply from Mars Station."

"We're listening, R.J."

"They are worried. No kidding. They have never heard of anything like what we have described. They want to know what your intentions are."

"Good question," I answered.

"Wait! There is one other thing. This is kind of humorous. Some ten-year-old kid, the director's son, said the wave we are talking about sounds like the field around an electromagnet. When power is applied it balloons out. When power is removed, it collapses."

We all went into silent thought-mode.

Elachia spoke first, "Well thank-you, Director's son! When you turn on an electromagnet, the field expands out to a distance based on the level of energy available to it. You turn it off and the field collapses in on itself. How could I not have thought of that? It's a wonderful analogy."

"But we know all about Earth's magnetic field," I said. "This is different. This would have to be a completely different kind of field."

"But it fits most of it, at least in some ways. When an electromagnet is shut off, the field around it does collapse in the opposite direct from when it formed! Just like we have been seeing." Elachia went to a portal and starred out into space.

"You're theorizing this field we've been seeing becomes energized and expands around the earth like a balloon, then collapses back on itself?" I asked.

Elachia came out of her daze and look around the cabin at us. She wrinkled her brow. "Of course there are still problems with the hypothesis."

"Please elaborate," said R.J.

Elachia lightly tapped two fingers against her lips then squeezed her chin and spoke. "It would mean the field is originating on Earth, not from outside which seems improbable to me."

"So Adrian is right? We're not talking about Earth's magnetic field?" asked Danica.

Elachia shook her head, "No, no. Earth's magnetic field protects it from the solar wind among other things. It wouldn't destroy and then restore Earth's surface. But I've never read of anything that would."

"Okay, but you've got a working concept of sorts, a big clue that maybe this is a localized event not a cosmic event," said R.J. "All you need now is a source."

"If this thing does originate on Earth, we might be able to find where it first shows up," said Danica. "Maybe we just need to keep looking for a specific place now that the second probe has crossed the halfway point again. We're coming up on Europe. It was overcast last time around. It's clear today and the probe *is* still sending."

R.J. asked, "Ela, assuming this expanding field theory is correct, any idea what we should be looking for on the surface that would suggest a point of origin?"

Danica spoke from behind us. "Wow! Look at this. Europe got hit the worst of all. There's damage everywhere!"

Elachia struggled. "Rowland, once again you're asking me to identify something completely unknown. How can you describe something or know its root effects when you don't know what *it* is?"

"So we just need to look for something unusual in the middle of everything unusual," I replied.

"I'm sorry," answered Elachia.

R.J. joined Danica. "Danica's right about Europe. There's widespread damage all across the west."

"If we were in closer we could do some surface scans that might show something," added Elachia. "But, I still wouldn't take that chance of getting closer. What other kinds of scans can you run with that probe when and if it arrives?"

"Very limited, especially since we don't know what to look for. But, if this expanding field idea is true, then there would have to be a specific point of origin, right?"

Elachia nodded, "Yes, I would guess that to be logical, unless the wave is coming from a point in space, as in the giant disruptor weapon Danica mentioned."

I looked over my shoulder, "R.J. there's still nothing on the long range radar, right? No other ships?"

"Empty space, Adrian."

"So with no ships out there, this has to be of Earth origin," I said.

"Still only guesswork," replied Elachia. "But, we have seen nothing other than the uniform damage all around the surface so far, which could also suggest Earth origin. A space-based weapon would likely affect only one area of the planet with each discharge."

I looked over at Danica. "Dan, where are we on the long distance video scans?"

"We're now over Russia, Adrian. Looks like the same damage and destruction everywhere."

"So if this happens again and we are watching the right place at the right time, we might actually see a wave created, or maybe the previous wave collapse down to a specific point?" I asked.

Elachia nodded. "You are proposing these events will repeat, and that as you say there is a central point of origin. We cannot say those postulates are correct. We could be searching for something that's not there, but at this point I don't see a better alternative."

"We *can* say this event has been repeating. There was already destruction all over the Earth when we arrived. The pirates went in and were destroyed by what appeared to be one of those events. That means there must have been at least two events so far, maybe more."

"Yes, yes I see your reasoning. Yes, there would previously have had to be more than one event," agreed Elachia. "But the problem is, does that mean there will be more occurrences, and how could you know exactly what area to be watching to see the next event originate, if indeed there is a next event?"

"We can only get one side of the Earth at a time. We can't send probe number two to the other side. There would have to be a relay station to receive from it and I certainly can't risk another of our two remaining probes to do that job. And, both would probably be destroyed by the wave we're trying to see. R.J. and Danica, you haven't finished recording western Russia, but have you seen anything unusual or just the same pattern of destruction everywhere?"

They looked at each other. R.J. answered, "Sorry, Adrian. But we haven't even looked closely at the southern hemisphere, and we still only have the long range stuff. The first probe hadn't even reached high orbit when it died."

Danica added, "I've been looking at some specific images, too. But, it's going to take a long time, Adrian. You see something that might be interesting but you spend time enhancing the frame. It's a slow process. The only thing that has stood out so far was France. At least I think it was France. It may have been Switzerland. I'm not so good with geography. Anyway, they got the worst damage so far."

"The worst damage? Can you put that up on the main monitor?" I asked.

It took her a few minutes to find the correct frame. I refilled my coffee and offered some to Elachia. She smiled and accepted. I sat and we studied the main overhead monitor. The video of Earth slowly turning switched off and a blurry still-picture of Eastern Europe came up. The picture moved around and finally stopped on a particularly marred section of terrain, then slowly began to pan westward. The area was scarred, fallen green woodlands, but as Danica guided the display, a very large patch of sand-colored terrain began to fill the screen, terrain that had formally been covered by forest. As we watched, a horseshoe shaped lake entered the image. It was brown water that should have been blue. As she adjusted the viewpoint on the barren area, it became clear there was indeed some type of epicenter to the widespread stripping of the land. A small, much darker patch of earth looked as though it might be a sizable crater.

"Something blew up here," said Danica matter-of-factly. "Maybe it was a nuclear power plant or something."

For some reason the image startled me. Something didn't look right. As I stared at the blackened shape of it, I called to R.J. "R.J., have you seen this?"

"Not until now. I was taking closer looks at Russia."

"What's the longitude and latitude, Dan?"

"That's easy. Forty-six degrees, thirteen minutes, sixty seconds north, six degrees, two minutes, sixty seconds East."

"R.J., do we have a navigation map that will show us what used to be there?"

"Sure. Hold on."

We sat back and studied the big patch of black earth encircled by ravaged forest. The blast area covered many miles in every direction. There were ragged edges to it. If there had been buildings within the perimeter, they'd been completely destroyed.

"It's Geneva," called out R.J. "Meyrin. Right on the border of France and Switzerland. Oh wait! It says here, the Centre World Pour La Recherché Nucleare! There *is* something here about nuclear. What is that? Hold on. I'm looking it up."

"Whatever it was, there's sure nothing left of it now," agreed Danica.

"There were a couple fairly large cities. How can there be not even a trace of those now? It also says WERN. World Center for Nuclear Research. Oh, I do remember this place now. Wow! This was that new gigantic collider completed a few years ago. The Higgs-something Collider, or something like that. This was the area where they built it. That's what used to be down there, along with those nearby cities."

Once again we all paused in silence and tried to imagine a research facility with cities and townships spread out around it in that charred brown space.

I looked at Elachia. "What about it? Could a collider test facility cause that kind of explosion?"

R.J. came over and stood beside us. "No way, Adrian."

Elachia joined in, "Rowland is correct. There are no large quantities of weapons grade material used in that type of particle collider. I am a little bit familiar with this installation. On my last visit to Earth it was well publicized. This facility was actually somewhat primitive compared to some on other worlds, but it is the largest ever constructed on Earth. Rowland is correct about colliders not creating massive explosions. Over the years the real fear concerning particle collisions is that microscopic black holes might be created. There were also myths about the creation of hypothetical particles called strangelets, particles that had mythological properties. But in reality, none of these dangers have ever materialized. There is no condition known where a collider could generate an explosion of the size we see here."

"Just the same, R.J., have either of you seen any huge crater areas like this anywhere else on the surface?"

"Not really. Not so far."

"So how about we gamble and keep both the Griffin camera and the probe camera on this area and watch it twenty-four-seven? Check me on this Elachia, if the expanding and collapsing field theory is happening here, then we should eventually see the field collapse and reset everything again, and just maybe we'll see it collapse into the collider facility?"

R.J. looked back over his shoulder. "Did you get that, Dan?"

"I'll set up the ship's autopilot if you take care of the probe," said Danica and she rose from the engineering station and headed forward.

R.J. said, "So now we have this possible collapsing field theory, but how do you explain a planet-wide destruction being reset to a previous state in time by it?"

"Let's take one preposterous idea at a time, R.J." I replied.

Chapter 13

With the Griffin tracking along Europe from long distance, and the probe re-vectored to allow it the same view, we settled in to watch and wait.

Surprisingly, we did not have long to wait.

As I poured myself coffee number four, Danica suddenly shrieked and pointed, "Oh!" as though she was trying to say something more but couldn't get it out. She pointed at the monitor set for wide angle. We all froze and stared up at the two monitors.

It was unmistakable and astonishing. The first wave had swept across the coast and resurrected everything in its path. Cities were restored to normal, forest land filled back in, trees lifted up. And to our further amazement, the wave quickly became an arc as it passed over the Atlantic and closed in on the Higgs-Englert Collider complex. It finally formed a collapsing circle and disappeared into the now reconstructed complex within surrounding forest and towns.

"I just don't believe it," cried R.J.

Elachia, standing alongside him, had to brace herself against the table as she shook her head in disbelief.

I opened my mouth to give a breathless, "Wow!" but did not get the chance.

A bright light flashed directly from the center of the restored collider site blossomed out leaving everything in its path barren brown ground. The circular line of destruction radiated outward, replacing all of society's architecture with carnage. The wave quickly disappeared off our screens on its way around the rest of the world.

Our probe went dead.

This time our stunned silence lasted. No one knew what to say.

Finally I had to ask, "R.J. would you check the camera time entries and see exactly how long between the first wave restoration and the explosion?"

R.J. appeared more disheveled than I had ever seen him. It took him a few seconds to come back to our deformed reality. He fidgeted around at engineering station B, finally looked up and said, "Six seconds, exactly." He looked at me in confusion as though he didn't know why I'd asked or what it meant.

I thought out loud, "Six seconds of normal Earth."

"What did they do?" Danica finally asked in exasperation.

I looked up from my own search for understanding. "R.J. how much time from when last destructive wave occurred?"

He understood immediately. He typed at the console. "Of course, we only saw the last one passing over the North America continent. It had already crossed Europe and the Atlantic, so if I calculate the speed of the wave and account for the amount of time it took to get there... Give me a few minutes."

I looked to Elachia. "The wave did turn into a collapsing circle just before it ended."

"Therefore, it really is a field effect of some kind," she replied. "The field hypothesis must be correct."

R.J. called out, "I've got it. I get approximately twenty-three point nine-something hours between waves."

"Can you be even more precise?" asked Elachia.

"Twenty-three point nine-nine-nine, if I figured it correctly."

Elachia looked at me. "A diurnal event possibly."

"A what?"

"Once per day."

"You're saying our world is being destroyed and rebuilt once a day, over and over?"

"So far it's a logical extrapolation."

"Well, I believe we have collected enough data here to confirm that we have no idea what's going on," I said.

"We need to collect more, Adrian," replied Elachia. "We need to watch the epicenter and set up for high speed recording before the next event. Then we can play it back in extreme slow speed to see how the event originates and what kind of emission it might be."

"I can't lose any more probes, Elachia."

"Yes, I understand. But I believe we have a foundation to build on now. Use Griffin's cameras with enhancement."

"Okay, but we should discontinue the Europe lock and go back to station keeping to monitor the rest of the world as it turns. If we were to keep our following attitude we'd come up on the terminator and I don't think passing into night would be helpful," I suggested.

"I agree, Adrian. We just need to be certain we are set up and ready to monitor France when the next event is expected."

I shifted in my seat and noticed Danica standing behind me. "I heard all that," she said, and she went forward once again to reset Griffin's autopilot.

R.J. left his engineering station, came over and hooked one arm around Elachia. "So back to blurry-eyed shifts studying long distance camera imagery?" he said.

"I'll take whatever shift nobody wants," I said. "But I'm sure we'll all be up and watching for the next event."

"Danica likes the afternoon, so that would put you on the graveyard and me on the evening. Elachia loves the morning."

"Maybe we should set the Griffin interior to reflect something nice that shows the passage of time. There's no telling how long we'll be here," said Elachia.

"What would you like, my love? Park or forest?"

"Perhaps forest with stream and waterfall to start?" she answered.

"As you wish," replied R.J.

Danica returned from the flight deck. "I'm slowly shifting us back to where we were. Did I miss anything?"

"You have afternoon shift," said R.J.

"Oh, yeah, that. Fine."

"You need to sleep Adrian, if you can," said R.J. "Staring at Earth images for six hours is brain drain."

"I'll give it a shot, but I don't know...."

Elachia laughed. It was the first laugh I'd heard in a very long time. "He is a mother hen, isn't he," she said. "Does the same thing with me."

"*You* deserved to be watched over," said R.J. with a touch of romance in his voice.

We all smiled at each other. It was also the first smile I had seen in a very long time.

So we went into surveillance mode, evaluating the info so far acquired, and studying long distance Earth images as the planet rotated in front of us, waiting for the twenty-four-hour period to bring another event. I could not sleep but I did get rest, locked in my sleeper cell the world outside shut out quite completely. There was the faint sound of waterfall. Stretched out there, I discovered the secret panic hiding within me, a desire to curl up in the fetal position and promise myself to never go out again. Hide under the blankets until the danger went away. Insurmountable problems often leave you feeling that way. Runaway, cover up, hide. Anything to put off facing a bad reality. Some people even jump off bridges, having decided that ending it all on their own terms is better than letting the monster get you. But, it's the worst mistake they could make. Fear and adversity are such devious deceivers. Halfway down from the bridge, you suddenly realize there was a better way out of the problem.

I got up at midnight, cleaned up and changed into a fresh blue flight suit, and found R.J. sipping tea at the table. He looked tired and ready to be relieved.

"Did I miss anything?"

"We transmitted everything to Mars Station. They thought there was some kind of mistake in the summery at first. They're studying it. They will pass it on so the other outposts know what's going on so far. They had nothing to offer except they described the situation as incredulous."

There was more fresh coffee brewed on the counter. I mentally thanked myself for overstocking. I poured a large cup and sat. "What else?"

"We heard from Captain Breen commanding Electra. He promised they were canceling their mapping mission and immediately returning here to help. The message took a while to get here, of course. He said it would be about three weeks."

"Nobody else?"

"I think they're all too far out. I'm kind of surprised we haven't seen or heard from the Nasebiens, though. They're supposed to be our guardian angels, right?"

"You do remember they sent us here?"

"That doesn't give me a warm feeling all over. Why was there no warning about flying into this mess?"

"Any interesting surface anomalies?"

"Nope. Surface destruction is normal now. All I've seen in the imagery is catastrophe."

"So maybe around noon today we see another event."

"There's something I've been thinking about all night. I think I can make a good case for it. Even Elachia went to bed unable to disagree."

I stretched in my seat to help wake up, sipped, and nodded, "You have my attention."

"We could make a landing down there."

"On Earth? You're kidding?"

"Think about it. The pirate ship orbited, landed, and did their dirty deeds, then took off. All of that happened before the field collapsed. It wasn't until the field collapsed and a new event erupted that they lost control and crashed. It's the same with the probes. Both of them flew inside the moon's orbit for several hours without a problem. It wasn't until an event occurred that they were taken out."

"So what are you saying? We can fly in and land as long as we get out of there before the next event?"

"Yes."

I rubbed my clean-shaven face and considered it. It took a minute or two. "Wow, what a terrible idea."

"Yeah, I have these brainstorms from time to time."

"Why would we do that?" I asked, although I already knew where he was going.

"We might be able to contact key people, tell them what we've found so far. Maybe figure something out."

"Yeah, what would we try to figure out?"

"Maybe figure out a way to stop that collider from exploding in those six seconds."

"The collider people are all dead. There's no one to talk to down there."

"We might be able to talk to them right after the first wave restores everything."

"In just six seconds?"

"I've been thinking about this all night. It's the only way."

I nodded, "It *is* the only way. But man, I can see a few problems with the plan."

"Which ones?"

"There's no way to warn them and get out of there in six seconds."

"Maybe we could get close enough to reach them by the comm system."

"What would you say?"

"Explosion imminent. Shut down immediately!"

"You know that has zero chances of working, right?"

R.J. nodded. "Absolutely no chance at all. Maybe we could land just before the six seconds, and warn them in person."

"Would we survive the restoration wave passing over us?"

"I don't know."

"Would the collider people believe us in six seconds?"

"I doubt it."

"Then we die with them. Over and over."

"Maybe we could land between events and rescue some survivors who know about that collider."

"Apparently I have the only functioning ship on the planet. What could possibly go wrong?"

"Yeah, I know. We'd be Noah's ark."

"And if we screw up and don't get out in time, or an event occurs early, we crash and die, over and over?"

"Another great idea ruined by a set of facts."

"Bet if I sit here with my coffee I could think of a dozen other bad ideas."

"Well, Captain Tarn, what are we going to do if we *don't* go down there?"

I thought for a moment and tried to sound enthusiastic. "How about this, we could wait for the six second window, fly in, and obliterate the collider facility."

"So then if that works, we will have killed several hundred people working there and destroyed an incredibly expense research facility that took years to build and we will then spend years trying to explain why after which we will probably be imprisoned for life or worse. Or, our weapons set off the same explosion, the wave then goes out anyway and we fall out of the sky."

"Over and over?"

"Over and over."

"Option two; we can just hang in here and wait for help to arrive." I raised one open hand for emphasis.

"Okay, and what will they do when they get here?"

"Evacuate survivors between events?"

"How many billion, even if there are that many?"

"You're the real spoil sport, you know that? Not me."

"And you're a ray of sunshine. Got any other ideas?"

"Yes, all bad."

"There's something else really weird I haven't told you about."

"Oh please, there can't be anything else."

"I did some image enhancement from the probe camera while we had it locked on the collider facility. There are three airports near there. In the images of destruction, one of those airports has three destroyed aircraft that appear to have been waiting for takeoff clearance. That means they were destroyed about twenty-four hours ago during the last collider explosion. When I look back at that airport during the six seconds that everything had been restored to normal, those three aircraft are again waiting to take off at the end of the runway, just as they were before the explosion. Do you see the problem here?"

"Please... continue."

"Those aircraft were scheduled to take off on a certain day, at a certain time. After being wrecked and then restored, they're back in the same place they started with the same people on board ready to go, but it is now a day later. And, each time these collider events occur, those aircraft become another day behind schedule. Earth is still moving in its orbit around the sun. Earth is still turning. For Earth, time is still passing. But for the people in that plane, time has stopped. They're now out of sync. Way out of sync. When they wake up in that plane after each restoration occurs, they think it's the same day and time."

"So no one on Earth is aging?"

"Correct, but that's only a small part of it."

"Have you explained this to Elachia?"

"Yes. She's beginning to approach this as a temporal event. But she still thinks it's more than that."

"So what about all the survivors who are down there wandering around during the twenty-four hours of the destruction period?"

"Time is passing for them, but they are just as out of sync. They have approximately twenty-four hours to survive in the apocalypse and do whatever they're doing, but then when the restoration hits it puts them back where they originally were for six seconds, then the next explosion makes them survivors all over again. I'm guessing they remember the explosion and surviving it, but I bet they don't remember any of the previous collider events."

"You're killing me, R.J."

"We have to make a landing and find someone familiar with that collider design!"

"I'm not convinced."

"We need more information. Where else are we going to find it?"

"Exactly where the hell would you want to go?"

"Maybe Space Center headquarters to start with. The Armstrong Building and Headquarters Building. Both survived the destruction as near as we can tell."

"You said to start with?"

"After that there are several university campus buildings around the country that appear to be somewhat intact and may be connected with WERN. At least I'll bet one of them has to be associated with the World Center for Nuclear Research organization. You mentioned who gets to be rescued. Maybe we can track down some high-grade physicists and gradually assemble a team to bring up here."

"Okay, that's not bad. But there are scientists on outposts in our system already working on our data."

"We've sent out everything we have, so yes they're already studying it. But anyone working with the collider test programs would not be out orbiting some other planet. The physicists on Earth are experiencing this mess firsthand."

"We'd need our two companions to agree to go down there. What about Elachia?"

"I have no doubt she'll sign on."

I leaned back and sipped my coffee. "Danica always goes."

Chapter 14

We gathered in the Griffin-late-morning with drinks and foods of our choice, to sit and watch monitors that would show us if another collider event would really happen.

Right on time, it did.

Just as before, the field collapsed and restored Earth's surface damage back to a pre-catastrophe state. It was a snapshot of our former reality, for a brief six seconds. Then, inevitably, the big burst of light mushroomed out from the collider facility into an expanding wave of destruction and desolation.

The apocalyptic magnitude of it seemed insurmountable. We tried not to look fearful. For a few moments we avoided eye contact with each other.

Elachia unexpectedly ruined our chances of gently explaining the previous night's plan to Danica. "So we have twenty-four hours between events. Are we going down there?" she asked.

"What?!" exclaimed Danica and she looked at me expecting disapproval.

"R.J. and I have been over this, Dan. It's that or do nothing."

"Where you going to land? What can you do on the surface?"

"We're thinking first shot would be KSC near the Headquarters Building to see if we can make contact with the Director."

"Oh really? You do know it looks like we'd be the only working ship on the entire planet?"

"I'm thinking you'd drop R.J. and me off and depart immediately."

"That doesn't work for me," interrupted Elachia. "I need to be on the ground with you."

I looked to R.J. for rescue.

He shook his head. "She's right, Adrian. She knows more than both of us put together."

"I can set up our hand scanners for customized subatomic analysis. There's a good chance we could learn about the nature of this field since it will still be active and we'll be inside it," said Elachia as though the decision had already been made.

I gave R.J. the, *you-sure-you-want-to-let-her-do-this* look. He raised one eyebrow and returned an, *I-can't-stop-her* shrug.

"Where would I retreat to?" asked Danica.

"Up and away safe where you could pick us up real fast," I replied.

"Are you guys actually talking about going down there now? I mean you can't risk getting into nighttime, right?"

"It could be now, or tomorrow afternoon, but not in the morning hours when the field collapse is coming due," said Elachia.

"We need to choose the best landing site and program it into Griffin. The scanners need to be set up, and we'll need to bring along a few other things. How long to do all that?" I asked.

"Tell me where to go. I'll plug it in. Thirty minutes tops," said Danica. "But, I don't like this. Not at all."

R.J. tapped at his tablet as he came over to me. "Here's Headquarters' satellite view. It looks easy enough. She could put in here on the west lawn. It's wide open enough that we could see if a mob was charging us or anything."

Danica came to look over our shoulders. "I'm on it," she said, and she disappeared forward.

Elachia had retrieved several scanners and took a seat at the table to work.

"So we've all agreed we're going?" I asked.

Everyone was too busy to answer.

We changed into cargo pants and shirts, lace up boots and utility belts. Gathered as much stuff as we dared carry in the event our visit lasted longer than expected. I also grabbed a medium sized disruptor and attached it to the back of my belt as well as tucking a small stun weapon in a lower leg pocket. When R.J. looked at me confused, I handed him one as well. "This is no different than landing on an unexplored planet," I explained. He nodded and accepted the weapon. Back in the living compartment there was a whole new atmosphere of apprehension.

Danica asked the awkward question. "Just one thing. We're going to fly into this field that damaged an entire planet. Why is it safe to do that again?"

We all looked at Elachia.

Elachia paused from her programming and looked up. "I don't know! It must be that during expansion the field is extremely harmful but once it has expanded to its full potential it becomes a steady state inert. And, yes those are just words. What did you expect?"

Danica joined in. "You know this isn't going to be fun, right Adrian?"

"Which part so I'll be sure to remember that?"

"We're not even going to a full orbit. We're going to jump onto orbit, dive right down and then fly atmospheric using the antigrav along with the orbital maneuvering engines. We never do that. It's always straight up to orbit with just a few seconds of OMS engines and then the same thing coming back down. We're going to actually fly around in the atmosphere on antigrav and OMS. That should really be something."

"Okay, it's going to be something."

R.J. interrupted, "We exit down the rear airlock ramp, Danica bugs out, then we go straight into the Headquarters Building and take the stairs to the eighth floor, right?"

I hadn't thought that far ahead so I answered while still considering it. "Right. Hopefully the communicators work down there. If they don't Dan, you automatically return in one hour for extraction."

Once again, the group became quiet and busy.

We strapped in for descent. I noticed Danica charging the main weapons.

"Why?" I asked.

"Can't be too careful," she replied, and I suddenly realized she sounded like me. The crew readied for the mission so quickly I hadn't taken time to have second thoughts. Suddenly there was an impulse to call out, "Hold on!" but I couldn't come up with a good enough reason to do so.

Danica brought Griffin to life, rotated around, set up for the quick jump and called on the comm system. "Anyone not ready?" she asked with a touch of daring. Without waiting she initiated the jump. For just a second the view screen blurred with a partial image of Earth along with a warped section of stars. We bucked onto orbit and again without waiting Danica rolled us to the right and twisted us downward in a reentry much too heavy handed, her usual style. Space jockey. I found myself thankful she had not plotted an even lower orbital segment.

Earth grew into full view now, our first full scale eyeball look at the surface. It was an ominous panorama. The ride suddenly became bumpier than it should have been. We were barreling through clumps of turbulence at altitudes where there should have been none. She dove us toward the Atlantic, leaving Europe behind. There had been no chance for even a cursory look back there. I'd never heard the OMS engines whine that loudly for that long. For all goods and purposes this was a test flight and Danica was our test pilot.

"We're way north," said Danica and she jerk-rolled us left. The inertia dampeners were handling the Gs, but anyone trying to focus out a portal was bound to get squirrelly eyed.

I glanced at the altimeter. We were holding ten thousand feet. On a wild chance I scanned all the comm channels. Static.

"You may have to help me find it, Adrian. There are no nav aids available at all," said Danica.

"Shouldn't be a problem. When we hit the east coast of Florida the VAB is hard to miss. The lighthouse is back on the coast too, along with the skid strip. You may want to ease off a little when we get there."

"Nag, nag, nag."

"Does the ocean look right to you?"

"I'd swear I've seen places where the waves weren't moving."

"Not a cloud as far as the eye can see."

When the first trace of landfall came into view, Danica nosed down and dropped us to three thousand feet and as we neared the coast, she spotted something in the water ahead.

"Can you make out what that is? It'll pass to starboard. Maybe you can get a good look."

As we went by, I felt a little touch of sick stomach. "It's either a cruise ship or a cargo ship capsized."

"Wish I hadn't asked," answered Danica. "So they're going to be righted and then capsized again with every new explosion."

"May be."

"Things don't look any better up ahead."

As Danica rolled to port to follow the coast south, we passed by a large marina. The long dock was completely on shore with dozens of watercraft still anchored to it as though nothing was wrong. There were other craft still in the water swamped or overturned and farther inland a few large boats were suspended in trees.

"I have no idea where we are," said Danica. "The compass seems to still be working, but still no navigation aids. It's definitely going to have to be visual."

"Just keep following the coast. KSC is impossible to miss from three-thousand," I replied.

"Wait, I'm thinking that's Savannah up ahead. The airport looks familiar," she added.

"I agree."

"The place looks like a mess from here. What's all those giant piles of junk stacked up around the city? What about those columns of smoke?"

"No idea."

From behind us, I heard a cry of "Oh!" come from Elachia as she studied what was left of civilization.

"Okay back there?" I called.

A few moments later, both Elachia and R.J. crowded inside the flight deck door and took a moment to stare out the forward windows.

"It's worse than we thought," said R.J. "We weren't able to get the full extent of it from pictures."

"We've seen people moving around within the city," said Elachia.

"Where are we exactly guys?" asked R.J.

"Coming up on the Florida state line," I answered.

"So we should fasten our belts and return our tray tables to the full upright position?" quipped R.J.

"I think Elachia should be issued some type of weapon," I said.

They exchanged questioning stares. Finally R.J. suggested to her, "Come back with me?"

Elachia balked for a moment then waved one hand for him to lead.

"Getting more populated along the coast," said Danica. "But it's not any better."

I tried to focus on the structures passing below us, but too much didn't make sense.

"Bodies on the beach, I think," said Danica.

"That's Daytona speedway coming up in the distance. It won't be long now. Get ready to slow it down."

"Got it." Danica reached down between seats, pulled out the landing checklist and handed it to me.

I skipped the challenge and response checklist method and just went through the whole thing myself.

"Shuttle strip in sight," said Danica.

"Okay, it's south of there. You'll see the big slotted roof right next to the O&C hangar."

"I see it. Heading for the west lawn. It's clear. Quite a few cars and vehicles in the rear parking lot. What a mess."

I called back to R.J. and Elachia, "Go ahead back you guys. I'll meet you in the airlock.

Deploy the ramp as soon as we're down." I looked at Danica. "You know that thing will retract automatically as soon as you leave the ground and the hatch will seal."

"Done this before, Captain."

"Yeah, but it's been a while." I pulled off my headset, rose and squeezed back and drew my comm unit from my back pocket. "How do you hear this?"

"Just fine. I'll climb to ten thousand and hold there as planned unless there's a problem with the anti grav."

"See you later."

"If I don't hear from you, I'm coming back down."

"Just be gone before the next event, no matter what."

"You guys just better be here. You hear me?"

I worked my way aft. She guided the Griffin down onto the grass with a slight rocking motion just as I reached the rear airlock. R.J. and Elachia were standing ready at the outer door. Elachia was now wearing a utility belt complete with disruptor.

R.J. palm-punched the big red button and the outer door slid aside. A second tap and the loading ramp jutted out and down. We had to concentrate on the steepness of the ramp as we marched down.

"Clear," I called.

The Griffin raised up a few feet, closed itself up, and then nosed up into the sky. I would have like to watch it climb but fear of our surroundings took precedence.

We turned and search the panoramic bedlam.

This was not our Earth.

Chapter 15

There were dozens of cars in the huge Headquarters' parking lot. Some were upside down, others on their side, quite a few more spread out over the grassy area beyond the blacktop. The Headquarters Building seemed out of proportion, almost like a cartoon of sorts. The windows lining each floor were frosted. Other buildings nearby looked equally obtuse. Stunted trees and landscaping foliage seemed to be half embedded in the ground.

There was not a soul in sight.

R.J. expressed concern, "Adrian, this could actually be an alternate dimension or something."

"It's like a macabre dream," added Elachia.

I raised my communicator. "Danica, you still have us?"

"Loud and clear, Adrian. I'm at ten-K, setting up hover."

"Well at least that's something," said R.J.

"We're here. We may as well have a look. Let's head for the building's back entrance."

So we started off toward the central rear doors of the building. The grass was crunchy beneath our feet, like walking on eggshells. As we neared the glass doors, there appeared to be busy people inside the building.

R.J. exclaimed, "They're all inside!"

We walked the winding cement walkway to the double doors, paused at the entrance, then pushed our way in.

Stepping through the doors, we found ourselves outside again.

After a brief reorientation, R.J. decided, "This is the front of the building! We've passed through the entire building!"

I looked around and realized he was right. "Okay, guys. Let's try again!"

We turned around and stepped back through the front doors.

This time it was an empty hallway with elevators. R.J. shook his head. "There were people in here a minute ago. We all saw them."

"Let me take some scans before we continue," said Elachia. She held her scanner out and slowly turned.

"There's a flashing floor indicator light above one of these elevators," said R.J. "If nothing electrical or mechanical works down here, what's powering that light?"

"We'll be using the stairwell," I said.

"Absolutely," replied R.J.

"There *are* indications of some sort of unusual radiation here," said Elachia as she continued to stare at her scanner.

"Let's get going guys. It's a long eight floors up."

We found the stairwell door at the opposite end of the hall. I opened it and peered in warily. The metal stairs looked normal. I led, Elachia merged between us, R.J. followed. But, as we started up, the steps felt like they were unevenly spaced.

"This really is just like being in a dream," said Elachia again.

"It looks okay all the way up," said R.J. as he leaned over the railing to see above.

We climbed to the third floor where R.J. called out, "Hold it."

I stopped and turned back to see what he wanted.

"Look here," he continued. "Look at this on the door."

There in the center of the door was a small plaque that read, '*Lobby.*'

He looked at me with a wrinkled brow. "I've gotta check this out, Adrian. It's a moral imperative."

"Okay, but we've got to stay together. We'll all go."

R.J. pulled the door open and we all bunched together going through. The door clicked shut behind us. We looked around and found ourselves back on the first floor.

"Is this really the first floor, or is it another first floor?" asked R.J.

"Back to the stairwell," I said.

We pushed back through the stairwell door. The opposite side of the door was still marked '*Lobby*' but looking down over the stairwell rail showed we were three floors up.

"Adrian, this is insane. Maybe we should abort," said R.J.

"There's been no danger that I can see so far, just a screwed-up reality. What do you think, Elachia?" I asked.

"Continue on, please," she answered. "I'm still getting interesting readings."

We continued the climb. The next floor's door read '*4.*' Looking through the small safety glass window in the door, the hallway beyond was deserted.

At '*6,*' something new stopped us. Through the window in the door, the hallway was populated by half a dozen people going to and fro as though it were a normal workday. R.J.

shrugged and waved a hand to suggest we go in and talk to them.

We opened the door to find the hallway deserted. Closing the door brought busy people back into view through the window. Several subsequent attempts yielded the same result.

We continued up.

The seventh floor was also deserted, though the hallway seemed to be out of square. We ignored it and continue to '8,' relieved that the floor was labeled correctly, and no other absurdities seemed to be present.

"Admiral Provose's office is the third door on the left," I said, and we headed that way.

I did not bother to knock. The knob on the double door turned open, but it felt funny like faint electricity was tickling my hand. We paraded in, past an unoccupied secretarial desk, and into the office beyond. To my surprise, Provose was there. We stood gawking at him sitting behind his desk holding a landline phone in his hand. He looked up as we entered and seemed to be searching the room.

As soon as he moved, we could see things were not as they should be. It was a strange, uncomfortable visual effect. With each movement, trails followed along behind him. When he placed the phone down, seven or eight hands and arms followed the movement, quickly catching up and blending together.

I took a chance. "Admiral?"

He looked up abruptly with another cascade of movement. He seemed to have heard something but clearly could not see us.

"Admiral Provose!"

"Hello? Is someone there, or am I talking to a mosquito?" His voice had a rapid echo to it.

"It's Adrian, Neil. Can you hear me?"

"Wait! Say that again!"

"Adrian Tarn, Neil. Can you hear us?"

"Adrian?" he stood and continued to search the room for us. The flow of following images made him difficult to focus on. "You sound like a buzzing insect, but I can make out what you're saying!"

"Neil, are you alright?"

Finally, he seemed to isolate our direction. He sounded exasperated. "Adrian, this is insane! I can't see you, but I can just barely hear you! Your voice is phasing in and out. Wait! I can just make out a faint wavy outline of you! There are others with you. As you can see, the Space Center has become multi-dimensionally corrupted or something. I do not understand it. It only just happened a few hours ago. I was in the security vault when it happened. Now nothing works. I can't even call out. I can't speak to any of my government contacts. I can see it's a disaster outside my windows, but I can't even go out there. Every time I try to leave somehow, I end up back on this floor!"

I spoke in a loud voice, "It was an explosion at the Higgs-Englert Hadron Collider, Neil. It has warped our reality. It is a worldwide effect."

"I can make out three of you now. It was a collider explosion? The entire world, you say? The new Hadron Collider? Oh God, now I understand! I was called to an emergency meeting of the National Research Council, the Division on Engineering and Physical Sciences last week. There was a petition to interrupt scheduled testing by the World European Nuclear Research Institute. WERN didn't like it but I was told that later they gave in. The testing was highly classified. A new particle or something. No one paid much attention to it. And you're saying that's the cause of all this? That experiment did this? What the hell did they do?"

R.J. cut in, "Admiral, do you know anything else about the experiment? We were outside the event horizon when it happened. We weren't affected. We're trying to help."

"I'm guessing that was Smith? Smith is that you I'm seeing? I see only faint blurry outlines."

"Yes, Neil. We're here with Elachia. Do you know what they were experimenting with?" said R.J.

"It was too classified. We weren't involved so we were not briefed. But there were rumors. The lead scientist's name was floating around. DeSortes, Doctor Andrea DeSortes."

"Oh my God," said R.J. and he held his forehead with one hand and looked at me in disbelief.

It stunned me for a moment. I pinched my eyes and shook my head.

"How did you three get here? It appears nothing mechanical or electrical works out there."

"The Griffin, Neil. We were outside the event horizon when it happened. We weren't affected. And we can't stay. We have to leave, or we will be caught by the next event. This catastrophe resets and repeats every twenty-four hours." I said.

"I don't understand?"

"Too much to explain, Neil. Unless you know something else, we've got to get going."

"What can I do? Can you assist us here?"

"We've got to find someone still alive who is associated with the Hadron Collider project, Neil. Do you have access to any of your science staff?"

"Unfortunately, I do not. As I said, I seem unable to leave the floor of this building and I cannot call out. I'm hoping some of my staff will eventually report in here or maybe cell phones will start working."

"Unlikely, Neil. There is an associate collider research facility in Texas. Maybe someone there can help. As I've said, our time here is limited. We'll try to return when we have more answers."

"Maybe I can accompany you."

"It is important that you remain on Earth for now Neil, and again we don't have time to explain."

"Well, let me walk with you. Maybe you can help me get off this damned floor at least."

I went to the door and held it open. Provose looked on like it was like a ghost opening his door for him. Enduring the tiny electrical shock from the handle was uncomfortable. The Admiral straightened up, rose from his seat, and his array of following images walked out past us into the hall. He turned and struggled to keep focus on our faint outlines as he recombined.

We headed for the stairwell door. The Admiral led the way and kept looking back. At the door, he pulled it open and held it. We passed through and gathered to watch.

"Okay, Admiral. Come on," called R.J.

A cascade of Admirals stepped into the stairwell and vanished, one at a time. To our surprise, the Admiral suddenly appeared in the distance at the other end of the hall.

He waved to us and held his arms up in frustration. We let the door swing shut and headed down the stairs.

"At least we were able to make contact," said R.J.

Elachia said, "The Admiral had the same faint, unfamiliar radiation signature embedded in him, the same one I see in the walls and furniture here. This wasn't a wasted trip."

R.J. replied, "Actually, we got some big ugly answers up there, didn't we? As soon as he mentioned DeSortes I had a great epiphany. You got that too of course, didn't you, Adrian?"

"You'll have to excuse me. I may be sick."

"What does it mean, Rowland?" asked Elachia.

"Dr. Andrea DeSortes was the woman scientist who led the Saturn Daphnis mission. She and her associate extracted that power source from the Daphnis ship, without telling us that was the real mission objective."

"But what was it?" asked Elachia.

I answered, "We have no idea. She called it Diamond Light. That's what it looked like too, silver light full of diamonds. It burned her associate badly. She stood back a safe distance while he did the extraction."

"So we know what the catalyst for this disaster was, and we know where it came from," said Elachia.

"Not sure how much that helps," I replied.

We reached the building's lobby and headed back outside. The world remained in just as much chaos as when we had entered. I drew my communicator, "Danica, I've left my comm open the whole time so you'd hear everything. Did you get all of it? And, we're ready for pickup. Onward to Texas."

"Yes I heard, Boss. On my way," replied Danica.

To the east, odd-shaped clouds were slowly moving toward us. They had a strange orange tint to them. Elachia seemed concerned, as I should have been. As soon as R.J. noticed he let out an, "Oh no!"

I searched the horizon and sure enough in the far distance a smoke stream of orange was rising into the clouds.

"It's hydrazine," said R.J. "Has to be."

"But they rarely use the stuff now-a-days," I said in a half whine.

"Satellites. The cheap ones," replied R.J.

I raised my communicator. "Danica, could you please be... prompt."

A faint laugh came back over the comm unit. I wondered if I should have been more explicit.

A black dot appeared in the sky above us and looked as though it was falling right at us. It increased in size and color as it came. We all instinctively backed away from the lawn.

She used both heavy thrusters and the antigrav to slow it. She was facing the wrong way for the rear airlock door. We would have gladly run around. Just a few feet off the ground she spun Griffin around so that the rear door was facing us then settled the ship with a tiny bounce. The airlock slid open and the ramp popped out and down. We ran in.

Danica brought it up to a hundred and held it there while I strapped in the right seat. As soon as Elachia and R.J. were secured in the engineering station seats we brought in the antigrav and headed up.

"Take it to ten thousand and let's head for Texas."

"We still have nothing but visual and magnetic compass for nav. Do you think you can find this place?" she asked.

I looked back at R.J. "Would you pull up a satellite map to the Desertron Collider site for us? Feed it up here to the nav display."

"There's bound to be good data available on the Desertron since they resurrected that project," said R.J.

"Would you guys keep all the cameras running on *save* also? We'll have extreme close-ups to study when it's time to leave."

"Already doing that, Adrian," said Elachia.

Danica glanced over, "So besides what I heard on the com, what else did you find down there?"

I shook my head. "It's like a fun house at a carnival. Nothing makes sense. We were very lucky even to talk to Provose. He's in his own little hell."

"Why didn't you bring him?"

"Didn't you hear us? When he goes through a door, he ends up back where he started?"

"What?"

"Exactly what I said. There's no better way to put it."

"Adrian, we do have a satellite map that includes the new collider construction," called R.J. "I'm sending it to your Nav screen."

I studied the map's topography as we sped across the torn-up landscape of Florida then out over the Gulf. There still was not a cloud in sight, high or low. A few minutes out over the ocean, Danica pointed to something. "What *is* that up ahead?"

I searched the rough water and spotted what she was asking about. It was some type of disturbance in the gulf. A big one. As we neared, it became clearer, a whirlpool the size of a football field.

"Do you see that?" called out R.J. as he studied the forward camera monitor. "It's like a hole in the ocean."

"Dan, slow us down. Let's orbit this thing once," I said.

It was massive and tragic. Had it not been so extraordinarily deep we would have been able to see the ocean floor. There were three boats caught in the vortex at various intervals. On the eastern outside border, the crew of a large fishing boat seemed to be fighting to navigate away from the current's grip. On the western side, what appeared to be an expensive yacht was caught midway in the swirl. It was nearly sideways to the pit of the whirlpool but making no headway out. But the worst was on the Northern inner edge. Some type of moderate-sized cruise ship, packed with people, was out of control and doing slow three-hundred and sixty-degree rotations as it neared the drop off. It was leaning to port badly. People were sliding off the low side. A panicked mass of others were running and climbing everywhere on deck.

"I can't look anymore," said Danica.

Elachia and R.J. sat in stunned silence behind us. We all considered attempting some type of insane rescue. No one suggested it.

"Let's get back on course," I said.

"Gladly," replied Danica.

We continued on in a heavy quietude as though we had just seen a movie with a bad ending.

"New Orleans should be coming up on our starboard side shortly," I said to break the gloom.

"I'm afraid to look," said Danica.

"Can you imagine what Dallas must look like?" called R.J.

"I don't want to," answered Danica. She tapped keys to bring up R.J.'s topography maps on her main nav display and began searching the distance for signs of land.

"I need some water. You want a drink, Dan?" I asked.

"Yes, but water will have to do," she replied.

I pushed up out of my seat and squeezed back between Elachia and R.J. at their stations. "Water break. You guys want anything?"

"I'm fine," said Elachia.

"I'll get it myself in a minute or two," said R.J.

As I fetched my water bottle from the fridge unit, R.J. moaned, "Man, what a nightmare."

I hurried back to find him staring at his starboard camera display.

"Yep, that's New Orleans," called out Danica.

I went to a starboard portal for a better view. Gulf ocean now occupied most of New Orleans. High rise buildings rose out of the water. The white dome of the Superdome sat just above the waterline. Debris was floating everywhere. No watercraft appeared to have survived the breach. It was a very calm, macabre vision of a drowned city.

"Uh-oh, got a little problem here," called Danica.

I climbed back into my seat, still not having tasted the water. "What now?"

"Turbine acting up. Main feed from the number two ball tank. I was expecting something like this. Running the OMS system continuously, those pumps have been cranking way more than usual. It's going to die on us. I guarantee it."

"Great. We'd still have up and down but couldn't go anywhere."

"Right. Using the light drive engines from a dead stop is never a good thing to do. You have a replacement turbine in spares?"

"Yes. That's the good news."

"So you can either put down somewhere to work on it, or go way up and do the same thing in a spacesuit."

"That's the bad news."

"Yeah, it is. If we do put down, which makes the most sense, you've got to make the switch and have us flight worthy before the next collider event."

R.J. came up between us. "I heard all that."

"Ever switched out a fuel turbine?" I asked.

"I was an inspector on that job a couple times."

"How long?"

"It was quite a few years back."

"I *meant* how long did the job take?!"

"There you go, ornery."

"For Pete's sake, R.J. Take a look where we are."

"There's Pete again. I can always tell when we're in trouble. Pete shows up."

"R.J. How long?"

"Several hours. It's an outside job. We'll be working into the dark. That is, if it still gets dark here on Earth."

"I remember now. It's a panel back by the tail. The compartment is lighted, and we've got spotlights to work in the dark."

R.J. pinched his lip in thought. "I'll call up the drawings and make a plan."

"Please do. Dan and I will need to find an isolated place to put down, somewhere we can't be seen too easily. Dan and Ela will need to keep watch with long guns while we work."

"I'm on it," said R.J.

As he headed back, I yelled to him, "Stun settings!"

It took longer to reach the coast of Texas than we expected. That was because the Gulf had swallowed up a good deal of the state. Houston was now shorefront property. Except for the high rises jutting above the water, half the city was now submerged. Our original destination was the Waxahachie area, south of Dallas, but we weren't going to make that. The ship was beginning to go through periods of shuddering and that's a very bad way to run on OMS engines. We needed an open area away from any roads and away from populated areas. If the work went past nightfall as R.J. had suggested, we'd have big lights set up, beacons sure to attract attention.

There was a lake on our charts, Sam Rayburn lake. It was long and narrow and pointed in our general direction. As we neared land, we could see it in the distance. Danica used it for a compass heading in the direction of Waxahachie. Within the surrounding forest there were patches of clearing beginning to become visible. For no apparent reason, the lake was bone dry. There was an old sunken fishing boat in the middle of it. No fish or other life could be seen anywhere. Vibration from the OMS was now too bad to continue. Danica pointed to a clearing not far ahead. I nodded in agreement.

The Griffin jerked and bucked down into an open area roughly the size of a baseball diamond, a field spotted with tall, brown grass. We settled onto gravel, grass, and weed. An off-roader trail ran through the middle of the place. When we had finished parking and the OMS thrust levers were pulled back to lower the sputtering whine, I nodded to her. "Good enough."

"I don't like this much," she replied.

I had to agree.

Chapter 16

All too often an unexpected job rears its ugly head, and to make matters worse every repair attempt goes ridiculously wrong. R.J. has a dozen motivational speeches for just such occasions. Success is the enemy of adversity. Patience is the surest remedy for frustration. Anger is undeveloped determination. I once thought of choking him as he stood over me dispensing those jewels of wisdom, but I feared he might have yet another to fit that occasion as well.

The utility ladder was buried in its compartment by ancient, unnecessarily stored items. When you extended the ladder, some type of ingenious, misunderstood clanking latches supposedly guarantee that it won't collapse under you sending you crashing toward the ground in a flat spin you cannot recover from. Having properly positioned the ladder, you are unavoidably frightened by each distrusting step above the extension joint. R.J. steadied the ladder and offered comical reassurance from below, "Don't worry, these never fail."

Fortunately, the access panel was high enough that I could stretch out and straddle the top of the spacecraft's body. It was a break-dance of sorts, sliding around in those positions, unscrewing fasteners and carefully stowing them in order. Panel removed, R.J. was required to come up the ladder to bring the thing down. He had the same look of misgiving that I had. "Don't worry, those never fail," I said.

"Touché," he replied. "It was funnier when I said it." He lowered the panel to Danica then came up and joined me atop Griffin.

"Crap," was the first word out of his mouth as we shined a hand lantern down into the dimly lit access compartment.

"Thank God we didn't try to do this in spacesuits," I added.

"Those six pressure lines are shown on a different section of drawing. That's why I didn't expect them. So much for detached schematics. In space we would have had to depressurize and disconnect them. At least here we have a slight chance of moving them out of the way enough to pull out the turbine."

"Yeah, but we bend one or make a hole and we'll be here for a very long time."

"Only until the next collider event. Then it will start all over."

"Well thank-you, Mr. Sunshine."

He opened his mouth, but I cut him off, "Don't you dare say ornery."

By the time we'd set up the proper tools and parts, the day's light was already beginning to fade. Staging spotlights took another forty-five minutes. Working hands or just fingers in the cramped compartment, underneath the crossing pressure lines, I began the removal of the old turbine pump assembly. Two and a half hours later the thing came loose so that I could wiggle it around in the tight space. We used cloth wrapped pry bars to risk pushing the pressure lines apart enough to just squeeze the damn thing out. It looked like a small, metallic football with a tube coming out of each end. We sat atop

Griffin exhausted, comparing the old unit with the new.

"They're the same, thank God," said R.J. tiredly.

I started to ask him if we dared take a break when Danica called out, "Adrian, you'd better get down here."

We looked up worriedly from our position and scanned around the open compartment, searching for anything that would cause Danica's voice to have a tone of urgency. Lights were on inside Griffin, but they did little to illuminate the area around us.

It took us a few moments for our eyes to adjust enough to spot them. Standing at the edge of darkness a few dozen feet away, three people, a man in tan work clothes, a woman in gray slacks and light blue blouse, and a teenager in jeans and a Cowboys T-shirt. The three weren't quite all there. They were faintly transparent like ghosts coming out of the night, and they stood staring up at the two of us. We hurriedly climbed down to join Danica.

I wiped my hands on my coveralls, leaned in close and asked, "What do they want?"

Danica held her weapon pointed toward the ground. "No idea. They haven't said anything. They're just staring up at the lights."

"Have you called out to them?"

"No. I'm too creeped out. They look like ghosts."

As we spoke, Elachia walked past us with her rifle slung behind, a scanner held out and scanning. R.J. immediately chased after her. The two reached the new arrivals, but the strangers ignored them. Elachia began a close-up scan. No words were exchanged. The family of ghosts did not seem to be aware of Elachia or R.J. As the scanning continued, the man of the group visually searched the area around Griffin and seemed to call out, but we couldn't hear a word he said. From our perspective he was mouthing the words, "Hello? Hello?" I could not tell the rest.

To my dismay two more people appeared out of the darkness. A man and a woman. The man was dressed in work coveralls, the woman in a very plain flowered dress. They were just as semi-transparent as the first three. They joined the others and again did not seem aware of Elachia or R.J. They began speaking to the first arrivals, and as before we could not hear them at all.

Elachia and R.J. returned. Elachia said, "They have a much denser signature of radiation than the Admiral had. If I had to guess, I would say these people were outside when the Diamond Light wave hit. They got a full dose. But that is still just speculation, of course."

"They can't see us?" asked Danica.

"I believe they see the bright work lights but not the ship nor us. I do not believe we can communicate with them. Our light must be bright enough to shine into their environment and it's probably the only functioning electric light on Earth right now," said Elachia.

"But that means we could communicate using the lights," said R.J.

"To what end, Rowland? It would be very slow, confusing, and difficult," said Elachia.

"She's right, R.J. Besides, we need to get this ship up before the next wave. We'd better get back to it," I suggested.

To our dismay, another individual appeared on the edge of the darkness, staring up at our light. He wore a gray businessman's suit that was dirty and in disarray. He spied the other semitransparent and went to them. A discussion ensued.

"It's getting worse all the time, R.J. Let's hurry up and get out of here," I urged.

R.J. nodded agreement. "Problem is, what we have left to do won't be quick, Adrian."

The idea of a break now completely discarded, we climbed up to the work area and proceeded with a touch more quiet nervousness than before. An hour into the work, there were now a dozen semi-transparents lingering around the Griffin. Two children chasing one another ran right through the ship's landing legs without ever knowing they had done so. The growing assembly spent most of their time calling out and staring up at our work lights. It was an odd tribute to life's most basic instinct. Most basic cellular life responses to light. Plants and trees reach for it. Insect life desire nothing more. And here we were, humankind, deprived of all our magic machines, gathering at the only remaining stimulus. A case could be made that it betrays our true simplistic, instinctive nature. But, since light has always been the most celebrated and accepted symbol of God, it could also be an example of our primordial subconscious allegiance and trust in Him.

At dawn the new turbine was in place. Our hands were cut and bruised. We began reinstalling the outer panel cover. We were now surrounded by a large fearsome-looking crowd. They had formed smaller groups within the larger. There was a great deal of wandering around. Although they still could not see us, the sheer number of them made me so nervous that I was fumbling tools and fasteners.

"Whatever you do, please don't drop a fastener," said R.J. "We can't fly if we're missing one." It was clear he shared my case of the jitters.

"Believe me, I'm with you," I replied.

"I could start taking down the lights, but I'm afraid of the effect it might have on our audience."

"Maybe when the sun is fully up it will drown out our lights enough."

"We could try shutting them down one at a time, too. I feel like turning them off will be like taking away all hope from these people."

"We still have time to make the Desertron site before we've got to get into space."

"Only if the new turbine works."

"Yeah, how long to run the calibration and systems tests?"

"Forty-five minutes probably. Why don't we leave these things on while Danica does that? We'll pull them down as soon as she's done. It'll be full sun by then. I wonder if they'll hear the engines?"

"Doesn't really matter. No other option. That's the last fastener. I don't know about you, but I'm beat."

"Tell me about it."

We left the lights and climbed down. To R.J.'s alarm Elachia, rifle still slung over her back, was winding her way through the crowd, scanning intently as she went. Danica remained close by; weapon ready. R.J. walked briskly through the crowd to his love and after a short conversation the two returned as Danica backed away.

"We'll leave the lights until Danica finishes systems checks," I said.

"That would be a kind gesture," said Elachia. "These people are all saturated with the unidentified radiation. They were all somewhere completely unprotected when it hit. As we speculated, they cannot see us at all, only the bright lights." As Elachia spoke, a young transparent child ran right through us, oblivious to our presence. Danica handed me her rifle and headed for the airlock.

I stood back by the tail, listening for the damning sound of dry turbine blades or failing pressure jets, but the Griffin hummed to life, giving cause for silent thankful prayer.

R.J. joined me. "I wish Ela wouldn't just jump into things like that," he said.

"Yeah, she's too much like us."

"She said she thought those people could feel her presence. There was body language and eye contact."

"With her, I wouldn't be surprised."

"Hear anything yet?"

"Just the APU warming up. She hasn't engaged fuel pressures yet."

"How are we on fuel, anyway?"

"We're okay. There was no orbital maneuvering leaving Enuro. We went to stellar drives right after escape velocity, so we arrived here still topped off. The last time I checked we were at sixty-four percent. We can make it to Desertron, leave, and still make another trip before we need to decide on refueling."

"That's good because we're not going to get any fuel around here. That's for sure."

Thirty minutes later, things were looking good. Danica came on the outside speaker system and announced all systems tests were good and she was just waiting for the program to finish running. I climbed back up and handed R.J. one spotlight at a time to lower to the ground. The lingering crowd became upset and began moving around more as though searching. Finished, I slid around on Griffin's smooth skin and began the fearful search with my feet for the top rung of the dubitable ladder. But as I found the first step, Danica came back on the loudspeaker.

"You guys better get in here," she said once again, and her tone sounded dark.

We gathered up our lights, collapsed the ladder, and headed up the ramp. In the airlock, things were quickly stowed. We emerged into the living area to find our already bizarre situation had suddenly become even more dangerous.

Chapter 17

A harsh, almost machine-sounding voice commanded us. "Just hold it right there!"

We had barely entered Griffin's living compartment. We were both weary from a long night of difficult work. My coveralls were thoroughly smudged with dirt and lubricants. R.J.'s hair and beard were back in Einstein-style. I looked up and focused on someone sitting with his back to a port window who should not have been there. He wore camouflage hunter's wear with a round soft rim camouflage hat. He had beard shadow, dark brows, and a long face, no hair showing from under his cap. He did not seem to have transparency but there was a strange, faint aura of gold around him that made his features a bit difficult to focus on. He held a disruptor rifle leveled at Elachia sitting opposite him. His rifle had the same strange glow. Immediately I felt R.J. catch his breath and tighten up.

Danica leaned over and called from the flight deck, "He came in while you guys were taking down the lights."

"Stay right where you are," said the machine-human voice. "We need to get some things straight."

I managed to control my anger. "Who are you and what do you want?"

"First things first, Captain Tarn. The ladies have filled me in on who you are. First I want you to know that this disruptor is set to kill."

"Take me instead," replied R.J. "There's no need to threaten her. I volunteer."

"Forget it, Smith. I know that the two of you value this drop-dead gorgeous woman's life more than your own. So I imagine you guys will not give me any shit as long as this kill weapon is pointed at her. My last job was security, so I know what I'm doing."

"The question is, *why* are you doing this?" I asked.

"You may think this weapon doesn't work. Take my word for it. It makes big holes in everything."

Elachia said, "I've scanned him. He has less than fifty percent of the radiation signature that the others have. That's why he can see us."

"Where did you come from?" I asked.

"Why am I not fading away like everybody else? I was on duty in the basement vault of the Cordon Financial Exchange building. I had to manually open that freakin' heavy automatic security door to get out of the place. When I came up to street level, the world was really screwed up all of a sudden."

"There must have been heavy shielding where he was," said Elachia.

"So what do you want?" I asked again.

"You will help me gather up a few things."

"Are you kidding me?" I said.

"Haven't you looked around, Tarn? It's a new world. There's no law and order anymore. The entire place is wide open for anyone to take what they want. Whoever gets the most will eventually run this place. I figure with this ship I'm way ahead."

I glanced at R.J. He seemed too frozen with fear for Elachia to speak. "What's your name? What do we call you?"

"You can call me Dutch. I don't want to hurt any of you but don't test me because I sure will. I could kill two of you right now and still get done what I need. I've got to keep this gun on the kill setting so you guys don't decide to rush me all at once thinking maybe one might make it. You test me, and some of you will die. You do what I ask, and nobody gets hurt. I'll even turn this ship back over to you when I'm done. You got it?"

I tried to put aside my desire to wring the living daylights out of him and instead sound sympathetic. "Dutch, you don't understand what's going on. This catastrophe isn't just happening to Texas."

"Okay, how far does it go?"

"It's worldwide."

"I don't believe you."

"There's no place to go, Dutch. There's no place to use what you take," said R.J.

"Right. Here's what we're going to do, and Tarn I can tell you're the most dangerous. So I should warn you right up front, if you try to do the get-too-close thing, I'll kill either you or her without any warning. I know how that crap works. We're going to fly into Dallas to my employer's CFE building. I have all the keys to the place, and I fixed the vault door shut but unlocked. We're going to load up with bars of gold, then you're gonna take me to some friends I have in South America. You do all that, and I'll turn you loose, no harm done."

We stood in exhausted silence. Explaining the facts of life to Dutch seemed an impossible task. R.J. was still fixed on the weapon leveled at Elachia. I wanted to get this guy so bad it was enough to make me cry.

Dutch persisted. "Remember, I can do this with just the doll up front at the wheel, but I'd rather have the help."

I tried once more. "Dutch, you've seen the people outside. Ghosts you can't even touch. Your gold may be in the same condition."

"Nope. I was in that vault. The gold was okay, but I stacked a few outside the vault just to be sure. We're good to go."

I called out, "Dan?"

She yelled back, "Yeah, I've pulled up the maps. The Corden Financial Exchange building is on them. There's a parking area about a block away that we can put down in if it's empty enough."

"Systems test?"

"Complete, all green."

Dutch straightened up and called out, "If you screw with me Dan, I'll kill one of them just to make a point."

"We only have about four hours to the next event, Dan. Let's go get his gold," I said.

"Hold on to something back there," she replied, and the Griffin power systems came alive all around us. The sound of the rear airlock ramp and door closing was followed by a swaying lift off the ground. Outside the portals the view changed as we rose above the trees, turned in place to a northern heading, and leaned into forward motion.

"What's the next event mean?" asked Dutch.

"Can we sit?" I asked.

"Those two seats in the back," he replied. "No closer. What'd you mean, the next event?"

We carefully took seats, I starboard, R.J. port. "It's what we've been trying to tell you, Dutch. All the destruction you see out there will go away for a few moments, then the explosion that caused it all will go off again and the world will be just as screwed up."

"You gotta come up with a better story than that, Tarn."

"Would you at least lower that rifle so you don't accidentally shoot Elachia?"

Slowly he lowered it toward her feet, not nearly enough to make a move on him but at least it wasn't pointed at her heart.

I tried to convince him again. "Dutch, we're telling you the truth. We have to be in space before the next event or this spacecraft will no longer function, just like everything else on Earth."

"Well then, you better get done with what I'm telling you to do, right?"

With the disruptor rifle lowered, R.J. had finally gathered himself enough to speak a second time, "Dutch, if this place is in Dallas, how did you get here?"

"I'm through pedaling that bike, I'll tell you that. You got anything to eat around here?"

Elachia answered, "Mr. Dutch, you should probably not eat our food. You are infected with radiation. Our food is not. It might not be compatible with you or there could be harmful effects."

"You guys are real jokers, aren't you? You don't even want me eating your food? I'm going to get up and look through this kitchen area over here, see what I can find. Tarn, if you try it, I'm sure to get at least one of you, probably two and she'll still be the first to go. Okay? You got that?"

He was very good. He never took his eyes off me more than a half second while keeping the rifle pointed in Elachia's general direction. R.J. kept giving me don't-you-dare glances. Dutch found the refrigeration unit and kept his gun steady in the right hand while pulling a sandwich out with his left. He sat back in his seat and like any good professional, unwrapped it with one hand while not taking his eyes off me, then raised the sandwich to his mouth.

Elachia was earnest, "Mr. Dutch, you shouldn't eat that. We don't know what it will do to you."

Dutch bit down on the sandwich, chewed and made a face of joy. It was an odd image of a man and gun with a strange faint glow of gold, eating a sandwich that did not glow at all.

Out the portals we were now flying over the south side of Dallas. It was so devastated it looked like a carnival that had been hit by a tornado. All of the buildings had that same sickly golden hue. Every so often I caught a glimpse of a body in the street. Some of the high rises looked twisted in place. Others seemed bent over. From time to time there were ghostly groups of people gathered in the street. Looking straight down. At one point I spotted a main roadway that ended in the middle of a parted high rise.

Danica called out, "Coming up on it. The parking area is open enough."

My mind began to argue that this was really going to happen. We were going to rob a private bank, but ironically in three or four hours, none of it would actually have ever happened. I had a sick feeling in my stomach at the thought of how impossible our lives had become. It was just like the lucid dream we had considered earlier. No way to wake up.

Griffin slowed, stopped, and rotated. She settled down into the stack of violated buildings and bounced slightly to rest in a parking lot bordered by cars piled up not far away. They looked as if a tsunami had struck. There was a long silent moment as Dutch finished his sandwich and stole glances out a portal.

"Perfect!" he declared. "Okay boys, here's the plan. You two will go bring the gold here while I sit with the ladies and wait for you. The CFE Building is the next big glass building over. There's a shopping cart I found that still works right outside the back doors to the building. The numbers for the pad lock are 8156. Leave the cart there, go in the building, take the stairs down. In the basement there's a cage door to get in where the vaults are. The lock code is the same, 8156. Inside the cage you'll see the big vault door. Just pull it open. You'll see a smaller vault door across the room. That's the weapons locker. It's locked. You'll find a backpack I left on the floor by the vault. It would be good if you could bring another one along with you. In the safe there are 400-ounce bars and 1000-gram bars. The big ones are 25 pounds, bring those first. Load up your backpacks, tote them up to the shopping cart and truck them here. It's gonna take at least four trips. Be careful not to overload the shopping cart. Okay, get going if you wanna get rid of me, right?"

Elachia tried again, "Mr. Dutch...."

He cut her off. "That was a good sandwich, Ma'am. A little heavy for my taste. You just sit quiet while these boys get to work."

R.J.'s face was flushed with restrained anger. There wasn't a thing we could do. We were trapped in criminal's fantasy. The guy wasn't too smart, but he was just smart enough to make it work. We had to bide our time for a chance. I stood and motioned R.J. to follow. We went to the rear airlock and tapped the outer door button. It slid open, followed by the ramp. Dutch remained seated, watching our every move. I shook my head, grabbed a backpack and trotted down the ramp.

At the bottom, R.J. caught me by the arm. "We can't leave them with him."

"He won't do anything to either of them as long as we're bringing him his gold. He knows if he messes with them we'll stop working. There's no way to get to him right now. Sooner or later he's got to make a mistake. We've got to play it smart. You understand?"

R.J. slowly exhaled. "Yeah, okay. I guess...."

As we looked around the arcane city, a group of transparent gang members came strolling down the street brandishing an array of weapons as though they were looking for trouble of any kind. They could not see us or the ship and just passed by swinging chain and tapping the tip of a samurai sword on the glowing pavement. It was another surreal sight that made us feel abandoned by reality.

We took the sidewalk to the CFE building. There was a slight upwelling to it, but everything Dutch had described was there waiting. The grocery cart parked by the back door had a label, "Save-A-Lot." No passcode was needed. The combo lock already had released. We followed the stairs down, pushed through the next unlocked door and entered the basement. The place was dark as night.

"We've got to block those doors open," I said. You get one, I'll get the other."

We returned to the hazy daylight and found glowing red bricks surrounding a wilted hedge. With both doors fixed open, light streamed into the underground chamber.

It was no wonder Dutch had been protected. The entire basement was actually vaulted. There were computer stations around the main room. Their screens were dark. The caged-in area was also just as he described. The vault door was the big round type, a foot thick. It had the same faint golden glow and pulled open more easily than would normally be expected. Inside safe deposit boxes lined one wall. There were shelves along the opposite wall. Dutch's backpack was on the floor with two large gold bars exposed. On a reinforced shelf nearby were more.

R.J. loosened up for a moment. "If I wasn't so damned scared there's a dozen comments I could make about this," he said.

"Our education counselors always said we'd end up in a life of crime."

"One of those guys suggested I was best suited as a domestic animal psychologist."

"Not so far off, if you think about it."

"What?"

"Well, you always seem to be right-on about the bad guys."

R.J. hefted a gold bar from a nearby shelf. "These gold bars feel like they weigh about half of what they should."

"Makes sense. They're only half here according to Elachia."

R.J. began loading his backpack. I dragged the one on the floor over and joined in.

"You know we've got to get this guy quick, Adrian."

"I promise you, we will. But even if we kill him, he'll be right back here after the next event."

"But we won't be. Where's all the little tricks you always have up your sleeve when I need one?"

"Funny you should mention that." I reached in my pocket and drew out my communicator.

R.J. stopped and raised his eyebrows.

"Danica always uses the headset. She never has it set on speaker."

"Why didn't I think of this?" asked R.J.

"Danica, if you can hear me do not speak. One mike click for yes. Two mike clicks for no. Can you hear me?"

There was a moment of silence then, *Click.*

"Has the bastard done anything to either of you since we've been gone?"

Click, click.

I looked at R.J. "How much time before the next event?"

R.J. glanced at his watch. "Three hours, forty-two minutes."

"Dan, R.J. says three hours, forty-two minutes before the next event. Let's agree right now that we will be in space before then no matter what it takes."

Click.

"Do you have a disrupter nearby and ready?"

Click.

"Do not make a move unless it's absolutely a last resort. He's bound to make a mistake before then."

Click.

"In the meantime, R.J. and I will try to work something out. We'll let you know."

Click.

R.J. took a deep breath. "I suddenly feel a little better about our chances."

"You know this guy isn't actually going to let us live when he's done, right?"

"Of course."

"Have you ever seen Danica on the firing range?"

"I don't visit that often."

"I have. She'll put a hole in this guy's head with a single shot in less than two seconds. But, I don't know if she's ever actually killed anyone. She might hesitate."

"A lot can happen in two seconds, but still that is reassuring to know. I now feel slightly better still."

"How many bars you taking this load?"

"Four I think. In case we need to drag this out."

"Good idea."

We slung our gold-bearing backpacks over our shoulders and headed up to the grocery cart. Eight bars were two hundred pounds as far as the cart was concerned. It sagged and resisted. We urged it along the cartoon land around us and found Griffin's parking lot too gravelly for the overburdened carriage. We hoisted our backpacks and headed up the ramp. Dutch was in the same seat, weapon still lowered in Elachia's direction. He became excited by the first backpacks-full and stood to watch us empty our gold. A quick nod of approval from him was followed by a terse gesture directing us to go get more.

On our way back with the second load, I stopped R.J. and said, "Stack the rest of it close to the door. If he asks, tell him no use carrying it any further than necessary. He'll hafta go out into the airlock to checkout his treasure."

"Seal him in and depressurize? Is that what you're thinking? What if he brings Ela with him?"

"Either way, we'll put him to sleep. If Ela is with him, she'll just get a very brief nap after which we'll keep the idiot unconscious until we're rid of him."

"Danica, you still with us?"

Click.

"If the asshole goes out into the airlock without Elachia, if you get the chance, snap the emergency pressure door shut and lock it, okay? No way he'll be able to get back in, and we'll take care of him outside."

Click.

R.J. noted, "I doubt he'll fall for that. As for your plan, we'd need to have them in the airlock with the ramp up and outer door closed. For some reason he would have to close the inner door himself. If we close it, he'll know we're screwing with him and he'll still have Ela as a hostage. Even then, the airlock pumps aren't that fast. It would take at least thirty seconds to bring the airlock down to high altitude pressures."

"Try to stay patient. He'll screw up. I guarantee it."

By the fourth load, the bastard still had not taken the bait. We had been up all night working on the turbine and were getting too tired to continue. Fortunately, after sliding the last of the load into the airlock, Dutch was apparently satisfied. He called us into the living compartment, but his position had changed. He was now standing aft, just inside the door to the airlock, one arm around Elachia's neck, the free hand holding the disrupter against her side.

"You guys take seats up front. Danica, get going. San Carlos, Argentina is where you need to be. I'll show you exactly where when we get there."

Danica wasted no time. She brought up the ramp and closed up. We lifted off and turned to a general heading of south as she called up maps. A moment later we were headed south.

"Now, Ms. Elachia and I are going to step back and take a look at your work and my future. I'm going to shut the door so there's no heroes trying to charge back there. Just remember, I can kill this one and still be ready for you two if you try. You just sit tight and we'll be right back. A man needs to count his winnings. In fact, sit down and fasten your seat belts."

We had no choice but to oblige him.

He dragged Elachia backward into the airlock. This time I was holding my breath along with R.J. Inside the airlock he took a quick look around, gave us a sick little smile then found the door button and tapped the door closed.

R.J. burst out of his straps and nearly fell over me charging the engineering station. He began hammering keys as fast as he could.

I raced up beside him. "For God's sake, you've got to do it slowly so he doesn't realize he's passing out."

"I know! I know!"

"You want me to do it?"

"Not on your life!"

R.J. called up one of the airlock cameras to our console display. Dutch was still appraising his take. He had Elachia by one arm. On a second monitor R.J. brought up the atmospheric readouts for the airlock. The O2 dial already was moving down excruciatingly slow with the helium feed increasing to match. There would be no loss of air pressure, no clue that O2 was being withdrawn.

Dutch surveyed his gold stash, still unaware of what was happening. We watched the monitors nervously, hoping he would not catch the first symptoms of hypoxia. Even experienced pilots often do not. Dutch finally looked up from his gold and turned his attention to Elachia. R.J. jerked to attention beside me.

There was a moment of resistance from Elachia as Dutch used one hand against her chest to press her against the wall. She was a little too much for him. He had to reach behind and place his rifle on a shelf to use both hands. A glance at the O2 dial showed it passing below fourteen percent.

"He's a dead man. He just doesn't know it yet."

"It's okay R.J. This is good."

"What the hell's so good about it?"

"He's so spun up for Elachia he'll never notice the lack of O2."

R.J. made a growling sound.

Dutch held her with both hands. Surprisingly Elachia did not seem as alarmed as she should have been. She had narrowed her stare and pinched her lips. Dutch did not seem to notice. He was too intent on his assault. He leaned in to force a kiss and missed when Elachia jerked her head aside. He pulled and banged her against the wall as punishment and took a wider stance for strength. It was a mistake.

Elachia's knee came up hard between his legs, hard enough to raise him off the floor for a second. There was the arching of the back followed by the classic keeling over forward as Dutch grabbed his shelved weapon and high-stepped with one leg around the room like a proud rooster. He held the injured nether region with one hand and stared at Elachia in disbelief and anger. He was breathing hard.

R.J. banged a fist against the console and exclaimed, "Yes!" as the O2 dial moved below twelve percent.

Elachia shrank back against a wall looking more defiant than ever. Both of them were swaying a bit. Dutch straightened up and thought to go at her but tipped to one side and had to catch himself. A second attempt caused him to fall the other way so that he needed both hands to push up against his weapon. Elachia's eyes suddenly rolled and she began a slow slide toward the floor. She seemed to have a secret smile on her face.

R.J. tapped at keys to speed up the gas exchange. At eleven percent Dutch began to realize something was wrong but his thought process was not working well enough to figure out what. Like most males, his most basic instinct continued to inspire him on. He took an awkward step toward Elachia, swayed and looked blankly around the chamber then tried for another step but fell back against the wall. Elachia appeared to be asleep. The O2 dial read nine-point-seven.

Dutch finally collapsed against a wall and folded up into sleep.

R.J. bolted. He yelled at me and pointed, "Fix it!" as he went. At the door he slapped the emergency open button, waited an excruciating sixty seconds, and dove inside the airlock to gather Elachia up in his arms while I fumbled around trying to remember how to reset the airlock systems to normal. R.J. came back into the living compartment carrying his Precious and looking like muscle beach. He placed her gently down on the floor, did not bother with an emergency O2 mask, and began carefully blowing air into her lungs from his own. I had to hurry back to the airlock for fear our jerk would start waking up. Zip ties from a nearby drawer fastened him up nicely. Feet joined to hands behind the back to ensure he would not be comfortable. It was all I could do not to bang him around while tightening him up.

A pang of new fear struck me. I looked at my watch. Forty minutes to the next event. I yelled, "Danica!"

"Already ascending, Adrian. You didn't even notice, did you? We'll make it. Get ready for the quick jump."

I made it back to R.J. just in time to see Elachia open her eyes and smile at him.

"Welcome back, my sweet," he whispered.

"Did you get him?" she asked.

"Oh yeah. We got him," replied R.J.

"Lucky for him," she replied.

The three of us broke out into low level laughter that was as much stress relief as it was consideration of what she was implying.

Chapter 18

We climbed away from the poor, fractured Earth, running from the monster that was sure to come. Danica had to scramble to find a clear route through the orbital corridors as I was not in the right seat to assist her. I hurried forward but the stars were already in the windshield by the time I got there.

"Jump!" she called and without waiting to be sure we were ready, she snapped us outward for just a second, just long enough to place us beyond the orbit of Earth's moon.

When we had settled into station keeping, and finished the neglected checklists, we gathered at the main table looking like four beat up, exhausted crew members, which we were. The door to the airlock had been left open with idiot still wire-tied on the floor. He was semi-awake but not yet coherent enough to speak. We took turns occasionally glancing uncomfortably in his direction.

R.J. ruffled his messed-up hair and asked, "Well, that was fun. What'da you guys wanna do now?"

No one laughed.

Elachia spoke, "As your self-appointed primary care physician I order you all to eat and sleep, ASAP."

"What about the bad guy in back?" asked R.J.

"The injection I gave him will keep him asleep for twelve hours. I will re-inject him as necessary," answered Elachia.

R.J. and I asked in unison, "You gave him an injection?"

"More than he deserved," she replied.

There was a moment of silence. It was only the second time any of us had heard Elachia speak with such cold intent.

Elachia continued, "Beyond that, we should review all that we have learned."

"I make the next event in three minutes," said R.J. He leaned forward over the B-engineering station and tapped in some commands. Our overhead monitors came to life with various magnifications of Earth. As the clock approached 11:59 A.M. we held our breath, and at the click of noon we watched the leading edge of an invisible wave collapse over earth, restoring everything in its path to a previous, pristine state. For six seconds there was a normal picture of civilization, a sadistic tease like a treasure just out of reach. That fleeting moment was followed by yet another bright flash of light from the border between France and Switzerland. A second wave burst from it and swept the Earth, leaving the same absolute desolation in its wake.

"I don't think I can take any more of this," said Danica and she shook her head.

"Why don't you go get some rest, Dan.? You've earned it," I said.

"If all of you will excuse me, I believe I'll do just that. Hopefully sleep will be better than living." She rose and headed back to her sleeping compartment.

Elachia said, "I believe the explosive wave we are seeing is both temporal and interdimensional. Also, I'm guessing there is a time signature in each new set of waves. I suspected all of this earlier, but I'm convinced of it now. During our visit to the Admiral, we saw normal human activity through a window in a door but when we opened the door the hallway was deserted. That evidence alone confirms a time component in the distortion caused by the wave. We were seeing people and activity from a different time. Everywhere we have investigated we have found people and objects in various states of transparency. In many cases they cannot see us. Using ourselves as the baseline for our dimensional reality, we must assume those people and objects are only partly present in our dimension. Because these people are clearly alive and reasonably well, their missing components must exist in an alternate parallel dimension. But that's not all we've learned. We find not only different levels of this unknown radiation infecting people and objects based on their location at the time the wave passes through them, we find that the resulting distorted reality caused by the wave is not constant from one location to another. We find areas nearly normal, and others severely distorted. The wave of destruction is not fluid. It is more like an unevenly mixed time-dimension stream. Yes, we have learned a great deal about this phenomenon."

I shifted in my seat at the table and rested my head in my hand. "I apologize for asking the obvious. How do we fix it?"

Elachia did not seem as fatigued as the rest of us, despite her recent brush with death. She paused for a moment then looked us both squarely in the eye. "I still do not know. I do not know if there exists a way *to* fix it."

"Then any suggestions about what to do next?" I asked.

"I believe the only option we have beyond transmitting our findings to Mars Station, is to continue gathering data and perhaps finding other temporal physicists for assistance."

R.J. spoke, "We have to return idiot and his gold back to Earth anyway."

"That's another issue," said Elachia. "I believe the consequences to his actions may be severe."

"You mean the authorities will eventually catch up with him if Earth ever gets fixed?" asked R.J.

"No, my darling. As I've mentioned before, because this radiation is temporal in nature it seems to contain a time signature. Mr. Dutch has now missed the last event. By being here in space with us, he missed being reset to Earth's six seconds of normal. The first wave did not put him back in the underground vault where he was when the first explosion took place. That means now, once he is back on the planet, the next collapsing restoration wave probably will not cleanse him of the radiation in his body because his subatomic signatures do not match the wave's temporal nuclei. Even worse, the next expanding wave will probably infect him again, adding to the radiation level he already possesses. Because he is out of sync, each subsequent wave may also result in an additional increase in his levels. The people we've encountered so far that were infected with nearly a full dose of Diamond Light radiation are almost invisible, so it's possible an individual with higher levels than that may no longer even exist in our dimension."

R.J. wrinkled his brow. "So you're saying because he missed this last event, he's going to be irradiated over and over? What can we do? Can we put him back in that vault? What should we do about this?"

"Folks, if we turn him loose, he's just going to start raping and pillaging again," I said.

"Oh, for cripes sakes," answered R.J. "So maybe we find a cell to lock him in somewhere?"

"That might work. Because he missed the last event, he would probably now be reset to wherever we leave him, over and over with each reset. I do not know what else could be done to help him," said Elachia.

I said, "When we make the next landing, we won't have time to screw around with him. And from what we've seen, it's more dangerous to us down there than we may have realized. We dump him off somewhere secure and get back to work."

"I agree," said R.J.

"Ela, not to belabor the subject, but would you have any suggestions at all on what we should do next?" I asked.

"We should continue with your original plan, Adrian. Descend to the Desertron collider facility and see if we can find any specialists there."

I nodded in agreement. "You know, I was exhausted after that turbine change-out. Now I'm wide awake on adrenaline. Did we leave any beer in the refrigeration unit?" I asked.

"Good idea. I'll see," replied R.J.

"Gentlemen, I will take the first shift so the two of you can get some rest," said Elachia. "If there are any ship alarms, I'll wake you both immediately. Also, I did not have a chance to thank you for saving me from that mad man."

R.J. handed me a cold bottle of beer. "Ela, I'm still not sure which of you we actually saved."

"Touché," I replied, and we clicked bottles.

Despite the turmoil, my compartment was a calming escape. I quickly fell into a deep sleep. It was the utter exhaustion from changing out a turbine followed by robbing a bank.

I awoke hoping it had all been a bad dream. My unchanged dirty flight coveralls assured me it was not.

R.J. and I gathered up front going through a bunch of overdue maintenance and periodic checklists. The new turbine had a beautiful graph readout that caused us elation. Our crew mates were sound asleep in their compartments. It was the first private time the two of us had found since the trip began.

"Have you thought about what you'd do if Earth can't be saved?" asked R.J.

"You got to be kidding."

"You know I'm not."

"You think the Nasebiens are going to leave Earth exploding over and over forever?"

"If the problem is unsolvable, I'd bet they'd send something and fire a quantum doomsday bomb at it and the solar system would be minus one celestial body and safe again for you and me. It will also have gained a new asteroid belt."

"Wow!"

"Yeah."

"Solar System Amputation, you're saying."

R.J. sipped his coffee and narrowed his stare. "Good comparison."

I pondered the idea for a moment. "You have a second home on Enuro, remember? You'd be okay."

R.J. glanced at me with sympathy and pain. "Yes and No. You have a home on Enuro also."

"Do I?"

"You just need to brush up on your golf game."

"My God, we've got to fix Earth."

"I hate to say it, but with all that we've learned I don't see a single possible way we can affect what is going on down there. Not even a long shot."

"There's got to be a more advanced culture out there somewhere that has an answer."

"More advanced than the Nasebiens? Those people, if you can call them that, are angelic inter-dimensional beings and they sent us here!"

"Well, that's pretty grim now that you mention it."

"We'd be neighbors on Enuro."

"With our past amputated."

"Musk City would become humanity's capital. Mars Station would be the center of the solar system. Human society would continue."

"There sure would be a big empty spot between Venus and Mars, though."

"Yeah, and a new asteroid belt where Earth used to be decorated with floating ugliness for years to come. I guess if there was ever a time to seek help from the Creative Force this would be it."

"Agreed."

We gathered up our misgivings and used the overnight time to catch up on things. R.J. went aft and replaced the O2 reclamation filters. I stayed forward and ran calibration procedures. Danica slept a double shift. Elachia was up by six, shifting from doctor/physicist to chef. She cooked up a breakfast that seemed better than we deserved. It even brought Danica, semi-awake, as she followed the smell to the kitchenette, still dressed in too sheer a wrap of light green nightwear, like a ghost passing by unaware of its surroundings. It was eight o'clock before we were all back to full operational consciousness, all of us that is except the idiot asleep in the airlock still guarding his gold. We sat and stood around the living compartment, finding trivia to speak about so the real subject matter could be put off just a little longer. When the subject of corrupted reality did finally come up, we all agreed to wait until after the noon event wave before attempting another landing. R.J. took some time to locate an appropriate Federal Correctional Institute just northeast of the Waxahachie Desertron. It had a large, secured, exercise area where we could deposit our drugged rapist-thief and his treasure, after which there would be great rejoicing.

The 11:59:54 explosion occurred right on schedule. I gave Danica a break and took the left seat. We dropped Griffin into the shattered Earth's atmosphere and dove across the western gulf. The correctional institute we'd chosen was so large it was impossible to miss. The buildings had largely survived the global blast minus most windows and doors. The walls and fences were still intact. There were many semi-transparent people within the main fence system, busily trying to find a way out. They did not notice us even as we kicked up dust to land. With all Griffin lighting shut off, we hoisted Dutch down the ramp and onto the brown grass and then threw his gold bars out around him. Finally, we were free to head for Desertron.

On the next leg we should have expected the unexpected. We incorrectly believed we had experienced all the absurd constructs the post-Diamond Light Earth had to offer. It is said that string theory demands many alternate dimensions. We suspected that quite a few irradiated people were partially existing in at least some of them. We should have carried out the hypothesis a few steps further.

As we approached what we believed to be the city of Waxahachie, our vision ahead became distorted. It looked like we were approaching a wall of water that went from ground level up to infinity. The blurry barrier was apparent enough that I pulled back the thrust levers and banked right into a holding oval so that we could study the thing before attempting to enter it.

"I'll be damned if I know what it is," said R.J. over our shoulders. "But I don't like it."

I looked back to find Elachia next to him. "Elachia?"

"I have no idea, Adrian," she replied. "A barrier of some kind?"

"So let's land close and disembark for a look. It's all farm and burned grassland around here," said Danica.

"I *have* grown to trust a woman's intuition," added R.J.

I came alongside the strange wall and lowered Griffin down. We settled onto a grass field and as the engines continued to whine down the four of us used the aft airlock to stroll down the ramp and approach the water-like rippling blur of wall. We stood within arm's length of it. Beyond the ripples we could clearly see the city of Waxahachie in the distance. Everything looked curiously normal there. Somehow the place seemed to have escaped destruction. Through the distortion, fine detail was difficult to make out, but the color and general layout of the buildings seemed to have been unaffected by the previous Diamond Light explosion.

Finally R.J.'s curiosity got the better of him. He tapped one finger against the wall. Circular ripples radiated outward from his touch.

"R.J., be...," I did not get the rest of the warning out.

He dared to put fingers into the blanket of distortion and pulled them quickly back for inspection. There seemed to be no damage.

"R.J....," I said in a scolding tone.

"We need to know," he replied.

"Rowland...," said Elachia disapprovingly.

R.J. held up one finger for us to wait. Without warning he stepped boldly through the veil.

The fact that we could barely make him out on the opposite side of the distortion caused me to flinch and without really thinking I leaned through after him expecting to grab him.

R.J. was standing just inside the distortion staring off into the distance at Waxahachie. I stepped in alongside him and looked.

Waxahachie had not been destroyed. It was a busy place. There were planes in the sky and trucks and cars on the highways. In the distance, people were on the move everywhere. A herd of cattle was grazing the grassland between us and the city.

R.J. looked at me. "Some kind of time distortion," he said. "Got to be."

"What makes you guess that?" I replied.

"The rest of the planet is in chaos. These people seem to be going about their business as usual. If they were aware of a global disaster there'd be panic everywhere."

"Okay, that's good, R.J. It's possible."

"This is the recent past," he continued. "That's my guess."

"That's still a big guess but either way I have the feeling we don't belong here," I answered.

"Maybe we do. If it's the past, maybe we can get word to Admiral Provose or someone else to stop the collider test."

"I hate it when you get a good idea that I don't like."

"It's worth a try."

"If you are right, how do we know this isn't the day when the collider first explodes?"

"We have to assume this is that day. We can't gamble that it's not. We have to be ready to get out of here fast."

"Hold on a minute." I drew my communicator from my pocket and on a long shot hope made the call. "Danica, Elachia, can you hear me?"

It took a moment of static, then to my surprise, "We have you, Adrian," said Elachia. "We can hardly see you, but you're coming through loud and clear."

"I know this sounds crazy, but we think we may have stepped back in time to a point before the disaster. We are going to try to make contact here and stop the event. You guys please keep Griffin ready to fly and leave us if there's any danger. We'll meet you back at this spot when we're done."

"We understand Adrian," said Elachia. "Keep the comm open. We'll be waiting. Keep us informed."

I looked at R.J. and with an expression of doubt and held out one hand in the direction of Waxahachie. "After you, sir."

We headed through the green grass toward the city, two spacemen in blue flight suits walking across an open field that existed only in the past.

"If your theory is right, that's pretty weird about the comm unit, don't you think?" I asked.

"Which part?"

"I mean, we just called the future on our coms and successfully spoke to people in it."

"Okay, yeah that's weird but I have heard stories of people who allegedly received transmissions on shortwave radio that were believed to have been from the past. And, if you think that's a brain-drain, think about this; what happens to we who are back in the past if we do manage to stop the explosion? The Griffin would be weeks ahead of us in a different timeline. Where would that leave us?"

"You had to think of that. Like my mind isn't overloaded enough already. I don't have my cell phone with me, do you?"

"No, I wasn't expecting to step back in time."

"That's okay. We can buy one in Waxahachie. All we need is our account numbers. And of course, there's more urgent matters at hand."

"Which ones would those be?"

"First we need to find out what day and time it is here. What if this place is only minutes away from the original collider explosion?"

R.J. stammered, "God, I should have thought of that but I'm catching up fast. Maybe we should just turn around and run."

"We've got to chance it. We might not get another shot like this."

"It's a really big gamble, Adrian. If that blast goes off while we're here, we'll become part of the never-ending story."

"Maybe we should hasten our steps I think."

There were high stacks of raked hay followed by invisible cattle fence outlined by a blue beam from emitters atop six-foot transmitting poles. It was an electrified threat that separated us from the divided four lane highway leading to the first shops a few hundred yards away. We came to a chest-high light beam and stopped to look in both directions for a different way.

"This is the only way unless we go way, way around," said R.J.

"You know about these fences? How bad will the shock be?"

"Significant but not debilitating. You go first."

"Thanks so much."

"Since you're ornery anyway...."

"Maybe you could give me a knee up and I could jump it?"

"You really want to be six feet in the air while you're getting a wicked shock?"

I grunted my displeasure, stepped back and ran as hard as I could through the fence line, grasping to the hope that perhaps electric fences in this time period would not affect me.

The thing shocked the hell out of me and electrified my hair as I fell through onto the ground.

"How was it?" asked R.J. as I brushed myself off.

"Significant but not debilitating."

R.J. rolled his eyes sarcastically. He did not bother to run. He dove forward and fell to the ground on my side. He stood, shook off the stun and tried to pat his hair down then gave me a victorious smile. We hurried along the busy highway toward civilization as we had once known it.

The traffic was a mixture of ground vehicles and floaters. There were fewer personal air vehicles here. The nearest business was a Mexican eatery. More than a dozen vehicles graced the parking area.

"It's lucky we got some sleep and personal grooming time in. Yesterday you looked like The Thing from outer space," said R.J. "You probably would have emptied the restaurant. It would have looked like a Japanese Godzilla movie."

"Me?! Your hair was bunched up like two horns and your beard was twisted into a point. You looked like the devil himself."

"Well we still can't go running in there screaming the end of the world is nigh."

"Right."

As we neared the entrance, R.J. stopped and straightened up. "Really now, how do I look? We have no money, no phones, and no ID. We can't tell these people the truth. They'd laugh us out of the place. We must be cautious."

"You want me to do the talking?"

R.J. slowly shook his head. "I'd better do the talking. I'll think of something."

"That's what I'm afraid of."

"You got a better idea?"

"Not offhand."

"Well I'm the cordial one. I should do the talking."

"You're saying I'm not cordial?"

"I'd never suggest such a thing, Worf."

"Huh? Who?"

We climbed the three stairs up to the porch entrance and had to hold the door for people coming out. They took suspicious notice of us, two grown men in flight suits with probably not a major airport for a hundred miles. They passed us cautiously except for their six-year-old son who considered us heroes.

Inside, the place was nice enough to make me want to sit and order. Floors, walls, and booths of deep oak. Wonderful golden lighting. A long bar with backrest stools. More servers than seemed necessary, all quite properly dressed and busy. Unfortunately, there was an unmanned greeter's pedestal which left us wide open to the entire dining area. A maître d' in dark slacks and a white, long sleeve shirt with a short western tie spotted us, looked puzzled for a moment, then charged over to seat us.

"Will that be two?" he asked as he tried to discretely sum us up.

Before R.J. could reply we were interrupted by an exchange of bartender to customers departing. As they passed by, they dropped their receipt on the floor, looked back but waved it off and continued out.

I spoke, forgetting to wait for R.J. "I'm sorry. We're not here to eat. Would you have a phone we could use?"

"Is everything all right?" he asked glancing down at our suits.

"We were on our way to Dallas and had a little engine trouble. Had to put down in a field out there. Just need to make a quick call."

R.J. stooped to pick up the receipt hoping the gesture would be reassurance that we were civilized.

"Adrian...," interrupted R.J.

"Hold on a second," I replied.

"I should let the Sheriff's department know," said the maître d' kindly as he pulled out his cell phone. "They'll need to make a report on this. Which field was it?"

"Not necessary, really. We can do that. All we need is...."

"Adrian...," said R.J. insistently.

I gave him the irritated not-now glance. "Sir, there's no need to report this. We'll fill out all the necessary paperwork ourselves. If I could just..."

"ADRIAN!"

I slumped my shoulders and spoke in a low tone, "Don't you see what's happening? I'm trying to stop a big matzah ball that's forming here!"

"Look at this receipt! Those people just dropped it on their way out!"

The maître d' began speaking into the cell phone.

I exhaled exasperation and took the receipt. The very top line had the date and time. It took me a moment to sync. Griffin's clock had remained on Eastern Time. Texas was one hour behind that but the time on the receipt was way ahead of our time. A quick mental calculation told me that if our step back in time had somehow brought us to the exact day of the original collider test, we now had about six minutes before the very first collider explosion.

E.R. Mason

We shared a brief, wide-eye moment of terror then both charged for the door nearly knocking down customers entering. We leapt down the stairs. R.J. grabbed my arm and stopped me. "We'll never make it on foot, Adrian! No way!"

I looked around with evil intent. There was a take-out window. Two old ladies were seated in an old pickup truck waiting for their order to be handed out. R.J. hesitated as I charged that way.

"Ladies, I'm very sorry. This is a public emergency. My friend and I are with Space Command and we need to borrow your vehicle."

The lady in the driver's seat raised her chin and looked away. "Oh, I don't think so," she replied defiantly.

Fortunately, she forgot to lock her door.

I yanked her door open and forced myself in, jamming her against her friend. I stomped on the gas but had to slow to let R.J. climb in the back. My two new friends began to shriek but as we bucked and skidded onto the road the shrieks turned into the most fowl-mouth cursing I'd ever heard, howling expressions of displeasure befitting any professional hockey player.

We sped the divided highway in the direction of the big haystacks. Unfortunately, there must have been a deputy nearby ready to answer the maître d's plea for help. And, of course in keeping with my bad luck, the deputy had to be coming from the opposite direction so that we passed him going much too fast with two cursing, waving women in the front seat.

I watched in my side-view as the deputy spud his back tires and swung the rear end of the patrol car around to pursue us. Of course, I had to get one that knew how to drive. If I could just make the hay field, perhaps he could not follow us off-road.

As the large piles of hay came in sight, we jumped the curb of the highway center divider, made a sizzling, crackling plow through the electric fence and hay, and bounced and banged along the field toward the distant, wavering wall of time. My prospects were beginning to look better despite the continuing chorus of foulmouthed objections in my right ear accentuated by a few weak punches to my right shoulder.

In the rear view, the deputy did not give up at the highway. He was ten car lengths behind us and obviously had off-road experience of his own. He was spinning tires to keep the abused patrol car straight. In fact, he seemed to be enjoying the chase. I joined in with my captives and cursed along with them.

The police cruiser was closing. For some unknown reason I decided driving right through the time wall would not be a good choice. I had to slow as we approached it. The deputy was now four or five car lengths behind. As we neared the barrier, R.J. made a grand leap from the truck bed. It was way too soon, and he had to run to catch up and pass us. He plunged through the time wall without ever looking back.

I tried to shoulder my door open, but it refused. The determined lady next to me suddenly reached under the seat and pulled out an old chrome-plated Colt 45 revolver and yelled, "Hold it right here!"

I yanked the thing out of her hand, jammed it back under the driver's seat, gave her a terse look, and yelled, "That's not nice!"

A second bang against the driver's door popped it open. I jumped to the grass, took two steps toward my time zone and heard, "Hold it right there or I'll stun you where you stand!"

I turned to face Mr. Deputy; his weapon raised in his right hand. It was a very old wire-fire stun gun, two cartridges in parallel.

But the deputy seemed distracted by the shimmering clear wall behind me, though he still managed the command, "Hands up. Now back away from the truck and the ladies, slowly," he said.

"Gladly," I replied, and hands raised I backed away right through the time wall and out of his world.

Chapter 19

R.J. was standing a few feet from the wall looking down at his watch, still catching his breath.

Half bent over and panting, I came up beside him and raised one hand. "No that's okay. I'm fine. Don't give it a second thought." I had to bend further forward with my hands on my knees.

Elachia joined us. "You two were *supposed* to update us. Rowland you worried me greatly. Did the two of you *steal* that truck?"

R.J. looked up like a teenager being reprimanded. Through the flowing window of time, the two elderly women were still sitting in the truck with the deputy speaking to them at the driver's window. R.J. said, "If it's today, then any second now."

There was a bright flash and the very first collider explosion wave burst into view in front of us. Although we could not see the wave, it moved across our field of view imparting a line of dead brown grass in its path. The ladies' pickup truck instantly turned to solid rust with an opaque windshield. The deputy was thrown to the ground. His hair turned gray and he looked old. He did not move. The wave swept across the killing field and left a brown cloud of dust where the restaurant and other buildings had been. The destruction quickly subsided to a still world of settling debris.

"Oh my God," said Elachia and she held one hand to her mouth.

R.J. looked at his beloved. "That was the very first wave. We just got to witness the beginning of the apocalypse."

Elachia nodded. "Now if we wait here for twenty-four hours, we will see the first collapse of the field and restoration of all of this."

I looked at Elachia. "Would it help to see that?"

"No," she replied. "Perhaps if I could leave a scanner in there to measure the leading edge of the expanding field but the device would probably be destroyed."

"You know something guys? I hate to say it, but we just changed the past," I said, half in thought.

"What?" asked R.J.

"The truck, those ladies, and the deputy. When the reconstruction occurs they will still be right here in this field. That's not where they would have been if we hadn't entered their time. We changed the past."

"A very dangerous precedent since you did not intend to change the past in that way," said Elachia.

"Explain?" asked R.J.

"Stopping the collider explosion is a risk that must be taken. But, changing anything else, no matter how insignificant, can cause a cascade effect that leads to some major change that could greatly affect the present."

"She's right," I said. "Two women were abducted at the restaurant. Their order didn't get delivered. A deputy was diverted to chase a carjack suspect. A framer's haystack was run down. His electric fence was damaged. There are dozens of things we changed. Here in our timeline they are now different. We were like elephants in a china shop. Let's get back on board and try to figure out what we're doing."

"That I'd like to hear," said R.J.

Inside, we gathered around the center table, water bottles in hand. Danica kept leaning over to look out at the blur of time wall. "It hasn't moved since we landed here, but I don't like staying this close," she commented.

"Which brings us to the dilemma at hand," said R.J. "We can't get to Desertron. From our previous imagery the place seemed intact but clearly now it's inside that time zone and it's been destroyed. So, where do we go?"

"My second choice was MIT, but we wouldn't want to fly there from here. We were very lucky not to fly through some other barrier somewhere. If MIT looks okay from above, we'd need to drop straight down on it to avoid running through one of these patches of insanity."

R.J. asked, "Ela, what would happen if this spacecraft flew through a time barrier like that one?"

"I would guess the same physiological effects that the two of you experienced while you were in there. But remember, we believe this event is both temporal and dimensional, so we know now there may be other envelopes of distorted environments very different from this one. There could even be some environments that we or this ship could not exist within."

"Would we have been destroyed by the explosion even though we were out of time?"

Elachia took a seat near a portal, gave a long exhale, and looked out at the wall. "I can only guess, but I would bet that we'd have been irradiated just like everything else. Certainly, you would never want to chance such a thing."

Danica added, "We only have a couple hours or so until sunset here. We don't have time to travel in this area anyway. We need to get into space."

"We should back out until tomorrow morning," said R.J. "While we're trying to figure all this out, we can look over the imagery again to recheck sites that may be mostly intact after the explosion."

"Dan, would you go ahead and do the launch procedures and I'll meet you up front in a minute or two."

Danica started to head forward but stopped and turned back to me. "Adrian, you know launches and landings are a big deal, never mind atmospheric flight. We've still been doing them like a regional carrier making short hops. No starship was meant for this kind of abuse. The turbine may have been just the tip of the iceberg. If we get a critical ascent or descent in-flight failure, it will be our own fault."

We all stopped and exchanged wary glances. A warning like that coming from a fly-by-the-seat-of-your-pants Danica was not something to be taken lightly.

I took a deep breath, exhaled and nodded. "That idiot and his gold didn't help our situation," I said. "From now on, we'll start being very careful about our reasons for landing. You're right, Dan."

Danica headed forward.

R.J. said, "I've been considering again why the Nasebiens and other advanced races are not helping us."

"It's possible they're letting us see just how bad screwing around with unknowns can be," I suggested.

"Or maybe there is no solution and they're letting us understand that before Earth has to be eliminated."

Once again, the idea brought sobriety. We paused in silence for a few moments.

R.J. continued, "Ela, with what you've seen now, can you imagine *any* possible way to neutralize an unknown radiation covering the entire Earth?"

Elachia looked at R.J. as though she felt the question was inappropriate. "A wave of equal and opposite atomic properties propagated around and above the world, which wouldn't stop the initial event from reoccurring anyway, so the question is moot."

I said, "As we've discussed before, it has to be the six-second window. That's the only thing that would do the trick."

"In six seconds?" asked R.J. "Okay, what about landing back here tomorrow, step through the time barrier, and try it again only this time make the call from one of our cell phones. We could show up earlier and have more time. And, maybe we could do it over and over until we got to the right people to stop the test."

Elachia said, "I suspect reaching the correct people and making them understand and believe might be unrealistic."

I considered the possibilities for a moment. "There will be military to contend with too. It would take several factions all agreeing to halt the test. What time did this Waxahachie explosion event occur, our time?"

R.J. looked at his watch and replied, "Four-something. We'd have to look at the onboard video to get the exact time. Waxahachie time was way out of sync. We could never be certain of what time it actually was in there even if we did come back."

I thought for a moment and said, "There's always that idea we knocked around about destroying the collider facility from orbit during those six seconds."

R.J. took a seat at the engineering station and began flipping switches. "We've been over this. If our particle cannon didn't do the job, we'd be caught in the collider explosion. We'd never have time to leave orbit."

"Yeah, we'd need prints of the facility anyway to know exactly where to target the place."

"And if we did fail and were destroyed by the explosion, we'd find ourselves back on orbit for the next six seconds. Bad way to die over and over."

"Right, and like we said before, even if we succeeded, we'd have killed a lot of people in and around that facility and then we'd have to try to explain it all."

"Still might end up being the only chance to save Earth," said R.J.

"It would be a one-shot deal."

"I definitely don't like that part." R.J. turned to Elachia. "Ela, is there a chance firing on that facility would work?"

Elachia took a deep breath. "It might but I'm not an expert at shooting things from orbit. The collider ring is deep underground. If you knew where to shoot could you aim correctly and fire at something underground in less than six seconds?"

"We may have to chance it. I mean, if there's no other way."

I rubbed my forehead and scoffed, "Yes, I can see it now. Honorable members of today's Judicial Hearing Committee; we had to kill those dozens of people and destroy the collider facility or life on Earth as we know it would have come to an end."

R.J. joined in, "And if we did fail, we'd kill them over and over for eternity or until Earth was vaporized by a more advanced culture's sanitation department."

Danica called back from the command seat. "Okay guys, are we getting out of here or not?"

Our little discussion came to another heavy and depressing end. I stood up, waved one hand in frustration, and headed forward.

One quick checklist later and up to a wide, following orbit we went, this time over Japan, an area just coming into morning light.

With all that we had learned, the orbital photography began to be much more discernable. Because we knew what to look for, we began to find many areas bordered by a distorted wall of alternate time and in some cases Elachia theorized the enclosed areas contained characteristics from alternate dimensions. There was no way to relate to some of the environments within them. It meant we had been crazy to attempt trans-surface atmospheric flight. It was just by luck we hadn't flown through some dimension completely incompatible with our own. After hours more of study and comparing notes, Danica and Elachia took rest shifts. R.J. and I sat on the flight deck, monitoring systems and exchanging pessimistic outlooks.

"Trying to find someone down there who could help was a long shot at best," I said. "Now? ...I don't know."

"I would have objected even before we began, but it seemed like the only option," replied R.J.

"I do not look forward to trying the Waxahachie thing again. For some reason my gut tells me that's not going to work. Beyond that, only thing left that I can see is the nuclear option."

"Bomb the hell out of the place for six seconds? Are we really going to give up on fixing things?"

"It's the only way I can see. Every time we make a landing there's a good chance of dropping into someplace fatal, and Ela was right as she always is. Just to blast the place we'd need diagrams for the facility to know where to set and lock the targeting system."

"We won't get that from Griffin's data base. We'd still have to go down there again."

"Yeah. We're choosing from crappy options because there are no good ones."

"Nothing electrical works down there. We'd need to find actual paper copies of the architectural and design plans. I'm not sure they even exist."

"Maybe we could find an opti hard drive with the data, remove the gel core and get our computers to decipher it."

R.J. nodded. "As you said, we're weighing bad options because there are no good ones. What's to say all memory hasn't been wiped down there? But I could attempt that. I did quite a bit of opti-drive code writing in my early days. I'm familiar with the gels. Except, as I said, they are just very advanced chemistry. They may all have been wiped by the wave."

"So, paper if we can find it, and gels as a secondary long shot."

"Hopefully I can at least find something in our records that indicate which subcontractors built the place. Even that's a long shot. All we probably have is the social media section."

"We can contact Mars Station and see if they or any of the other outposts have anything on it."

"All this to blow up our friends and neighbors."

218

"We can always change our minds before we pull the trigger."

"You know we've got to try the Waxahachie thing again before we even consider doing this, right?"

"That ought to be a riot."

"In case we fail, I'll go start the search for possible collider blueprint locations."

"In case we fail?"

R.J.'s late night research showed that the offices of WERN, the primary operator of the collider, had all been destroyed in the initial explosion. But there was still a chance. WERN had set up a library extension in the main Geneve Library near the University of Geneve. Although the area around the collider was essentially brown dust, much of Geneva seemed to have remained intact at least to a degree. The Library and University were located within a large desecrated park-like area where a landing would not be difficult. But, in the middle of Earth's massive desolation it seemed like we were looking at another unlikely chance.

At 0400 Danica relieved us so that we could sleep until Earth's terminator moved past Texas to again reveal the wreckage in that part of the world. I got up intending to shower but became concerned about Griffin's water supply. I went to the Environmental Control and Life Support Systems station in Griffin's med lab and checked the Water Recycling System readouts. The ECLSS components were all operating perfectly. The WRS was okay as well, but water reserves were down to fifty-five percent. A five more percent decrease meant tapping into the Contingency Water Containers located just behind the aft airlock wall. The CWC's weigh about one hundred pounds each and refilling them was something I did not care to think about. I skipped the shower.

We waited for the day's big event then set up for the second descent to Waxahachie using the friendliest flight path the navigation display could show us. With Danica in the pilot seat we started down, hoping for the best. She dove us directly at the coast, so steeply it gave a roller coaster effect. She leveled off and slowed just as I was about to beg that. We strained our eyes, watching for ripples in the distance, distortions that might suggest another bubble of displaced reality. The world passing below us was the same destroyed topography as the day before. Drained lakes, flattened forests, residential streets with homes missing, other homes minus rooftops, dead vehicles on the roadways.

Our luck seemed to hold. As we approached the Waxahachie area, we began to see the shimmering curtain of time barrier. It had returned right on schedule. Beyond it, Waxahachie did indeed seem to be restored to a period in time before the first collider blast. Danica turned us sideways to the wall and settled down quite a bit farther away this time. As Griffin whined down into park mode, we looked at each other. No explanations were necessary.

R.J. leaned into the flight deck. "So it's there. The twelve-o'clock reset wave restored the bubble in time again."

"And we're early. We should have a lot more time in there to reach the right people," I added.

"May our powers of persuasion be with us," said R.J.

"At some point we're going to need to think about thruster and OMS fuel," said Danica as she flipped switches on her panel.

"I've been trying *not* to think about that," I replied.

She gave me a cautionary stare with raised eyebrows.

We gathered in the living compartment where I immodestly pulled on civilian jeans and a blue collared work shirt. R.J. was wearing his trademark farmer's coveralls. We strapped on two wrist watches, one for Griffin time, the other for best-guess Waxahachie time and pocketed credit cards and ID. As R.J. had said, we were much earlier this time. We set the Waxahachie watches for three hours before the next time-warped explosion would again decimate Waxahachie. That allowed us a safety margin.

This time we dressed in common street clothes, along with cell phones and debit cards. As we readied, I took a quick look around the cabin. "So as planned, Dan stays in the control seat and monitors separation between the wall and the ship. Elachia monitors our coms and body cams. We look average, and we've got our IDs and all four cells. We were kind of stupid last time, but we're prepared this time. We've got a good chance. Right?"

R.J. smirked. "I could make an argument that we're still stupid."

Elachia ignored his comment. "Just remember, nothing is carved in stone here. Everything in there could be different this time. You won't know until you're inside. If I say abort, it means we've seen something from here that is catastrophic. Exit immediately. You two *will* comply, won't you?"

R.J. nodded, though it was not actually a question.

"I will, of course," I joked.

"Gentlemen, please take this seriously. If we were to lose the two of you, I don't know what we'd do."

I said, "So our very first job is to try the cell phones. If they do not work, the next priority is to quickly confirm what day and time it is in Waxahachie."

Danica took her place in the control seat as the three of us headed down the ramp and across a stretch of brown grass to the wall.

"Remember, say the time into the comm as soon as you know what it is so I can track it for you," said Elachia. Her voice had taken on a terseness.

I said, "You know, I'm suddenly starting to feel pretty optimistic about this. It's going to work."

We exchanged glances. R.J. nodded that he was ready. I gave an artificial smile and we pushed through the strange fabric of time.

The world of destruction was indeed gone once more. We stood amid knee-high grass. In the distance, cattle again grazed in a field of green.

"Okay, cell phone number one." R.J. drew out his first cell and began typing. I did the same.

With phones to our ears we looked at each other and both shook our heads. We offered repeated greetings into the phone but received no reply.

"That's so weird," said R.J. He pulled out his second phone and began dialing once more. I followed suit.

"Are you getting the same damn thing?" he asked after repeated hellos. "It sounds like someone answers but there's no one there."

"Definitely Twilight Zone," I replied.

R.J. pocketed his phone. "I have this weird feeling that our cells are trying to call satellites in the future, satellites that are no longer working. Well anyway, looks like we've got a walk ahead of us. At least we have the time now."

I searched the distance and pointed. "Hey, look over there to the left."

"Yeah, what?"

"That's looks like a gate. It's out of the way but I don't relish the idea of charging through that electric fence again. Let's go use the gate."

"Your plan has merit, sir. Lead the way."

The trek to the gate was quite a bit farther than the fence had been. We had to avoid spots of fresh bovid fertilization. At the gate, we were in luck. No lock. I unlatched it and held it open with a low wave for R.J. He gave a slight bow and passed through.

"You really are optimistic, aren't you," he said as a matter of fact.

"We could go sit and have a cup of coffee in that restaurant and still have plenty of time to phone the right people to get the ball rolling. There's no way we can lose."

We walked the divided highway toward the restaurant. Few cars passed by. Not far ahead the farmer's tall haystacks sat in the field, undisturbed. In the restaurant parking lot we could see some of the same vehicles that had been there last time. We had just a hundred yards left to go.

R.J. stopped suddenly and stared toward the restaurant. "Hey, that's weird."

I stopped and looked for something out of place. "What!?"

"In the drive-through.... That truck looks just like the...."

"No, that's not the same truck."

"There's two people in it."

We began walking again, quickening our pace.

"It does look like two women," said R.J. His voice had raised in pitch slightly.

"No way," I insisted.

As we neared the farmer's hay stacks, R.J. abruptly stopped again. "If this is really that, then we're out of."

Before he could finish speaking, the restaurant door burst open and out flew our earlier counterparts, nearly falling down the steps as they began to head for the farmer's field. They stopped abruptly, had a quick, fierce discussion, after which the other Adrian Tarn lurched around and headed for the two women in the pickup truck.

R.J. spoke without looking away from the distressing scene. "We are so screwed."

"My God, we're out of time. I don't believe it."

"Believe it."

There were a few seconds of argument at the driver's door of the pickup truck after which it was forced open as the earlier Adrian Tarn pushed his way into the driver's seat.

"We have only one chance," said R.J.

"I slowed the truck way down when I hit the haystacks," I replied.

We both began running as I spoke. I was outpaced by R.J. by three yards, which surprised me to no end. We stole glances to watch the beat-up pickup squeal out of the parking lot with the other R.J. holding on for dear life in the back.

Elachia's voice cut in on the com, "Rowland, what's happening there?"

"No time, Ela. Standby."

I reached the fence and chose not to slow. I barreled through it, stiffened from the electrocution, then fell into one of the hay piles. R.J. landed alongside me a second later. We both frantically pushed up to look again for the truck, our only chance to escape the next collider explosion.

The thing was bouncing more and much higher than I remembered. The expression on the other Adrian Tarn's face was one of wide-eyed determination. The old lady seated next to him was hitting him repeatedly with her hat. I'd forgotten that as well.

The abused truck came at us like a runaway and plowed into the haystack just beyond ours. We charged at it. I managed a death-defying leap and white knuckled grip on the side of the bed just behind the wheel well. R.J. dove forward in a one shot catch of the closed tail gate.

We both pulled and swung in, gasping for breath.

The other R.J. was peering over the cab of the vehicle. He hadn't seen a thing. A loud squeal of tires caused us to look back at a patrol car behind us and following.

The other R.J. turned, spotted the cop, and declared, "Oh crap!" Then he saw us.

He held to the top of the cab as the truck bucked and jerked him around. He decided we were of greater interest than the cop car.

"Oh... my... God...," he said, his voice shaking from the rough ride. I could see the gears turning in his head.

My R.J. held on and looked at me in earnest. "We need to get set to jump out on the passenger side. That'll put the truck between us and the deputy."

The other R.J. stared at us and yelled over the whine of the trucks straining engine, "I don't get it? Oh! Wait... You idiots came back and tried again, right? It's the only possible explanation."

"You'd better not change anything," yelled my R.J.

"Right. But at least I know I'm going to make it out of here."

"Unless now we screw you up somehow. You better pay attention," added my R.J.

The other R.J. nodded and turned back forward, but he couldn't resist periodically looking back at himself.

The deputy was closing in. R.J. and I braced against the side of the truck bed, ready to bail. As the truck skidded on the dirt to a stop, the two of us flew out, ran forward falling and bursting through the curtain of time. We both fell prostrate on the ground, our hands and arms breaking the fall.

I looked back to be sure my entire body was through. Without getting up I asked, "Okay, are we double screwed again. Did those other two come through the barrier with us? Are there two of each of us now?"

R.J. was still panting. He rolled on his side and shook his head while catching his breath. "I don't think so. I think those other guys went through the barrier and back to yesterday."

A concerned feminine voice spoke from above us, "Are you alright? Were you injured?"

Still breathing hard, we rolled on our sides and looked up at Elachia.

I said, "I think we're okay, but we wouldn't want to do that again."

Elachia held out a hand and helped R.J. to his feet. She then offered me the same.

We brushed ourselves off and as we did so, a bright flash came from within the time barrier. The wind of destruction blew by leaving the land beyond desolate. R.J. shook his head and exhaled a deep breath. Dejected and without speaking we all headed back aboard Griffin.

Chapter 20

We brought Griffin to a geostationary position over Geneva and waited for surface light. We anchored directly over the rubble where the collider facility had been. As we came into sunlight, a surprising number of intact buildings dotted the landscape below. The collider zone was an ellipse of barren ground, but outside that were quite a few large buildings that seemed still to have intact rooftops.

We roused Danica and Elachia early, 04:00 Griffin EDT. Danica appeared in a new blue flight suit, Elachia a deep purple body suit laced with white. They sipped coffee and reacted to the new recon plan with a solemn silence. Geneva was in full daylight. A spiral deorbit was our best chance to avoid zones of time and dimension corruption. When the girls were ready, we began our descent expecting a good five or six pre-explosion hours available to search for blueprints. Geneva time was six hours ahead of us. That meant the original event had occurred at 6:00 P.M. their time. It was now nearly 11:00 A.M. Geneva time. These people already had begun their share of the nightmare from last night. Those that had survived must have had an unthinkably bad night. Telephoto images revealed a Geneva that was dusted with brown, but otherwise roughly intact. The only mystery was; there were no signs of people, semitransparent or otherwise.

The spiral descent went smoothly enough. At one point, far in the distance, we watched a cloud of satellite debris whiz by. But as we passed into the first thin layers of atmosphere, Griffin began a kind of shiver I had never felt before. It continued through the thermosphere and faded away below fifty miles.

R.J. clicked on his mike, "Okay, what was that about?"

"Please tell me that was not a barrier wall like the one around Dallas," I added.

"I believe it may have been exactly that," answered Elachia.

"So, have we jumped back in time again? Are comm systems working down there? Can we get a date and time?" I asked.

Danica looked at me from the pilot's seat. "Abort descent?"

"Not yet. We're already there. R.J., you getting anything from down there?"

"Static, Adrian. On all channels."

"Continuing descent until you say no," said Danica.

"Anyone have an opinion?" I asked in frustration.

"Keep going," said R.J. "What will we do otherwise?"

I wanted to say, *"Go to Enuro and live out our lives?"* but I didn't. "Okay, you heard him, Dan. Find us a place."

The Geneva park site was spotted with quite a few naked trees. There was an open area bordered by a large cluster of them in front of the library. With her usual skillful tact, Danica dropped us down seemingly too fast but then gently slowed to the ragged brown grass and teetered us to a landing.

As I stood, I called out, "Weapons all, folks."

With Danica keeping Griffin ready, the three of us met in the aft airlock, weapons clipped to our belts. Elachia was already staring down at her scanner. As soon as the door opened and the ramp dropped down, the world became uncomfortably eerie. We marched down and stopped to take a careful look around. Beyond the bare trees there were buildings three-hundred and sixty degrees around us. Paved walkways led to them. For some reason the place looked like the spooky woodland Dorothy had faced in the Witch's forest. The stone buildings had dark ivy or vines growing up the sides. In some places there were large roots wrapped around some structures. Windows were broken here and there. A steam vent was drifting upward not far away. When I stared too long at any open window, it seemed as though something moved within.

"I've never heard a silence like this," said Elachia.

"Contradictory statement, my love," answered R.J.

"No, just listen. It's as though there is less than silence here."

She was right. It was almost like something was being taken from the ears rather than put into them.

"Ela, I think you should get back aboard," said R.J.

"Absolutely not. Can you two be certain of which drawings are needed or how long might it take to find them?"

"What do you think, Adrian?" he asked.

"I think that's somebody's shoe over there on the walkway."

"And I think I see a shredded windbreaker over there on the left," he answered. "Maybe these were people running away."

"Let's err on the side of caution, okay? Set your weapons to heavy stun and keep them ready, okay?"

"Are we really dedicated to this mission enough to remain here?" asked R.J. but he already knew the answer, so none was given.

"That's the library, through those trees," said Elachia. "I have to say, even the trees do not look right. Should there be all these vines climbing the sides of the buildings?"

"There are live ferns over there, like you'd see in the Amazon. That can't be right," added R.J.

"I know why it's a weird silence," said R.J. "It's because there's not a living soul in sight."

"Could that be someone sitting on that park bench?" asked Elachia.

"Let's go. R.J. you keep an eye on our six, okay?"

"Right."

We approached the park bench that Elachia had noticed. It was not a person sitting there. It was some kind of strange cocoon-like egg-shaped husk the size of a large suitcase. We paused to stare for a moment.

"Any idea what it is, Ela?" asked R.J.

She looked at both of us with misgiving. "We know we passed through a layer of some kind. This does not look like anything that belongs in our world, or at least our time."

"We're in some kind of shift," said R.J.

"But we know the event has already happened here," I said. "We can't get caught by the explosion. Let's keep going."

The remaining stretch of park yielded more signs of past humanity. Torn clothes, a baseball cap, a purse, other items that appeared to have been left behind by people in a hurry. Fortunately, we saw no areas with bodies or blood.

At the library's entrance, the main hall was blocked by overturned furnishings. We had to divert through a small restaurant. Tables were turned over; food was scattered everywhere. We had to move debris to get through the exit door at the far end of the place. It brought us back into the hallway, beyond the cave-in of debris that originally had blocked us. Dirty blue carpet led to three silent elevators. The hall opened to a large multi-floor reading room with decorative catwalks to reach the upper levels. As expected, there was no power anywhere. To our good fortune there were giant windows all around the place. We had forgotten headlamps, but we had glow sticks in our flight suit leg pockets.

Between the silver doors of the elevators was a six-foot tall directory with too many listings to count. As we looked for the best category sections a buzzing sound came from the reading room.

Suddenly Elachia let out an, "Oh!"

It flew by us at eye level. It was an insect the size of a small bird. It had ant legs, four black, narrow, long, fluttering wings, the head of a fly, and a tail with a stinger. It was not interested in us and passed on by.

"Definitely not Earth-like," said R.J.

"We are inter-dimensional," said Elachia, matter-of-factly.

"Like I said, watch our six, R.J."

"Absolutely," he replied.

We forced our attention back to the directory and found what we were looking for in the fourth floor listings beside the 'PREMISES PROTECTED BY VIDEO DETECTION' sign.

4TH FLOOR

ADMINISTRATION
CONFERENCE ROOMS
PHYSICAL RECORDS
LARGE PRINTS
ARCHITECTURAL DESIGN
ELECTRICAL DESIGN

"That's definitely the place," said R.J. "That blocked open door over there is the stairwell."

I cautiously approached and peered through the open door. There was an unpleasant smell coming from somewhere.

R.J. leaned in next to me. "Anything?"

Moving into the stairwell, I sidestepped around the stairs and looked behind them. There in a neat pile were three human legs cut at the hip, still wearing pants leg and shoe, leaking a small amount of red. I backed out and stopped R.J. from going to look.

"Okay, what?" he asked with Elachia looking on intently.

"Parts of people that didn't make it."

"Crap. It had to be that...," said R.J.

I yanked my comm unit from my pocket. "Dan, you still have us?"

There was an excruciating pause. "This place is giving me the creeps, Adrian."

"Close up and take off immediately. Hover at one hundred and standby."

R.J. nodded. "Good thing we weren't burning the OMS engines when we came in. You can hear those for a mile."

"Yeah, whatever did that in there, it was brutal," I added.

"Oh, for Pete's sake," said Elachia, and she forced her way past me to inspect the remains.

"Damn, you've got her using that expression now too," declared R.J.

Elachia returned appearing unmoved by the carnage. "The limbs were removed using some form of spiked tool, or by some creature with that type of mouth or claw."

"Would you two please set your disruptors to kill. I'll keep mine on heavy stun. If mine doesn't do the trick, then you guys have at it."

R.J. balked for a moment then looked pleadingly at Elachia. "Please do," he asked.

They both adjusted their weapons.

"We'd better pick up the pace," R.J. suggested

Next there was a blood trail coming down the carpeted steps. We kept to one side to avoid stepping in it. At the second-floor level, the door was cracked slightly open. That caught me by surprise and caused me to jerk my weapon forward at it. To our astonishment the door slowly pushed open and a young female human inched out and let it shut.

She appraised us with distrust and spoke in a low tone, "What are you guys doing? Why didn't you go with the others? Didn't anyone tell you? Are you crazy or somethin'?"

I guessed her to be seventeen going on thirty. She was of the evening persuasion, the association they call future Goth. A black, slant cut tank top that declared *'FUTURE CORPSE,'* fit tightly over pale white skin that glowed gold from Diamond Light radiation. Her hair had been dyed deathly gray. Heavy lipstick, a small tattoo on the right cheek that reflected the two large red and black ones on each arm. She had hip hugger black leather tight fitting pants that barely covered her crotch. She had a switchblade belt buckle. Black lace up boots came up to the knee.

"You speak English?" asked Elachia.

"I'm from Orlando. My parents are temporarily working here for their company."

"You were saying.... Didn't anyone tell us what?" I asked politely.

"To get to the tunnels! In the basement! The sewer system! There are still some around! Don't you know that?"

"Some *what* around?" I dared to ask.

"The centipedes! The three of you banging around will bring them for sure! Are you all crazy?"

"We're not from around here," said R.J. in his most comical tone.

Elachia took over. "What's your name, dear?"

Goth looked up and down the stairwell nervously. "Elvi. You guys can't tag along with me. You need to get down to the basement."

Elachia persisted. "What about the centipedes, Elvi? Why are you afraid of little bugs?"

"Little!? They come up to here on me!" Elvi held one hand at breast level. "How can you not know that?"

Elachia continued, "We just landed here in a spacecraft. We're trying to fix what happened to Earth."

"Well, good luck with that!"

"We need to get to the fourth floor to get some drawings. Are there centipedes up there?"

Elvi continued to look around worriedly. "There's at least two in this building. They stay on the move. They could be anywhere."

"Elvi, why haven't you gone to the tunnels?" asked Elachia.

"I'm looking for my sister. She's not as good at hiding as I am."

"All the people here are down in the tunnels?" asked Elachia.

"The ones who haven't been eaten or stored. The word was, get to the tunnels and head for downtown. There's soldiers there. But the bugs picked up on people running there and followed them. There were hordes chasing them."

"So, we need to avoid these centipedes at all cost?" asked Elachia.

"Are you kidding me? Once they lock onto you with those teeth you have no chance of getting away. People are carried off kicking and screaming because the worst is, they don't kill you right away. They have little places set up where they either eat you or they store you up for food for later."

"We have weapons with us, Elvi," said Elachia.

"Good luck with that too."

"If you help us get to the fourth floor, we might be able to fix all this," said Elachia. "Could you help us get there? Maybe we can help you too."

Elvi seemed very resistant. Elachia smiled at her.

"I'll go a little ways. But I've got to go down and get to the next building over. Sabrina must be over there." Elvi thought for a moment then pointed up. The four of us followed her.

Elachia tried to calm her. "This all began for you last night, Elvi?"

"At dinner time for a lot of people. First thing, the big boom that echoed for a while. Lights went right out. Wind like an A-bomb. That was the real bitch of it. Then they found out generators wouldn't work either. Batteries were all dead. People would kill you for a candle. No moon even. Fucking pitch dark unless you had fire handy. Can you imagine? Nobody could find out what was going on 'cause there were no phones or computers. It was a bad night. People started disappearing. Nobody could do anything. When the sun came up there was all these vines and other crap on everything. Then real quick we found out why people were disappearing. The centipedes. There was other stuff too, but they were the worse. Thousands of 'em. Every time they discovered a group of people hundreds would show up. It was a massacre over and over. All you could do was hide and hope. Finally, word got around head down to the sewers. Keep the covers in place and the doors shut. Okay you guys, this is it. Fourth floor entrance. Don't go skipping in there just yet."

My comm squelched on. "Holding clear at one hundred, Adrian. Ready for a quick extraction."

"Standby, Dan."

Elvi very gently pulled the door open a crack. She smelled at the opening, then made just enough space to see in. "The main study area is okay, but we need to check all the resource rooms."

Elachia asked, "You sound like you know this place?"

"My friends and I meet here all the time. It's the last place our parents would come looking for us, plus the librarians treat us like okay kids. You guys got to be real quiet until we check the side rooms, okay?"

We eased into the main study room. Somehow the architecture had remained reasonably intact and was so beautiful I had to stop and look. Computer stations along the wall on deeply carved oak desktops. Giant picture windows looking out over the park made up the south wall. Thin, light-brown carpet on the floor. An exit at the opposite side of the room. Beside it, a large air-conditioning intake grill had been punched out of place and rested on the floor leaving a big hole. To our right, five other rooms with directories beside each door. The entire ceiling, cracked in places, looked like it would have been softly illuminated had there been power.

R.J. got ahead of me, moving against the right wall to lean around and peer into side rooms in search of predators. Elachia stood close watching him intently.

Elvi did a slow walk around and came back to us. "They've already been here. That's good. The smell is fading so they've been gone a while. You guys better get doing what you want 'cause they could show up anytime."

So we did. Elachia and I spread out and began looking at directories. All rooms cleared, R.J. joined in.

"It's this one," called Elachia. "Architectural."

It was a large, deep side room. Tall, very thin pull out drawers in tan cabinets where marked, "*large prints*." There was a computer station in the center of the room. We quickly learned that the cabinet doors and drawers were locked. There was an automated system setup. You had to request a specific item after which the computer would pop the correct drawer or door open.

"We need something to break in," said R.J. as we stood looking at the first possible cabinet. "We need a pry bar."

"There's a pedestal sign out there that says, 'Quiet Please.' We can break the leg off it and hammer the end down with the base," I suggested.

Ten minutes later we had a four-foot pry bar, and like bank robbers in a vault we began prying down and open drawer after drawer looking for our version of treasure.

It began to take longer than we'd hoped. Thirty minutes into the caper we had found many drawings for buildings that no longer existed, proposed future facilities, and rejected drawing proposals. Finally, we opened a drawer that had a red warning card atop the contents:

CERN PROPRIETARY DATA
CLASSIFIED
LEVEL 4 CLEARANCE REQUIRED

We pitched the sign aside and furiously began rolling up the 24X36 inch drawings.

To our great misfortune, we were interrupted.

From the main study area a loud rattling began to come from the ceiling. Elvi appeared in the doorway with big eyes, holding her first finger against her lips. We gathered at the door, staring up at the ceiling. It was then I noticed the air conditioning vents built into the ceiling lighting. A vent near room's center began to rattle. Elachia came quickly over to join us. We detached our weapons from our belts. The vent rattled furiously. This could not be Elvi's centipedes. The vents were only twelve inches square, far too small for a chest-high bug.

But as we watched, the vent broke away at three corners and swung down and open. Centipedes, two feet long and twelve inches wide began to ooze out and fall to the floor. The first landed on its back. Dozens of little legs wiggled and searched until the gray-green body was knocked upright by the next plummeting centipede.

R.J. and I reacted almost in unison. We fired on them. The disruptor beam stopped them immediately and turned their bodies to a smoking brown shell. We killed four. No more appeared overhead.

Elvi was furious. "What are you doing?! Do you know what you've done? All we had to do was stand perfectly still! They don't have eyes! They can only detect movement and smell. They could crawl right over your shoe and not know you're there." She looked at me angrily.

"Not my shoe," I replied.

"They can only smell fear! All you had to do was stand there!" she continued.

"They would certainly have detected me then," said R.J.

"You guys still don't get it. They can talk to each other. They're like ants. Now these dead ones have told the main colony that people are here. The whole bunch will be coming now. You're on your own. I've got to get to the tunnels."

Elachia said, "We can take you anywhere you need to go. We could drop you on a different roof if you'd like."

"These things climb up the sides of buildings like it's nothing to them. I have a plan. You guys better get going. It will be a swarm here."

Elvi headed for the door.

Elachia called out, "Elvi, what's your last name?"

"Dorran," she replied as the door closed behind her.

I pulled out my com. "Dan?"

"Go ahead, Adrian."

"We may need a hasty pick up from the roof of this building. Be ready, okay?"

"No problem. That all sounded very ugly."

"Call for you in a few minutes, Tarn out."

We scrambled. We bumped into each other trying to stack the drawings together in one pile. Elachia took over rolling them up and securing them with tape found in the computer station desk drawer. It looked like we were getting everything on the collider from foundation drawings to basement power facilities, cable routing, tunnel boring, and the main control room.

My comm squelched to life. "Adrian, I'm hovering fifty feet above your roof. I see your problem and it's as bad as she said. They are on the roof. Ugly little beasties. Four of them. They must have climbed up the back wall. They keep looking up at me and showing their teeth. What do you want to do?"

"Crap," said R.J. once more. "We're going to have to go out a window."

I winced and clicked on the com. "We'll have to go out a window. You'll need to come along side on this floor. We'll either ramp or jump in."

"Wait, let me take a look around your floor," answered Danica.

"Let's gather this stuff up and see about making a hole in a window," I said.

We stacked our drawings onto Elachia's outstretched arms and headed for the big windows. We'd need to use the aft starboard airlock door and ramp. That meant the Danica would need to nestle Griffin alongside the picture windows with the airlock door toward us. We took a position about twenty feet from the best window and checked the settings on our disruptors.

"Just one of us should do it, don't you think?" said R.J.

"Piece of cake," I replied.

I stood sideways, held the disruptor with arm fully extended, and fired at the window.

A three-second burst left the window unscathed.

"Wow! I'm impressed!" said R.J.

Aimed and fired again, this time a good ten seconds.

Still not a thing. Not a hole, not a burn mark. Nothing.

"Okay, I'm with you," said R.J. He stood alongside. We pointed weapons together and fired.

Twenty seconds of disruptor resulted in no apparent window damage.

R.J. went to the target area and studied it. "It's faintly fogged. It's not even warm!"

I joined him. "Reinforced storm windows. The new kind. Reinforced transparent aluminum."

As we stood considering it, Griffin dropped down into view. Danica rotated the ship so she could see us. She waved through the forward portal. The comm squelched on. "Better pick it up, guys. There's more of those things showing up down there. A lot of them."

"Dan, we can't break the damn window. You're going to have to do it."

"Really!? Wow! That's a new one. Where do you want it?"

"Right where you see us now."

"Gonna be overkill. You know that."

"Yeah, we'll take cover in a back room. Go ahead and engage the particle cannons."

"I'll have to back away to get weapons convergence. Standby. Say when you're ready."

R.J. gathered up the prints from Elachia and we headed for the side room farthest from the target area. The door had been blocked open. We shut it and gathered around the small rectangular door window.

"Ready on this end."

"They're climbing this wall," warned Danica. "First burst in 3, 2, 1, execute."

For the first time in my life I watched the Griffin spacecraft, pointed right at me, particle cannons glowing yellow red bursting light so bright it made my mind wish I could see it again.

Wavering balls of plasma shot from the two cannons. The left-hand window in the study area exploded, then erupted into cookie-sized fragments that scattered like bullets in every direction. They embed in our door sounding like rounds from a machine gun. They ripped the ceiling to shreds, disassembled most of the room's furniture, and formed little piles here and there.

There was enough smoke that it made us wait to open the door. As it cleared, we dared to step out in time to see Danica maneuvering the Griffin sideways to us, edging the ship closer and closer to the very large hole in the side of the room.

"Last time I could see, they already had overcome their fear of the blast and were heading back up the side of the building," said Danica.

The long, rolled up drawings became awkward. There were too many for R.J. to maneuver easily. We climbed and pushed our way through the debris to the windy opening in the glass. Danica had extended the ramp straight out but because of Griffin's swept wings the ramp could not get all the way to us. There was a three-foot gap between the ledge and the ramp.

With a strained, worried look from R.J., Elachia went first. R.J. stayed so close to her he was almost a hindrance. She stepped sideways across with no problem and then with a nervy little act turned and looked down over the edge.

"They're coming up, you two. Watch it," she commanded.

We leaned out and looked down. Four big ones had made it to the second-floor windows. R.J. looked at me in annoyance. I fired downward and watched the four fall back to the ground, dead.

"Watch it, Adrian. They've started down from above also. They're still on the roof," said Danica.

We looked up just in time. I fired at one that had nearly reached us. The thing plummeted past us. Others were looking over the roof edge, considering the attempt.

"You next," I said.

"You next," he replied.

"I'm the Captain," I replied. "Hand the drawings over to Ela and then go."

"Ornery," he replied. He tightened up his grip and handed the drawings across the gap to the brave Elachia waiting on the ramp. He took a moment to fire on centipedes that had begun the trip down from the roof. They fell past us, legs still wiggling. I took out four more crossing over the third-floor windows.

"It's getting busy," said R.J. and he jumped across.

"Will you guys please get to it. How long do you expect me to hold in this tight?" called out Danica with notable irritation.

"Sorry Dan," I replied. I made the small jump and hurried into the airlock. R.J. slapped the big red button for emergency close. As we did there were two big bangs on the top of the ship, centipedes that had decided to tag along.

"Grab on, you guys," called Danica and we barely had time as she rotated the ship almost straight up, dumping our unwanted passengers. From there it was a quick ride up and out of Earth's atmosphere, past some visible debris that appeared to be from the One-World Space Station, to a point well beyond the orbit of Luna. There, after settling the ship in, we all once again took to the bottle and glasses of ice, celebrating our perilous retrieval of treasure, and by necessity putting off any consideration of what we planned to do with it.

Chapter 21

We drank more than was proper, an escape that was perhaps becoming too frequent. It was a group effort to rid ourselves not only of the vision of the centipedes, but the smell from them that seemed to have come back with us. Elvi had mentioned it, but for some reason it hadn't been too noticeable until after our return. It was possible we were becoming too loose. Corrupted reality was taking its toll. There was an atmosphere of what-difference-does-it-make underlying each spoken word. When we all began to get tipsy, we banded together and cooked. It became a large dinner around the main table with desperate jokes and forced group laughter. It was The Last Supper before the unthinkable. Afterward, we drank some more.

When finally fatigue overtook anxiety, I ordered them all to bed, promising to wake someone to relieve me at midnight, a promise I did not intend to keep. I wanted them to sleep away the real-life bad dream. We had handled insanity well. The centipedes never really came close to having the upper hand, but the prospect of what might have been challenged the imagination.

R.J. was the last to give up and go. We clinked glasses. He took his with him. I sat in the pilot's seat, watched Griffin talk to me with indicator lights and scrolling display screens. She was good company. Believing spacecraft or aircraft instruments is something that requires educational faith and absolute focus. No matter what you feel, you must trust those instruments. Many an aircraft has come out of the clouds nose down and into the ground because the pilot believed his senses rather than his attitude indicator.

Around three o'clock, it became regrettably necessary to change my serving to coffee. Not such good therapy for the stomach, bourbon followed by coffee. I wormed my way tiredly out of the seat and had to hold onto things to make my way to the kitchenette. Could I actually fly Griffin having imbibed this much? I had no doubt. Thank God the new coffee brewers only take ten seconds. With an ungodly amount of creamer added to reduce the acid, I warmed my hands on the ceramic cup, my special cup with the old Sabre Jet Aerobatics Team logo on it and dared a sip. From the corner of my eye, I thought I saw someone sitting at the table and scoffed up a sarcastic laugh at my imagination. Clearly there had been one bourbon too many.

But when I looked, there was actually someone there.

I jumped and spilled some of the coffee. A moment was needed for the adrenaline to help focus.

My hand wet with hot coffee, I demanded, "Who are you and how did you get on this ship?"

He had sandy hair in a butch cut. He looked to be about my age, tanned skin, a bit weathered. He wore an odd, deep purple suit that looked like fine, lightweight medieval body armor.

Suddenly my fatigue was gone. Adrenaline was peaking. I insisted, "Who are you?"

"Please, being here is very difficult for me. All this heaviness. It's exhausting."

I dared a step closer, keeping ready for combat. "Last time, who are you and how did you board us?"

"My name is Aries, Captain. Take it easy. I'm here to help you."

I quickly looked around for others. He seemed to have come alone.

"No, it's just me, Captain. You have a very big problem. I will help you fix it."

"How did you get here? There are no reflection alarms on radar. No boarding alerts."

"The Nasebiens contacted us through several rarely used channels. It's highly unusual, but then this is a highly unusual situation."

"What are you talking about?"

"Why don't you sit? It would take part of the stress of being here off of me."

"I believe I'll stand for the moment, if you don't mind."

"Earth is in bad shape, Captain."

"Tell me about it."

"I will. Some very naughty children played around with something that they knew they shouldn't. That's usually how these things begin."

"I'd feel better if you were in restraints."

"You're partly responsible for this, you know. At least, you were involved."

"I don't see a weapon on you. But I have one stored within arm's reach. I'll bet you I can have it pointed at you before you can stop me."

"You took an expedition to Daphnis, the satellite embedded in Saturn's rings."

"So?"

"Something was recovered from Daphnis and brought back to Earth. A celestial element known as Diamond Light."

"Okay, you've bought yourself a minute or two. Keep going...."

"I have some experience with Diamond Light. In my reality I transport extracted Diamond light to the proper destinations. Diamond light could also be called the Z particle. It's the last element on the infinite periodic table, not exactly the same scientific table Eartlings are familiar with. It is an element that remains stable in all dimensions and believe me that's saying something. There is nothing else like it. Are you sure you won't sit, please?"

I pulled out a chair, put down my cup, and slowly sat keeping within reach of the cabinet that held the disruptor.

"Anyway, these naughty children brought Diamond Light back to Earth and somehow managed to extract a particle group from the containment for use in your primitive Hadron Collider. We were shocked that they were able to do that. Naughty children are often remarkably devious. The naughty children were beside themselves trying to understand what they had found. And, I can understand the military supporting them. A source of infinite, inexhaustible power and more. Have you ever seen the old Earth movie Forbidden Planet, Captain?"

"First movie I ever saw."

"Remember how on the planet Altair the people became so advanced and powerful they could create whatever they wanted just by thinking it?"

"Yes."

"Diamond Light could provide that kind of power on Earth. You think Earth is ready for that?"

"Keep going."

"It's not entirely the fault of the naughty children. That ship sleeping in Saturn's ring was actually part of a Diamond Light transfer task force. It's considered the most valuable commodity in the cosmos, yours *and* mine. Pirates from outer dimensions are always trying to intercept shipments, and since Diamond Light is superbly difficult to harvest, shipments often come under attack. That's what I do. I get the Light from point A to point B. I'm actually a Captain much like yourself. So, the task force for that Daphnis ship came under attack by a large pirate group. This all happened ages ago, of course. There were problems defending against the attack. The battle wasn't going well for either side. It was decided that the ship carrying the Light would secretly break off from its escort, hopefully taking the pirates by surprise and leaving them behind. Unfortunately, it didn't work. More pirate ships entered the fray and noticed the Light ship breaking away. There were several jumps into other dimensions to escape but at least one pirate stayed the course. The Light ship dove into Saturn's rings to hide. It readied its weapons for defense. The pirates finally found it. There was an exchange of weapons fire. The pirate ship was crippled and spun down into Saturn but not before getting one last shot off that caught the Light ship directly in the bow. You know the rest."

I stared back at him, still wondering if he should be believed.

"As you can see, that ship should never have been there in the first place, but it had been lost.

Exhaustive efforts were made to find it. All to no avail. Which brings us back to the present."

"That all fits, but assuming I believe it, how do we fix this?"

"I would call it the Great Leap of Faith, if I may."

"Go on."

"To correct the Diamond Light cycle on Earth, you must volunteer to die."

"Really? That's the best you've got?"

"Yes, and you'll probably need to die more than once, even many times."

"You've got to be kidding."

"Six seconds. When the Light field collapses and resets everything back to almost normal, at that moment a Diamond Light particle group is racing around that collider on its way to collision. You will have six seconds to stop that collision from happening."

"I still don't see how."

"It will take a number of attempts to interfere with the particle's trajectory so that it misses the collision. The particles will then continue on into space until they find a compatible star core to migrate to."

"And I have to die to do this?"

"It's much more than that. You also have to convince two of your associates to come along and die with you."

"Oh, come on, please...."

"I cannot help you convince the others, by the way. I'm expending enough energy just projecting here right now. I could not endure a meeting with two more. You will need to convince them I am real and that what I'm saying is the truth."

"You're leaving me with nothing here. Can't you reappear later and speak to them one at a time?"

"Too much exposure for me. I can only commit to maybe one more meeting between the two of us. If this mission is accomplished, my associates will be able to remove the remaining core of Diamond Light and transfer it to an appropriate destination. Right now, nobody can get close enough to do that. Afterward, a higher court will conduct an investigation to find out how the naughty children were able to extract Diamond Light particles but no one from your Terran System will ever be aware of that."

"And exactly how can the path of the Diamond Light particle stream inside the collider be redirected?"

"I'm not a physicist. I can't explain the subatomic properties of Diamond Light. No one can. But the collider diagrams you now have should provide enough information for you and your crew to determine a way to interrupt power to the collider in such a way as to interfere with the particle stream. We expect it will likely take three of you to divert the particle stream trajectory. As I've said, you will need to modify the collider facility's power systems to do it."

"We'll be able to make changes to that system?"

"Yes, during those six seconds all Diamond Light energy will have collapsed back into the collider."

"And we'll be able to do it in six seconds?"

"Unfortunately, no. That is why you must make the ultimate sacrifice. The idea is actually rather simple. First, you and your team must find and be in just the right place in the collider facility's debris field. You will need to find a way down to the lower levels and be there before the Light field collapses and restores everything. Your team will take specific positions where a power control area will reform after the restoration. The collapse of the field and subsequent restoration will not affect you since you were not saturated with Light radiation during the previous explosion. The facility will reconstruct around you. You cannot attempt this plan in the main control center. Too many moving people, too long to access computers. If you positioned yourselves correctly, you will end up standing in one of the collider's power control console areas. The collider will be restored and operating again right in front of you. At that time, you'll have six seconds of access to those power control consoles but, by the time you are oriented and focused enough to do anything about it you will be too late. The next explosion will happen. The three of you will die. Twenty-four hours later, you will be resurrected in the same exact location, ready to try again. You will remember that this is not your first attempt. In fact, you'll know that you may have already attempted to stop the explosion and failed many times. In either case, you will have a new six seconds to begin again."

Aries paused and reached into his breast pocket. "There are actually only two reasons I was assigned to thought-matter transfer here. These gyres are one of those reasons."

Aries drew out three small coin-sized objects. He placed them on the table in front of me. They glowed and appeared to be slightly translucent. Just looking at them seemed to interfere with my thought process.

Aries continued, "Don't ask me to fully explain these. They are some kind of dimethyltryptamine device, an entheogen. Supposedly they affect your pineal gland somehow. You wear them over your ajna. Sorry, I mean in the center of your forehead. They induce some kind of psychoactive substance. If all of that sounds confusing, I'm with you. My associates had to force-feed just that much info to me. I'm just a roc-jock like you. The bottom line is, these things will allow you to remember past lives. When you guys fail at your mission, and you will, you will wake up at the next six second restoration back where you started. Obviously if you did not remember the last attempt you would simply begin again, make the same mistakes over and over, failing again and again. These DMT devices will allow you to remember what happened during the last six second attempt so that you can correct where you failed and continue on. Does all that make sense to you?"

"Nothing makes sense to me. We're supposed to swallow these?"

"Absolutely not! Sorry, too much ethereal information at once. Once you are all in position in the collider power room, a few minutes before the first restoration event occurs, you each press one of these against your forehead. It will stick. In fact, it will be difficult to remove after that. Do *not* put these on way ahead of time. If you do, you may begin to recall previous lives and believe me, you don't want that. Want to add guilt from a previous life to what you have now? I don't think so. And there are also all those long-lost loved ones to remember. Those kinds of memories are for people who have earned their way out of the life-death cycle. The human mind was not designed to handle that kind of transcendental memory. So do not put them on early. Trust me. But with these, in the collider power console area at every new six second interval you will remember what you did last time and hopefully you will find a way to shut down collider power. Got it?"

"What a wonderful solution you've come up with! And we're not busy anyway.... You said there were two reasons you came here. I'm afraid to ask about the other."

"The other was to tell you that firing on the collider will not work. It will set off the same explosion that we are now dealing with."

"Do you have any good news?"

"If you think about it, your team will actually have all the time it needs to find what has to be shut down and quickly get to it. You'll have as many six seconds intervals as needed."

"And in between, we'll be dead for twenty-four hours."

"Yes. Most likely you will be unconscious, asleep during that period and will simply wake up during the restoration. If you do regain consciousness during the twenty-four-hour void you must be careful to remain exactly where you are and remain ready no matter what happens around you."

"Wait a minute! If we regain consciousness after our death? How can we regain consciousness after we're dead?"

"Come on, Captain. No one actually dies. I though you knew that. For a human, death simply means withdrawing to a much larger, truer existence."

"You realize that when you leave here, I'm going to decide this was all just a real bad bourbon dream."

"You have advanced degrees in electronics and electrical systems. Commander Smith has degrees in several related fields and his wife has studies far in advance of both of you. You are the perfect team for this extraordinarily difficult mission. That's why you were chosen. Diamond Light effects are extremely hazardous to the Nasebiens and many other advanced races. They cannot even enter within the boundaries of the Sol system. Were they to transit anywhere past the Oort Cloud, they would be severely harmed in ways you cannot understand. It is up to you, Captain. Set up for it, and I'll try to visit you once more later, but only if that's needed. These explosions are affecting other dimensions in ways you cannot imagine. There is nothing in your life more important than doing this."

"Including staying alive?"

"A trivial concern at this point."

"You realize if we fail to stop the collider we'll die over and over forever."

"We probably will bring in another human team should that happen, but it will be much more complicated with your team being in the way."

"This really sucks in every way possible; you know that?"

And with that, he was gone.

Chapter 22

I tried to find the best time to tell them. It had to be all together because I was not going to try to answer the absurd kinds of questions they would have more than once. They were all already upset at having been allowed to sleep all night. R.J. looked particularly refreshed despite Elachia's compartment having been designed for only one person. They brooded around grumbling. I sipped coffee at the table and smirked, looking drunk from fatigue.

"So now we know we can't trust you," said Danica as she poured herself a cup.

"Funny you should put it just that way," I replied.

"We can't discuss shooting up Geneva until you've slept," said R.J. "You're in no condition to make those kinds of decisions."

"I know how much *I* drank last night," added Elachia. "How much did you drink?"

"Boy, you guys aren't making this easy."

R.J. knew me too well. He stopped wiping off the counter and stared. "Making what easy?"

To the best of my ability I told them the story of Ebenezer's ghost, the tale of the naughty children, and the path to uncertain redemption. They all stopped what they were doing, and it

E.R. Mason

took a very long time for anyone to speak or even move.

"Had you been sleeping before this happened?" asked Dr. Elachia.

"It wasn't a dream."

"No proximity alerts at all?" asked Danica.

"Not a one."

"If there really was a guy, he didn't even tell you where he was from?" said R.J.

"There really was a guy. He left us these little coin-things. No, he didn't not tell me exactly where he was from."

"So the bottom line is, one of us is supposed to drop the other three off at the explosion site and leave them there to die?" said Danica.

"Not exactly," I replied. "*You* are supposed to drop we three off and then get the hell out of there."

"Fuck that!" answered Danica.

"Wow!" said R.J. "I've never heard her speak like that!"

Surprisingly, Elachia let out a laugh.

"And this guy that may or may not have been on our side said this is the only way?" asked R.J.

"The only way," I answered.

"Wait a minute, wait a minute," declared R.J. "Ela, is that even possible? Could we divert a particle stream without having access to the control room?"

Elachia answered reluctantly, "Yes, if we could interrupt or vary power to one of the dipole cascades in time."

"Why doesn't this guy really do something to help us?" demanded Danica.

"He did help us. He told us what to do," I replied.

Danica scoffed.

Elachia said, "We *would* have to face the fact that this could not be done the first time around.

We could never find the right positions, focus on them and switch off the correct power circuits in the first six seconds."

"And I'm assuming we don't actually have six seconds. The final one or two seconds would be too late," added R.J.

Elachia said kindly, "You did not think before you spoke, Rowland. Those particle streams are traveling at approximately the speed of light. It takes about 80 microseconds for the particle group to complete a single trip around the ring. That means in the last second, the particle stream will circle the ring more than eleven thousand times. So even if we eliminate the magnetic steering in that last second, that should work."

"It's a stupid idea," said Danica.

"As I'm thinking about this, there's something else," said R.J. "The power rooms must be on the lower levels, so we'd have to search around the explosion area and try to find a way underground. From there we'd have to make our way and find an appropriate power room, a room that's still in good enough shape that we'd have places in the clear to stand. Who knows how deep that is. There'd be destruction all along the way. It could take hours or days."

"Yeah, and if you didn't get there and the next explosion happened the whole thing would be useless and you guys would be trapped down there," complained Danica.

"Unless we could get back to the ship in time," said R.J.

"Adrian, are you really for this?" asked Danica.

"He's been awake for probably forty hours and he's hung over. He doesn't know what he is," said R.J.

I returned an unsteady stare. I must've looked something like Stan Laurel because they all stared back at me with the consternation of Oliver Hardy.

Elachia said kindly, "Adrian, why don't you go to bed. Do you want me to give you something to sleep?"

I stood, and with my best Stan Laurel smile raised my chin and marched off to my sleeping compartment.

In retribution for my having allowed them to sleep all night, no one gave me a wake-up call, and someone snuck into my compartment and shut off the alarm I had set. Twelve hours later, I opened my eyes, wondered who I was and where I was, then pondered the failure of my alarm as reality began to seep back in.

It was 10 P.M. Griffin time. After an extravagant, irresponsible, long hot shower, I found a fresh green flight suit and headed for the kitchen.

I passed Danica on her way to her sleeper, a book in hand. She gave me a flat smile and wiggled her fingers at me. In the main compartment, R.J. was studying drawings at the table. Elachia was in a seat opposite him with drawings spread out on the floor.

"We're hoping we find something that will prevent us from doing this," he said as I searched the refrigeration unit. "Never mind the fridge. Danica left you these." He held up a dish of cinnamon buns. I grabbed coffee and snatched them away.

"Did she *bake* these herself?"

"The pastry ship didn't go by this morning. So, yes."

"Oh man! Good. Oh man."

"You can have them all. Ela and I have already stuffed ourselves."

"Making any progress there?"

"Yes. We don't have to worry about getting trapped underground. We have a plan."

"Really."

"I believe stark terror prevented us from thinking about it before. It's simple. The events occur around six P.M. Geneva time. We get dropped off at the site in the morning, carefully work our way in and after four hours of spelunking we leave, and Danica drops down and picks us up. In other words, assuming we don't get all the way in, four hours will leave us plenty of time to make our way back out and take off. We'll wait until after the next event, then go do it again knowing exactly what to expect and bringing along exactly what we need to get past obstacles. We'll do that as many times as it takes until we have found a way to where we need to be and can get there in the time we have. Ta-da!"

"So, helmets, headlamps and pickaxes then?"

R.J. scoffed, "Are you kidding? Try full face masks with oxygen. I'm embarrassed to say Elachia had to remind me about fuel and gas contamination. You know the hazardous stuff they've got down in those support rooms and tunnels that feed the collider? Tons of helium 4 used down there and who knows what else."

I looked over at Elachia. "Are you optimistic about any of this, Ela?"

She looked up from large schematics on the floor. She sat back for a break. "There is too much to tell, Adrian. There are no less than ten different test stations set up along this collider ring. The ring is at least one-hundred and fifty feet below the surface. We could never have destroyed it from orbit. I have been studying the primary area of destruction. It is a very large crater, but it is easy to see that the source explosion took place at the Merlin test station on the southeastern side. There is a newly made gravel chimney dropping down into the earth there. That's where the greatest amount of damage will be. Fortunately, there are nine other test stations we might access even though all of the surface buildings have been destroyed. There was also a central power station in the middle of the ring that distributed the high-power lines to substation points around the ring. We may find access there also."

"You're saying we would have to climb down more than one hundred feet?"

"If I understood correctly, we need a reasonably intact chamber to take up positions before the restoration takes place, a chamber that can be restored around us without affecting us, and one that gives immediate access to a part of the power distribution system that can interrupt the collider. So yes, it means that we'll need to descend to the collider ring level. Were we to chance being in the right place anywhere else, we'd face the possibility of having a wall or equipment form right where we're standing. That would be a fatal error."

"Have you found any places in the videos where we might be able to get down there?"

"Yes. There are several exposed shafts. R.J. is working on special scanning that will reveal some subsurface imagery. It should help narrow our search."

"And if we do find a way down, can we really shut the test down in time?"

"As Rowland would say, there's good news and there's bad news."

"What's the good news?"

"It's only half good news. The facility has three separate power systems. They have main power from the French, an alternate main power from the Swiss, and they have a battery backup power system designed to give them time to shut down a test if the two mains both fail. If we can shut down all three of those substations in one area in time, it's likely the particle groups would disband making collisions very unlikely."

"That's the good news?"

"The bad news is, one of us must be at each of the correct power control racks, and those panels must be shut off in the correct sequence to disrupt the particle stream."

"In six seconds...."

"Well, if we can accurately locate where each of the racks will appear after the restoration, and we can be standing in those exact spots, we should have a chance."

R.J. tried to sound comical, "There's always C4!"

"What?"

"C4. When the collider appears after restoration, we jam a bunch of C4 explosive against it, stick in an igniter and blow the place up!"

"You mean blow ourselves up?"

"He's not serious," replied Elachia. "It is not a viable plan. Subtract the time to do those steps from our six seconds and we'd be much too late."

"Do you guys have any idea when you'll be ready to try this?"

Elachia answered, "Tomorrow morning, Geneva time. That is if we keep working straight through. By then I'll have identified the exact power console designations, and Rowland should have his subterranean mapping done. We'll know which shaft to attempt first. Let me ask you, what do we have for climbing gear?"

"We're pretty good in that department. We can use space suit tethers along with a long length of nylon line I have. We also have a power ascender used to cross over long tethers to other ships. If we set up a pulley feed tether, the ascender will hoist us up and out, no climbing required. We can use our emergency O2 masks for the tunnels."

"What do we have for explosives?" asked R.J.

"Explosives?"

"There's bound to be superstructure blocking the way at points. We'll need to blast it clear remotely."

"Hmm, not so good on that one. I just don't carry that kind of stuff unless it's specifically needed for something."

"That's okay. I'll hunt around in our chemical supplies. We can make something."

"Tomorrow morning Geneva time then."

R.J. said, "You know, there's always a chance we might be able to shut the collider down on the first try and walk away heroes."

It was a nice attempt at encouragement, that none of us believed.

Chapter 23

We suited up and stowed gear, and through the portals watched the day-night terminator line slowly move away east of Geneva. Down and down the ship went, with us scanning for ripple barriers left behind by the Light Wave creating border zones of other-worldly intrusions, all the time hoping there would not be giant centipedes searching the tunnels.

But no such barriers were detected and as we descended there were no signs of snake-like vegetation or man-eating bugs, even though the Geneva library complex was not that far away. There was nothing but miles of disrupted dirt and sand. Griffin kicked up a wide tall cloud as we settled, powder so fine it would have worked in an hourglass. It gave me concern for Griffin's intakes.

We wore brown cargo-style clothing. Many pockets to hold tools and other human essentials. We wore high lace up boots with reinforced toe covering. Oxygen masks hung down on our chests. O2 canisters sat in pouches on our back. We used spare foam helmet liners for helmets and strapped work lights to our foreheads for headlamps.

Danica left her command seat and came back to wish us luck as Griffin sat idling. "See you in eight hours or less," she said, and she made it sound like a warning as she tapped the ramp and outer door to close.

Packs hanging from our shoulders, we backed away from the liftoff cloud but couldn't really escape it. We had to hold our masks against our faces while we followed Elachia through the sandstorm in the direction of our fractured shaft of choice. Danica had put us down roughly a thousand feet from it. It was like walking on the dry sand of a beach.

The closer we came to the shaft the more ominous it looked. It was wide enough to lower a tractor trailer into it. A jagged piece of cement shaped like an arrowhead pointed upward just below the rim of the big hole. Sand would periodically waterfall down at points around it. It wasn't safe enough to get close to the edge without safety lines, and the flattened world around us offered nothing to tie off to. But we had expected that. We drove iron bars into the ground as deeply as possible. I tied off to one, went to the edge and leaned out to look down.

"I do see where the service ladder starts. It's a good hundred feet down but the tunnel walls look solid there. We're in luck. It's here on our side."

"We're in luck, you say?" remarked R.J. sardonically.

We set up the clothesline feed and lowered the power ascender down to the bottom. We each tied off to a separate iron stake. I insisted on going first. Because both of them were smarter than me, it bothered me that they did not object.

Rappelling is actually a great deal of fun unless you are descending into a dragon's mouth, which I was. It's always nice to be able to look down and see you are nearing the bottom. In this case, there was no bottom. There was only the beginning of a rebar ladder embedded in a violated cement wall. The power ascender waited there, swinging slightly at the end of its line. Darkness waited beneath it.

But the rebar looked secure when I arrived. I grabbed on and pulled myself in, stepping on the ladder rungs for support. I clicked my comm button. "Danica, you still receiving us?"

"Five by five, Adrian. Everything okay so far?"

"One hundred feet or so down. No problems."

"As planned, you do not need to press your comm keys. I've set you all on constant com. We'll all hear everything everyone says."

"Very good. Ela, R.J., I'm on the ladder. It seems solid."

"On our way down," replied R.J.

A further inspection with headlamp revealed long cracks running up and down the shaft walls. In places, chunks had fallen out leaving a small waterfall of sand sprinkling down. Cool air was rising from the shaft. It smelled funny. Below, within the black hole, I could barely make out fallen superstructure beams stretching from one side to the other. With surprising agility Ela dropped down alongside me. I climbed down to make ladder room for her. She held to one rebar step and pulled herself over like a pro. R.J. dropped down a moment later and worked himself into a position above her.

"The power ascender better work," said R.J. "That'll will be a long climb out if it doesn't."

I called out, "We can use a Prusik if we need to."

"Oh, yeah. Still...," he replied.

When everyone was unhooked and secured to ladder rungs, we started down again, one step at a time, testing each with great care. There were fallen beams to climb past and large cracks in places, but the rungs held.

R.J. finally called out, "I can see the bottom."

We stopped to look down at the pile of debris half buried in sand. Our headlamps cast eerie shadows within the broken pile. We climbed down to it, stood on powdered sand, and turned within the spectacle of rubbish to study the place.

"This was a test interface room alongside the main collider ring!?" I asked.

Ela nodded. "That's what's buried below our feet. We need to access the service tunnel to the west. That will be right over there." She pointed to the opposite side of the shaft.

R.J. reached behind and unhooked his folding shovel. He climbed and pushed his way there and began to dig.

I had neglected to bring a shovel but when I turned to look at Ela she was smiling and holding hers out to me.

The dig took twenty minutes of the four hours we'd allowed ourselves. We finally uncovered the arched ceiling of the main service tunnel. Sand began to stream down into the black hole beneath it, confirming the passageway was still open. But as we made a space large enough to crawl into, we were staring into such an absolutely dark abyss, it made us dread going in. We tied off two short lines and with a last look of resolve I slid feet first, face down, into it.

Our dread had been well founded. My first sight after focusing my headlamp, was a body twenty feet away. It was gathered up in the fetal position, charred so badly it had been reduced in size. But even through its dark, flaky appearance, the wide-eyed look of surprise death was still clearly visible. Surrounding that frozen stare was the arcane disaster we'd expected. Large cables strewn everywhere. Pieces of superstructure leaning against displaced equipment shelves and consoles. Small waterfalls of sand leaking through cracks in the ceiling. The continuing channel of carnage led into the main passageway.

R.J. slid down beside me, scanned with his light and stood absorbing the tomb-like adornments of the unstable artery we were determined to traverse. He noticed the first victim.

"We expected this," he said.

Danica's voice came over the com, "Expected what? The body cams are crap."

"Just some debris from the explosion," I replied.

"You're looking good, Ela" said R.J. and he stood ready to catch her as she slid down.

I took a position opposite him and helped guide her to the floor. She turned and scanned the tunnel and quickly saw the body but paid no attention to it. "Can we get through?" she asked.

"With some climbing, as long as we're not blocked farther up ahead," I answered.

"We've already used more than an hour of our planned four hours. We should get going," said Elachia.

The first three obstacles were main support beams laying forty-five degrees across the tunnel. We went over two and under the third. Dirt and sand rained down on us.

Elachia paused to study the next stretch of tunnel. "We can't even see the collider ring yet. It's buried along the shaft to our left. That's why you see the continuous flow of cabling coming down from the ceiling and running into the sand. For all we know there could be power substations buried in there along with the collider but there's no sense in randomly digging to find out. We need a more open section of tunnel where we can tell there are rows of consoles that follow along the ring."

R.J. said, "You know, we're very lucky this place isn't in a dimensional warp like we've seen before. Imagine trying to get through here with giant centipedes running around, or time shifts happening."

"Don't be too sure, Rowland, dear. This is the center point of the eruption of the Diamond Light. We can't know what might be happening around us. Let's keep going. Watch for signs of the collider ring."

We came to a complete blockage of more iron and cable. We could see openings overhead, but they were too small to fit through. There were two spots on floor level that looked like they might open up with some digging. We were lucky. It only took a few minutes to shovel a hole in the loose, golden sand and crawl under the debris.

Beyond the latest blockage, we found a new puzzle. The tunnel became a sort of Y, with a second section of tunnel opening to the right. The new right-hand passageway was fractured from the ceiling to the floor on the right side, but easily passable.

"It must be a cable service tunnel," said R.J. "Do we ignore it and go on, or what?"

"We've got to split up," said Elachia. "If the main tunnel is blocked up ahead, we will have wasted too much time following it. We need to check both passageways and meet back here."

"Better keep in frequent contact on the coms," said R.J.

Splitting up made me even more apprehensive, but I had no good argument for Elachia's plan. "So, you two take the service tunnel and I'll cover the main."

"If there's any trouble we run back to this point and join up," said R.J., as though he felt guilty about sending me off on my own.

"It seems safe enough so far," I replied. "If one of us finds what we're looking for we can just join up at that spot and start figuring out which consoles are the right ones."

They nodded and with last looks headed off into the dark tunnel, their headlamps dancing.

My solo sojourn soon became macabre again. More black charred bodies with looks of eternal wonder on their half-skull faces. There were six of them this time. They had been running. Clothing and sex were not recognizable. I had to step over one to get through the stacked trash. Maybe this many meant there was a workstation nearby.

Fifteen more minutes of spelunking the morbid subterranean graveyard brought me to a very open chamber that seemed to go beyond what I could see. The collider shell was completely exposed now on my left. Up ahead there appeared to be dirt-covered workstations. I thought to trot ahead to inspect them, but something stopped me.

A sound. Coming from somewhere ahead. An image of a four-foot centipede popped into my head. I took a position behind the last of the dirt-covered steel stations, drew my disruptor, and watched from the shadows.

There was a light! A beam bouncing off the tunnel walls.

Voices! At least two.

Stunned, I watched as two men in yellow and red security coveralls came into view. They had headlamps and handheld big beam flashlights. They wore fluorescent chest belts with glow stick pads attached. Both had holstered weapons. Lace-up black military boots completed their uniforms. Breathing masks dangled against their chests.

It took me a minute to believe it. As they neared, I finally stepped out, hands raised, "Hey! Where did you guys come from?"

It made them jump. They both slapped their holsters, but my raised hands reassured them. They pointed their lights in my face so that I had to squint.

"Identify yourself," called one.

"Tarn, Adrian Tarn."

They relaxed. "Oh! Captain Tarn. We were told by Mars Station to be on the lookout for you. Glad we caught up with you."

"Who are you?"

"We're Space Systems Homeland Security. Our task force came in last night. We did not pick up your ship on scans, but they probably have by now. We're here to set things right."

"You know at 6:00 P.M. this place is going to hell and if you get caught up in it, you'll be trapped?"

"Oh yeah, we're fully briefed on the Diamond Light loop. We're already set up to break the cycle. There's nothing more that you need to do here. You need to get back to your ship and get outside the event horizon. Do you need anything?"

"You're with who again?"

"Space Systems Homeland Security, Tango base. We've been on the problem since it began. We were outside the blast area. Somehow, we missed hooking up with you guys. We were busy."

"So that's it? You're set to interrupt the explosion after the next field collapse."

"Exactly right. We have operatives who know how to divert the particle stream almost instantly. There won't be another explosion. But, if you would, please head back to your ship and let us get on with it."

"Sure, okay. I just can't believe I'm getting off this easy. Thanks for everything. You have no idea how glad I am to see you guys."

They nodded and headed back the way they had come. I turned and in a daze from relief shook my head in amazement at our luck. Halfway back to the separation point, I ran into Elachia and R.J. coming to find me.

"The other tunnel is a dead end. It will take explosives to open it. Tell me you had better luck," said R.J.

"You're not going to believe this, but there are two Homeland Security officers back there that want us out of here now. Their agency is taking care of the problem."

"Oh my God! So, we don't have to commit suicide? Danica we're ready for extraction. Let's get out of here. Time to hit the Culatta Blue, and watch the show from outside lunar orbit," said R.J.

We worked our way back. At each blockage we helped Elachia through, followed by R.J., then me. I pulled myself through the final dirty hole and stood to brush myself off. We had arrived at the spot where the tunnel divided in two different directions.

R.J. stood watching as I brushed off. "Ours was a bust, Adrian. The other tunnel is blocked up ahead. It would take explosives to open it up."

I looked up at him inquisitively. "You already told me that, R.J. It doesn't matter now."

"What do you mean I already told you that? You just got here. What do you mean it doesn't matter?"

"R.J., you're losing it. I told you, the Homeland Security guys are taking over the mission. We're out of here."

"What Homeland Security guys?"

"Okay one of us is mentally AWOL. I told you, Homeland Security is set up to interrupt the collider operations. We're done here."

"Wait a minute, wait a minute. When did you tell me all this?"

"Back in the main tunnel when you guys met me back there."

"We haven't been any farther than this junction. We just got back from the branch tunnel."

"R.J., the three of us just climbed under that fallen stanchion right there."

"Elachia and I have not gone through that opening. This is as far as we've gotten."

"Elachia, would you straighten him out for me, please?" I asked.

"He's right, Adrian. This is as far as we're come. We've been in the other tunnel until just now."

"Okay, let me try this once more. I met two Homeland Security guys about a hundred yards ahead. Halfway back I met you two coming to find me. The three of us came the rest of the way here."

"Never happened," said R.J.

"So, who came back with me?"

"You came back alone," said R.J. "No one came under that pylon but you."

"Something's definitely wrong with one of us," I said.

"Got to be you," said R.J. "I have Elachia."

"Or maybe both of you just had some kind of stress amnesia or something," I replied. "I'm not making this all up, you know."

R.J. paused. "Danica, have you been monitoring?"

"Every minute."

"Did you hear Adrian tell us about some Homeland Security people a few minutes ago?"

"Yes, but no one answered him."

I said, "R.J. mentioned Culatta Blue. Didn't you hear him say that? Or the Homeland Security people, didn't you hear them?"

"Nope. It was like you were talking to yourself."

I shook my head. "I don't believe it!"

"What about these Homeland Security guys?" asked R.J.

"They said they were from Space Systems Homeland Security, Tango Base or something like that. They knew we were in the area but had not been able to make contact. They were based outside the event horizon, so they weren't affected. They're set up to interrupt the collider test and reset Earth to normal. They asked us to leave as soon as possible."

"Are you sure?" asked R.J.

"What do you mean?"

"You thought you were with us back there. Are you sure those guys were real?"

"For cripes sakes, R.J."

"Wow! Cripes sakes is it? That's like a whole level above Pete's sake."

"Are you suggesting we climb all the way back there to see if those guys are really there?"

"We have less than two hours if we stick to our plan," said Elachia. "Did you ask Danica for extraction after all that?"

"The other R.J. did."

"Danica, did you hear the call for extraction?" asked Elachia.

"I heard Adrian talking to someone, but no one asked for extraction."

"We've got to go back there," said R.J.

Danica cut in, "I'm giving you guys two hours more, no longer. Then I'm coming down."

R.J. shook his head. "You *know* your story isn't making sense, Adrian. We have to see if those guys were real. We have no choice."

I shook my head in dismay. "You're thinking I imagined the two of you on my way back?"

"I keep telling you we were never there," answered R.J.

Irately I replied, "Okay, you guys want to climb back through that mess, let's go."

So, we went. Once again Elachia led so that we could assist her over and under obstacles. It was a twenty-minute struggle to make it back to the open tunnel where I had met the security team.

"This is the place?" asked R.J.

"They came from up ahead," I answered.

"Well this *is* the type of area we've been looking for," said Elachia. "That long row of racks sticking out of the sand looks promising. There are almost certainly power control panels in some of them. It would help if I could identify each of them. I know which ones we need."

"So, this *is* where a Space System Security Team would set up shop to stop the collider then. Do you believe me yet, R.J.?"

"I want to believe you very badly," he replied.

Movement from farther ahead caught my eye. "Well then, you're in luck. Here they come again," I replied.

The same two security men appeared, headed in our direction. When they noticed us they picked up their pace. As they approached, they spotted me and became stern-faced.

"Captain Tarn, I thought we had an understanding. You were to evacuate this facility," said the first man.

"My apologies. Colonel is it? My friends here wanted to be absolutely sure you were who you say you are."

"Space Systems Homeland Security. Delta Base dispatch. The three of you have got to vacate these premises immediately."

"May I ask your name, Colonel?" said R.J.

"Colonel Reeves Walker, at your service. Now, would you please expedite your departure?"

"And you, sir?" said R.J. to the second officer.

"Captain Mars also at your service, Mr. Rowland."

Elachia asked, "Gentleman, would it be possible to see how you're setting up to control the collider operation?"

Captain Mars answered, "I assure you, ma'am, we have introduced an inductive control console that will divert the particle cluster away from the collision point with seconds to spare. I wouldn't worry about that if I were you."

"But could we see it," persisted Elachia.

"If it will get rid of you guys, I supposed that could be arranged. It's just around the ring area over there," answered Colonel Walker.

The Colonel motioned to his assistant and they led us deeper into the tunnel way. Around the first bend we spotted a new, single position console with a man seated at it wearing a white lab coat. The Colonel brought us alongside and motioned Elachia to inspect the device. Elachia and R.J. leaned over for a close look at the readouts on the equipment. Elachia moved around behind to check the interconnections. When they were done, they both came to me and nodded.

Colonel Walker spoke in a noticeably more terse tone, "Now lady and gentlemen, I will ask you for a last time to please clear the area. If you refuse, or you choose to return once more, you will be taken into custody and *we* will remove you to a safe distance from the planet." The Colonel placed a hand on his holstered weapon for emphasis. "Are we in agreement this time?"

The three of us nodded enthusiastically and turned away. We headed away at a brisk pace. When we were well clear, R.J. grabbed our arms and stopped us.

"It's not real," he said.

We formed a small, closed circle and talked in low tones to avoid attracting attention.

"What was your first clue?" I asked.

"Well for God's sake, there's power to that console coming from the collider power bus. There can't be any power coming from there."

"Maybe they found a way," I suggested.

Elachia shook her head. "It's a false console. There's nothing on that panel related to collider operations. There's no interface with the collider ring. It is what you Earthling's call a *sham*."

"Do you really think those guys are legit?" asked R.J. "You, the most distrusting, skeptical person on Earth?"

"For Pete's sake, you might as well have added *ornery*, R.J."

"But do you believe them?"

"Absolutely not. They blew it a minute after we found them."

"Why?"

"Colonel Reeves Walker. How could you forget Reeves, R.J.? Reeves Walker flew with us on the Nadir Mission. And the other guy, Captain Mars. That was the name of the Captain of the Star Seven, our luxury cruise that nearly got us killed, remember? Where we met Elachia and Fantasia. I admit the Mars name is a bit common, but Reeves Walker is not a common name. What are the odds that we get both a Reeves Walker and a Captain Mars stopping us down here?"

R.J. lost his train of thought and looked lovingly at Elachia. "I'd fly that Star Seven mission a hundred more times if I had to."

Elachia returned a Mona Lisa smile.

"Okay you two. You can get a room later. What's going on here?"

R.J. snapped back to reality. "At the risk of offending passivism, I suggest we return with guns a-blazing and get real answers to our questions."

"You want to risk a gunfight with Elachia here?"

"You stay and cover her, and I'll go on ahead. There's only two of them. I should have the element of surprise."

"Okay, okay. *You* hang back and take care of Elachia. I'll go secure our SSHS friends and then call you to come join us."

The two of them looked at me with guilt and gratitude. It made me cough up a low laugh. Their expressions turned to comical disapproval.

I stealthed along, weapon drawn and held out of sight behind me. I kept to the cave-in and equipment along the collider ring. Approaching the area where they had set up the console seemed too easy. There was no sign of them now. I came out of hiding and walked around freely. Their shiny new console was nowhere to be found. There were footprints in the dirt and sand but they looked like ours only. As I stood trying to understand, a loud crash came from farther along the tunnel. I took a position behind dirt and steel and watched and waited.

What came around the curve and into sight was the last thing I wanted to see. It was three feet tall and eight to ten feet long; a centipede with its spiked teeth bared. There were two more following along behind it.

I backed away. When there was enough distance for concealment, I ran back to our meeting point. R.J. and Elachia stared inquisitively as I struggled to catch my breath.

"You're killing me! What happened?" asked R.J. impatiently.

"The Homeland Security guys and all their equipment are gone. They've been replaced by centipedes."

"Oh crap, not them," complained R.J. "How many?"

"I saw three but there's sure to be more."

"They can move through this tunnel wreckage a lot better than we can. Let's start backing out of here right now before we have to race for our lives."

"I tend to agree," I replied.

We started a quick walk out, looking behind as we went.

"All the new equipment was gone?" asked Elachia.

"It's all gone. There are no consoles there now," I answered.

Elachia stopped. R.J. stopped with her. With my best arm gestures, I begged them to continue.

"That was a false console," said Elachia.

"What?" I asked.

"There were impossibly heavy power cables connected to the power bus and communications rack behind it. There never was a new console there."

"We did all see it this time," suggested R.J.

"You can't just jack into a system like that. The cabling is too heavy and there were too many lines."

"We could talk about this aboard Griffin," I said meekly.

"There was no console and no Homeland Security people there," insisted Elachia. "Danica, did you hear the Homeland Security men when we were talking to them?"

"Nope, all I heard was you guys."

"Adrian, you went back there to see if those guys were for real. Now you're saying everything we saw is suddenly gone?"

"Amigos, we need to keep walking. Three-foot-tall centipedes, spiked teeth, probably dozens of them...?"

"I believe we are being tricked into leaving," said Elachia. "I believe there's no real danger."

"Tricked by who?" I asked.

"I do not wish to speculate yet. But we should go back," said Elachia.

Danica cut in on the com, "You guys are nuts. ...Just sayin'."

"Danica, are you sure you didn't hear the Homeland Security men?"

"Nope. Just you guys."

R.J. said, "Admit it Adrian. You do agree something's wrong back there. You said so yourself."

"Yes, but that doesn't mean there isn't a herd of giant centipedes headed this way waiting to tear us into pieces for dinner. I saw them. If there's too many they'll overrun us."

We stood in a tense moment of silent impasse.

R.J. said, "That girl Elvi, she said if you stood perfectly still they can't see you."

"You really want to take Elachia back there, R.J.? From here we could probably make the ropes in time, but if we go back in it's slow going. We won't be able to make a run for it fast enough."

"Ela could continue on to the rope lift and wait for us on the surface."

"No, Rowland. We're running out of time. I'm the one who needs to locate the proper equipment racks. I must go with you."

Another moment of silent impasse.

Danica cut in once again. "People, you have less than an hour left to explore if you want to keep the four-hour safety margin for extraction."

R.J. turned to Elachia. "What do you say, my love?"

"I am certain that we are being tricked. We must go back."

I shook my head and gestured in frustration with one hand. Reluctantly, we headed back into the tunnel.

Chapter 24

No one dared speak, as though evil might hear us. We stayed as close to the side walls as possible, always using cover whenever it was available. The trip back in took only fifteen minutes. We hid behind the same fallen stanchion and like any good comedy team, stared from above or below each other, craning our necks to see in the direction of the expanded tunnel section.

There seemed to be no roaming gangs of centipedes. There was no SSHS console where it had once been, and no sign of Homeland Security.

After five or ten minutes of watching, R.J. finally stepped out and casually searched the area with his weapon held down. He turned to look at us, raised his arms in exasperation, and of course that was when it happened.

From behind him a horde of centipedes making squeaking sounds of delight came charging around, led by a particularly large leader focused exclusively on R.J., spiked teeth open anticipating the first bite.

I stepped into the open and fired as the bug reared up to drop onto him. The creature took my disruptor beam mid-section, and was completely vaporized from it. A split second later the centipede mass overran us.

E.R. Mason

Strangely, Elachia seemed unconcerned. She did not call out or use her weapon. She stood her ground behind the debris barricade as I struggled to climb up the broken cement wall nearby. The herd flew past us, jamming the tunnel way until it was almost full. The passing lasted only ten or fifteen seconds before the last of them wiggled through the hole in the tunnel blockage just beyond Elachia.

Amazingly, Elachia remained unscathed. I jumped down and searched for R.J. He was standing in the same spot, not a mark on him. An expression of both stark terror and relief was fixed into his face. He began to search himself with his free hand expecting areas of mortal injury.

I looked to Elachia. She straightened up, gave a long exhale, and shook her head. She tucked her weapon back on her belt and headed toward R.J. "It's alright Rowland, dear. They were only mirages."

For a moment R.J. looked at her like he was still going to cry out for help, but he managed a quick manly recovery and asked, "Are you okay?"

"We're all fine," replied Elachia. "We were under attack by our own imaginations. Nothing more."

R.J. embraced her as though it was a necessary reassurance for her, although clearly it was a gesture he needed. I came up beside them still searching the area.

"Never mind, Adrian. Don't worry. There won't be any more of those. We've lost our fear of them," said Elachia.

"Maybe you have," I replied.

"It is only yourself you need fear now," continued Elachia, and she paused to check R.J. over a little more closely.

282

"Ela, I think a further explanation might be helpful," said R.J.

Elachia nodded. "I once reviewed a case study of a person who suffered from lucid dreams. Actually, this person would dream even while he was awake. Whenever he was faced with doing something he did not want to do, his imagination would conjure up his worst fears in such way that the unwanted task could not be done. Does that sound familiar to either of you?"

I raised an eyebrow. R.J. stared blankly.

"We are faced with a task that no one would ever want. And, this area has been affected in such a way that our worst fears can somehow be realized purely through imagination. Security people that the two of you would normally trust have warned you to leave. Frightening creatures we recently encountered suddenly returned to chase us away. All these things generated from our own minds to help us avoid doing what we must. Do you understand?"

"Whoa," remarked R.J. "That's bizarre."

I considered the idea. "Now that you mention it, our benefactor, Captain Aries during his late-night visit did mention that Diamond Light had the power to create anything a person wished for."

"We thought this place was free of dimensional or temporal warp, but obviously it is saturated with the effects of Diamond Light. We must control our thoughts and feelings here. Some apparitions could be more dangerous than those we've already seen."

Danica cut in on the com, "Ten minutes guys. You're supposed to start back in ten minutes. I'm on the checklist to come down."

It snapped us back to reality. I searched the tunnel area. There were twelve, partially buried equipment racks lined up together along the collider tube.

"So, are those the ones, Elachia?" I asked.

She placed an affectionate hand on R.J.'s shoulder and turned to look. She walked to the first rack in the group and with one hand began to wipe away dirt and dust from the console.

"The ID Plates have been stripped of print, but I can tell from the large power breakers these must be the right ones. I'm just not sure which is which. We need to shut down three of them in a certain order. The battery backup supply has to be shut down first. Then the secondary, then the main. We can't be sure which are the correct racks until the next wave restores these rack labels."

"We can get that from the drawings on Griffin," said R.J.

Elachia shook her head. "No, we can't, Rowland. The drawings all have TBD for the specific rack locations. Even if the positions were listed, those details are almost always unreliable. The only way is to read the rack's top part number label after they are restored."

I asked, "So in six seconds we need to read the labels, find the right ones, figure out the shutdown order, and trip the breakers?"

"I know that's not what you want to hear Adrian, but that's correct," answered Elachia.

I looked at them dejectedly. "You guys know what that means, right?"

"No way we can make it the first time around," said R.J.

"We knew what we were getting into," said Elachia.

"We may at least be able to find the right positions on the first try," said R.J.

Danica cut in once again, "That's it guys. You're past your four-hour tour. You now have less than four hours to climb out of that pit and get aboard so we can jump to a safe distance."

The three of us stood silently exchanging stares. No one spoke. It went on too long.

Danica transmitted, "Guys? Did you hear me?"

The silent standoff continued.

Finally, I couldn't take it. "You two are going to make me be the one to say it, aren't you? We're all thinking the same thing. Is there any reason for us to return to the ship?"

An annoyed Danica interrupted, "What? What are you talking about?"

R.J. looked lovingly at Elachia. "Can we do it? Can we last here for several hours without monsters from the Id attacking us?"

Elachia spoke grimly, "There's no choice, my love. Regardless of what we do, or where we go, that situation will likely exist. Maybe we can clear away enough sand and dirt that I can recognize one or two of the racks we need."

For no particular reason, I turned away from the others. "Danica, drop a communication buoy in geosynchronous, and park the Griffin beyond lunar orbit. We'll be remaining here for the next event. Keep your comm lines open. You should be able to hear us during the six second intervals."

She did not reply but we heard her curse under her breath.

I tried to change the moment. "So, twelve consoles. How should we set up for the next wave, Elachia?"

Elachia looked at me then went to the line of equipment racks. "Maybe if I study these more, I can isolate some of the exact breakers we need to trip. Give me a few minutes."

R.J. came and stood next to me. "A three hour wait for the inevitable, hanging out with charred bodies all around us. I'd say we've been in worse situations, but I can't really think of any."

"Well, theoretically this can only kill us for twenty-four hours."

"Is that supposed to cheer me up?"

"At least the centipedes haven't shown up again."

"Waiting to die among the already dead in a chamber of nightmares. Personally, I believe we've hit a new low, as impossible as that seems."

"How's the psychic link you have with Elachia?"

"We're sharing each other's strengths."

"I wonder...."

"What?"

"If we *do* go through a period of death, and it lasts about twenty-four hours, will you two be in touch during that time?"

"God, never even crossed my mind. Maybe she will know."

Elachia paused from studying equipment and looked back at R.J. "I do not know," she called, and returned to her work.

We stared over at her, waiting for more explanation but none came.

"How come she's more casual about this than I am? Maybe we ought to do something like see what's farther ahead while she's trying to figure out those racks," I said.

"Lead on," replied R.J.

Beyond the control area and cabling, the tunnel continued to be reasonably open. There was still wreckage everywhere, but no additional bodies. Cracks in the overhead could be seen here and there in places where the suspended ceiling had collapsed and disintegrated. Sand rained down from some of the cracks. We used our hand-held big beams as we dared to go deeper.

Not far ahead there was a large tipped over console, face down. Beyond it, fractured I-beams and stanchions again crisscrossed the tunnel. We decided to head back.

But as we turned to leave, a voice called out. "Rowley, wait!"

R.J. stiffened and spun around. An elderly woman in a long, flowered dress with a matching flowered apron held up one hand toward R.J. Her hair was in the traditional gray bun, her pale face fully aged, a smile fixed in place. She hurried to catch up as fast as an elderly person could manage.

R.J. stood in shock and began to stutter, "Mu...Mu...Mother?"

"We need to talk, Rowland."

R.J. looked at me in desperation.

All I could do was shrug.

"You are not my mother. You should go away right now," said R.J. with exasperation.

"Rowland, you should not be doing this. There is no reason for it. Take your bride-to-be and get home."

R.J. looked at me. "Okay. I'm concentrating that she isn't real, but it's not working."

"She sure looks real," I replied.

"Rowland, one person can do this job. You don't need to be here. Just tell him the names of the consoles and he can switch them off by himself. You and that lovely woman can leave and be safe."

R.J. frowned and looked at me. "I'm really sorry, Adrian. I'm not thinking that at all. I wouldn't leave even if I could."

"She may have a point," I replied.

"No way. If something happened to one person making the attempt that would leave only two left to try again. Let's keep walking. Maybe she'll go away."

As we approached the equipment rack area, Elachia glanced up and spotted the old woman following close behind R.J. She straightened up and came to us.

"Mrs. Smith, it's such a pleasure to meet you," said Elachia as she approached.

We stopped. R.J.'s mother gave a great smile and held out one hand. As their hands met, the old woman gently faded and disappeared.

"Oh, I am so delighted," said Elachia. She gave R.J. a hug and went back to her work on the equipment.

R.J. and I went to a spot in the debris as far from bodies as we could get. I leaned against steel; R.J. sat on a fallen stanchion.

"Want to talk about what just happened?" I asked.

"It was a perfectly accurate representation of my mother. As you know my mother passed several years ago. But strangely enough, Ela just now got to meet her exactly as she was. It pleased Ela greatly. And I think as soon as they met, there was such a positive atmosphere it extinguished my subconscious mirage, at least that's the explanation I felt from Elachia as she went back to work."

"Well I hope that's the last of it."

"I wouldn't count on that."

"Maybe we should start going over exactly what will happen in our first six seconds."

"Yes. So far it's looking as though Ela won't be able to ID the exact racks we need."

"There are twelve racks over there. That means we've got to take positions where we are evenly spaced in front of those twelve racks. We'll each be looking at the rack IDs. As soon as the restoration takes place the three of us will each, as quickly as possible, get to one of the racks we need. Elachia will already have shown us how to spot the right circuit breaker switches and we'll know what order they've got to be shut off in. The person with the first breaker will call out and switch off. The person with the second breaker will hear him, switch off, and call out. The person with the third breaker will then switch off. The collider collision won't happen."

"In a perfect world," replied R.J.

I nodded. "In a perfect world."

"So, let's consider the worst-case scenario."

"Okay, let's say we spot our racks, start to get to them and the explosion occurs. We're dead for twenty-four hours."

"That's my least favorite part."

"Okay, we're out of commission for twenty-four hours. The restoration happens. We already know where the three racks are, but we've only tried this once. The first person gets to his rack, calls out and switches off. The explosion happens. We're out of commission for twenty-four hours."

"I wish the worst-case scenario didn't sound so likely. Keep going."

"Third try. Restoration happens. The first person reacts quickly this time and shuts down. The second guy calls out and shuts off his. The explosion happens. Fourth try. We wake up. The three of us are quick this time. We shut down all three. Explosion canceled."

"And yet, there is still room for error in there somewhere."

"Very funny."

"I wasn't trying to be."

"Which of a thousand errors were you thinking of?"

"Reaction times, identification errors, equipment problems, interruptions."

"Any suggestions?"

"Yes. We should practice this. We'll at least know exactly how much time each step will take. We can also maybe come up with some contingency plans for problems that might crop up."

"Good idea, sir."

R.J. stopped abruptly and pointed off to the distance. "Oh brother, here we go again."

A big man dressed in Special Forces apparel was suddenly headed our way. He had short, dark brown hair receding in the front. Weathered face from too many combat assignments. I recognized him instantly. Wilson Mirtos, a very close friend who had saved my butt on more than one occasion. The best of the Special Forces crowd.

Wilson came up to us and stood smiling. "Now I don't want any trouble here. I'm taking you guys out of here, right now."

R.J. looked at me, eyebrows raised. "Obvious it's your fantasy this time, not mine."

"Go, away, image of Wilson."

"I'm not kidding around, guys. I'll carry you out of here if I have to."

I looked at R.J. "Can he do it?"

"How should I know? But I suspect he can."

I called out, "Elachia, we need you over here."

Elachia slapped the dust off her hands, stood up from a crouched position in front of a rack, and came to us. She appraised Wilson. "Oh hello! You're quite a big one, aren't you! I'm Elachia and you are?"

The image of Wilson seemed off balance. There was a faint translucence fading in and out.

Elachia continue, "These men do not require your assistance, sir."

Wilson disappeared.

Elachia avoided looking at me as though she feared embarrassing me.

R.J. had no such restraint. "So, you begged Wilson to force us to leave?" he asked with a smirk.

"At least it wasn't my mommy," I replied.

Elachia interrupted, "I am unable to identify these equipment racks. They are all basically copies of each other. They have no manufacturer's tags and the rack IDs are charred blank. We have no choice but to wait for the restoration to read the ID labels and find the three correct consoles."

"Couldn't we just shut down power on all twelve racks?" asked R.J.

Elachia shook her head. "There are two large breakers on each rack. That's more than twenty-four breakers and as I've mentioned earlier, using the wrong order we could end up causing the emergency battery power to kick in and once it does it's possible we might not be able to shut it down. But since you asked, I do think we need to go over some basics to be sure we're all on the same page."

"Please do," I answered. "We been talking about practicing."

Elachia began, "Okay, during our first six seconds we will already be positioned evenly spaced in front of the twelve racks. When the restoration occurs, we'll be studying the rack labels to find which of the three needed racks is nearest each of us. Immediately, the person closest to the battery power rack will get there, shut down the breakers and yell, '*Clear*.' By then, the other two should have found their racks, and they will quickly shut theirs down. If we're very lucky, it's possible we could do all this on the first try. If we do not succeed in time, we'll be caught in the explosion and trapped in the twenty-four-hour cycle."

"That's the nice way of putting it," said R.J. dejectedly.

"Rowland, please," answered Elachia. "Stay focused. When the restoration occurs again twenty-four hours later, we will find ourselves back in those original positions. All the equipment racks will be up and running again, and if our benefactor Captain Aries was telling the truth, we will remember everything that happened during the previous six seconds. We will already know where the three equipment racks are, and the person nearest the battery power rack should be able to get to it quickly and shut it down. By then the other two should be in position to shut theirs down. Did I leave anything out? Does everyone agree?"

"We might make it the second time around you're saying?" I asked.

There was long, silent pause as though once again everyone was facing the fact that either way our deaths would probably be required.

I said, "We've been thinking we could practice doing this in six seconds. What do you think?"

Elachia nodded. "I was going to suggest that, although I fear it will show us what a bad lot we have drawn."

We went to the burned out, half-buried racks and she used them to teach us how to identify the correct ones along with the order in which breakers needed to be switched off. We each had to cover four of the twelve racks in such a way that we could get to the correct circuit breakers as quickly as possible. Each rack was thirty inches wide and six or seven feet tall. That meant the twelve racks spanned thirty feet along the collider ring. As we took positions a foot or two in front of them, more cold emotion set in. The first glance showed we were a good ten feet away from each other. It was very possible one of us might not have a needed rack in our group of four and one of us might have two or even all three target racks. That meant those of us with no rack would need to quickly shift over to the correct group. If all three racks were located on one side, the person farthest away would have to cross twenty feet to get to the critical rack group, otherwise the person in front of that group would need to tackle two power downs in six seconds.

We began with Elachia's theory that each of the three power control racks needed other support racks alongside it, which made it likely there was one critical rack in each of our groups. She randomly chose three racks to be the ones we needed. We would pretend we did not know which rack was which. We set up R.J.'s wrist comm as a stopwatch, programmed it to beep the *"you're-dead-alarm,"* after six seconds. We took positions. R.J. triggered the timer, and we acted out our parts.

The first results were depressing. It was necessary to wait until the battery backup rack was spotted and that person called out, "I'm One!" Shutting down that rack was followed by the call, "Clear," which meant the remaining two of us could power down our racks.

The first few tries took us six-point-seven seconds just to identify the battery console rack and shut down its breaker switches.

Annoyed, we took a break.

R.J. said, "On the second try, like we've been saying, we will all remember the previous attempt, and we'll know which of us got the number one rack. That person won't have to call out. They'll just immediately shut down the four breakers and call out, '*Clear.*' The others will be

E.R. Mason

ready and shut down theirs. We should try that as a practice run."

So, we did.

After a couple test runs, we had that down to five-point-four seconds.

Cautiously optimistic, we took another break.

"See? That works," said R.J.

"With half a second to spare," I said, still sounding fatalistic.

"Better than six-point-seven," argued R.J.

Elachia tried to be reassuring. "We've proven that we can possibly do this the second time around. We can reset the world to almost normal. The clocks will all be wrong. People will have missed many days. They will find themselves out of time for everything. But the world will recover."

"We need to practice the alternate scenarios," said R.J. "Like if two of the needed racks are in one group. We've got to be ready for that."

"There is one other thing we haven't talked about," I said.

"Which is?" asked R.J.

"These bodies lying all around here. They will be living, breathing people when this place restores. They may get in the way."

Elachia thought for a moment. "I don't think they will have any real impact during just those six seconds. They'll already have been busy. They'll be busy again when the restoration occurs."

"Maybe," I replied.

"I think she's right," said R.J. "I don't think any of them could even get to us in those six seconds."

Danica squelched in on the com, "Communications buoy placed. I'm moving out beyond lunar orbit."

"We're making progress, Danica," I replied.

"Right," was the sarcastic response.

With solemn optimism, we continued practice. We ran every possible gambit we could think of. We died make-believe deaths a dozen times, always earnestly struggling to make the six seconds. As the time of Earth's restoration approached, we moved as far away from bodies as possible and sat on sections of destroyed architecture. We rested. There was nothing left to say, and nothing left to do but wait for those first six seconds.

Chapter 25

As the zero-hour approached, time itself became a contradiction. There was a deep urgency to be ready for the quick flipping of switches, but at the same time, there was a competing emotional aversion to the tragedy that was about to hit us. As previously instructed by Captain Aries, we pressed our memory tablets onto our foreheads and wondered if we'd done it correctly. We stood in spots where we had cleaned the painted concrete floor as much as possible.

A cynical Danica counted us down. "Two minutes guys. ...Sixty seconds. ...Ten seconds."

And it hit us like an earthquake. The ground shook as the field collapsed over us. Vision blurred in color and form. A strange, malevolent tingling formed on the crown of the head and descended over our bodies like a decontamination shower. Atmospheric pressure seemed to be fluctuating all around us. The air smelled like burning plastic. As the tingling left my feet there was a strange inhuman howl as a great blast of silver light burst out from every direction.

Instantly everything around me was restored. And instantly, all the preparation we had done went straight to hell.

A woman with her dark hair in a bun, dressed in a white lab coat was standing so close to me, had she materialized a few inches closer she would have been partially inside me.

It took me at least a second to regain my composure. I couldn't help it. As I tried to identify the consoles in front of me, a male voice from somewhere behind yelled, "Halt!"

A second later, far to my right, R.J. called out, "I'm One!"

The woman standing so close beside me suddenly became alarmed at my presence and grabbed my arm.

At the same instant, R.J. yelled, "Console is locked out! It takes a key!"

Before I could respond, I heard the sizzling pulse of a disruptor being fired and to my near right Elachia grunted and fell to the floor.

There was a tremendous bang, so loud it broke both my eardrums. Concussion followed instantly, crushing my body. I flew backwards into a wall as we joined the charred bodies on the floor.

Darkness and absolute silence.

There was a feeling of timelessness. There was an endless emptiness in every direction except for a small round golden light a million miles away. The biology required to form thoughts did not seem to exist. I was egg-shaped with currents of life flowing within. I could not move because there was nothing *to* move. Although I could not form thoughts, occasional thoughts passed by, seemingly of their own accord. I suddenly realized I felt pretty damn good. Weightless exemption from all concerns. My horse had won the race. I had the high score on the video game. I graduated with honors. The slot machine had paid off big. I intercepted a pass to win the big game.

Time was no longer passing. It was meaningless anyway. It was wonderful. Existence with no outer attributes. No memories to avoid. No contemplation of what should be. No fear.

Suddenly for some reason it alarmed me that I knew who I was. But that particular awareness came from a completely new perspective. It was more like what I had become than who I was. Or, it was a perception of who I had always been. This space seemed like the best possible place to sleep. Finally, really catch up with a big sleep. I drifted off.

Something was gently pulling at my feet. Then my legs. I began a slow turn. Although my eyes seemed to be closed, I could still see a deep vortex forming below me. It was a blue whirlpool. I was being sucked down into it. I began to feel weight. My downward velocity picked up enough that there was something like a G-force forcing everything up to my head. Suddenly I seemed to be standing.

A blast of white, florescent light blinded my eyes. There was noise coming from everywhere. Machines running. People calling out to each other. There was cold air and pressure enveloping me and the smell of oil and machines. I could not remember from where I had come. I remembered only my previous death. It made me choke in fear.

It took at least two seconds for full awareness to return. On what must have been the third second, R.J. desperately called out, "I'm One! I need a key!"

At the same instant the woman in the white lab coat grabbed my arm, and a voice from behind yelled, "Halt!" Elachia withdrew her hand from a console to avoid being shot again. I forced myself to read my rack identifications. None of them were racks needed for shut down. As disappointment set in, I heard R.J. yell, "Crap!" and the big bang painfully burned us.

The bright white fluorescent light erupted around me once more. Instantly I knew this was the third time. It required perhaps a second to become human. R.J. yelled, "I'm One, but I need a key!" Elachia did not attempt to touch her console. The woman in the white lab coat grabbed my arm. A voice from behind yelled, "Hold it!" Elachia began scanning the area for a key. I knew none of my racks were the correct ones, so I began reading those in front of Elachia. She had two. The rack to her left, the one closest to me, was one of them. I knew she knew. If we'd had the time, she'd take the far rack, knowing I'd move over to the rack closest to me. But our seconds had passed. I tensed up. The ear-shattering blast hit. Fire engulfed us.

Bright fluorescent light slapped me in the face. I was no longer sure which attempt this would be. "R.J. yelled, "I'm One, but I need the key!" I desperately decided there was always a chance he would spot the key in time. With the woman in white holding my arm, I forced my way toward Elachia's left-hand rack and noticed her positioning herself in front of the rack on the right. The voice behind us yelled, "Halt!" It took me two full steps to reach the rack, dragging the woman in white along with me. The brave Elachia disregarded the warning and rested her hand on the upper circuit breaker, hoping for R.J. to call out, "Clear!" The bastard behind us fired. His aim was high. It caught Elachia in the back of the neck and knocked her forward into the rack. I took pleasure in knowing the next blast would kill the shooter. It did.

The blast of fluorescent light forced us alive again, death still imminent. "I'm One. Still no key!" was R.J.'s quick call. Once again, I could not recall exactly how many times we'd done this, but his call out had to mean the key was not anywhere around R.J. The woman in white had me by the arm. The voice from behind yelled, "Stop right there!" I knew I needed to take two long steps over to Elachia, but without a key, it would be a useless march ending in a disruptor bolt. I looked for a key. To my sick surprise, six inches away from my face, on a small silver chain hanging from the neck of the woman in white, was a shiny red key. I flushed with embarrassment, and anger. In one swift motion I ripped it from her neck and as she yelled in protest, flung it in R.J.'s general direction. It flew passed Elachia and skidded on the floor toward R.J. They both saw it. There was no chance he'd recover it in time but now we all knew the key had been found. The voice behind us called out, "*I said...,*" but the big bang cut him off.

Awaking to the bright light began to invoke more anger now than anything else. Far in back of the mind was a resignation to what's-the-use–we'll–never-make-it, but it was being kept at bay for the time being. R.J. sounded tired when he yelled, "I'm One. Key!" White lab coat grabbed my arm. I ripped the key from her neck and used a hook shot to lob it over Elachia and toward R.J. He was ready for it. It fell short and skidded along the floor to him. Elachia stepped forward to her equipment rack and when the voice behind us yelled, "Halt!" she raised her hands to avoid being shot, but she was close enough to hit her three circuit breaker switches if the "Clear," came. In those same seconds I dragged White Coat along with me toward my equipment rack. Although the lady in white resisted, she was hardly strong enough or weighty enough to even slow me down. In those last three seconds, the voice behind yelled, "I said stop!" and without waiting, he shot me in the back. The blast hit high, and I fell just as the much bigger boom ended the entire affair.

Bright lights. Alive again. The bitch of it was, there was no time to think things through. We couldn't reason out the situation and decide on the best way to proceed. There was no time for that. The six seconds required us to instantly try something or die. I knew I had found the key and thrown it to R.J. several times now. It was infuriating that to this point we had never heard him call out, "Clear!"

"I'm One. Key!" called R.J. This time I ripped the key from White Coat's neck, hooked it over to R.J., and stood watching just to see how well that worked. The key fell short again and slid along the tiled floor. R.J. dropped to one knee to pick it up. It took him microseconds to fuss with the chain and draw the Precious in. He leapt up to his rack and had to lean in and fumble again to align the key with the lock. He jammed it in place, turned it, and as his mouth opened, grim death arrived once more.

Bright lights and noise. It was clear skidding the key and chain across the floor would not give R.J. enough time. I needed to put it in his hand. It would need to be an underhand throw. If Elachia continued to take her position in front of the equipment rack that would leave her backfield open. Only the defensive lineman,

White Coat, would be running interference. Ripping the key off her neck seemed to displease her to no end. A wiping right palm to her head would force her to my right and out of the way. I could be throwing in the same motion. I'd wasted two seconds thinking it through. It would take two more to move her and make the throw.

"Halt!"

I ripped the key with my left hand and swiped her aside as I made the throw. The aim was good except this time it went high. It flew passed R.J.'s face before he could react. Our eyes met for a split second and he understood.

Then we died.

The fluorescent light of life brought a new, more promising six seconds. This time I ripped the key off of White Coat within the first second. I swiped her out of the way in time to see Elachia moving close to her equipment rack. The voice behind yelled, "Halt!" but due to my manhandling of White Coat, the shooter sounded like he was addressing me rather than Elachia. I ignored him and underhanded the key and chain toward the open hands of a waiting R.J. I was on target this time. He caught a section of the chain, deftly pulled it in, fumbled, and shoved the key into the lock, twisting it with all his might. He slammed down on the three circuit breakers and for the first time yelled, "Clear!" It was the most heartening cry I have ever experienced. Elachia dropped her hands to her circuit breakers, shut down the first, and as she slapped down on the second, I realized I was late starting my move to the third rack. I pushed off of White Coat and lunged for position. The voice behind yelled, "I said hold it right...." He fired without finishing. The shot glanced off my left upper arm, the one I planned to use for the shutdown. It spun me and prevented Elachia from making a move.

We all died.

New light again brought new hope. Same throw to R.J. and with adrenaline accuracy he pulled it in. Again, Elachia managed to shut down her two breakers, but this time White Coat managed to get a handful of my shirt and was dragging along behind as I moved for position. I had my hand on the first breaker when Shooter caught me square in the middle upper back throwing me into a pile up with White Coat and Elachia. I heard Elachia curse just as the fireball arrived.

The next life-light brought intense determination. Another spectacular overhead catch by R.J. In his fastest time yet he proudly yelled, "Clear!" Once again, having yanked White Coat's key off caused Shooter to switch his attention from Elachia to me. I dragged White Coat along in what seemed like a choreographed dance with Elachia. I reached for the upper breaker with my left hand as Elachia screamed, "Clear!" a proclamation so overwhelming to the three of us that I nearly jumped. As my fingers touched that first breaker, a thought so devious it would have befitted any superhero villain popped into my head. In the same shut-down motion, I swept my right hand behind White Coat and scooted her behind me. The Shooter fired in that same instant. The shot caught White Coat in the back and as she fell, my fingers dropped down to the final circuit breaker. But Shooter happened to be a talented fast gun. His second shot caught me in the back of the neck before I could swipe down on that last golden circuit breaker. It was excruciating. I had missed grabbing the ring on the merry-go-round, dropped the game winning catch, my horse had fallen off in the fourth turn, power failed on the video game console, the slot machine took my last coin without paying off, I failed English and did not graduate with my class.

The world went dark.

Bright lights and noise. I tried to flinch into readiness, but my body wasn't working. Something was different. For some odd reason I recalled Bill Murray in a very old classic film declaring, "Anything different is good."

Something was definitely not right. I clearly remembered on the last attempt not shutting down the final breaker but there were no white ceiling light panels here, only a chandelier. The open room was far too large to be the collider tunnel. The place was pristine, like a waiting room for Heaven. Had we died too many times, and this was some sort of purgatory? Had we failed to save Earth? Would I now have to account for the way I'd lived my life, or face what kind of person I'd been? I tried to squirm in reaction to the thought, but nothing below the neck seemed to be functioning at all. I gave up and waited while pondering my fate.

Chapter 26

I was in a bed with clean white sheets and too many white pillows. I was naked, I could feel that much. I suddenly realized there was a faint feeling of electricity flowing in my arms and legs. A few noises echoed throughout the room. I tried to move my head to look around, but my neck only partially responded. The room was Victorian style. I could see that much. The noise was someone softly banging trays.

Abruptly a smiling face appeared over me. It was almost an angel. It was the most beautiful face I had ever seen... again.

Fantasia kissed me on the forehead and smiled. "You look fully conscious. Why is it I keep ending up with you looking up at me from a hospital bed?"

"Where am I?"

"You are in the Chateau Fantasia, if I've translated that correctly."

"What happened?"

"That is a very long story. You saved the Earth. The entire thing was recorded from your body cams. It took the authorities several weeks to understand it all. There was quite a bit of chaos from the lost time. Some people even died from that, but the clocks have been reset, the lost time accounted for. Things are slowly getting back to normal there."

"Weeks to understand it? How long have I been here?"

"Well, it took a week to prove to the government you weren't terrorists, two weeks for Danica to fly you here to Enuro, and you've been comatose for three weeks, so you've been out of it for six weeks."

"What's wrong with me?"

"The security guard shot you, don't you remember? He had the weapon set on heavy stun and that would have been okay except he also had it on narrow beam. He said he forgot to widen the beam after target practice."

"That guy was good...."

"It nearly killed you. You took the beam in the back of the neck. Your nervous system was locked up tight. It's amazing your heart kept beating."

"I shoved that woman in the white coat into the line of fire. Is she...?"

"She took the narrow beam also. Several weeks of recovery but she's okay. She was hit in the left lung. Not nearly as serious as you."

"I can't move anything."

"Yes. I'll be exercising you myself daily. The muscles will learn they're okay. And, there is something else we need to discuss. I hope you're in an understanding mood."

"How many times did we die?"

"I haven't heard yet. They haven't finished calculating Griffin's time base."

"It was too many. I'll tell you that much."

"The three of you are so heralded on Earth now you'll have trouble even visiting there. They're marking the day of recovery as a worldwide day of giving thanks."

"Oh boy...."

"But as I mentioned, there is something else."

"We're joined... aren't we?"

"You guessed it. You've sensed that already?"

"It feels like the only pleasant sensation I have."

"I apologize for the inappropriateness of bonding without your consent, but it was absolutely necessary."

"But how...?"

"It wasn't easy. Elachia administered an injection. I had to stimulate just that one part of you, and you were only semiconscious. You certainly would be justified calling it rape."

"Don't make me laugh. It might hurt."

"R.J. joked that if anything on you still worked, that would be it."

"I'll get him for that."

"Ah, feisty. That's a good sign."

"By the way, I'm not ornery."

"Who said you were?"

"R.J. said you said...."

"Then he made that up."

"Well, that's two I owe him."

"I hope you're not mad about me taking advantage of you."

"It's got to be every teenager's greatest fantasy; we had to sleep together to save his life."

"It may sound like a joke but it's not. Had I not merged my nervous system with yours it is doubtful you would have survived."

"Does that mean you shared my pain?"

"A little."

"Liar."

"I didn't mind. Really."

"So, what happened? How did we stop the collider explosion?"

"I've already told you too much. I promised R.J. he could do the filling in. He's having tea in the garden with Elachia."

"Are they okay?"

"I'll send R.J. in."

My neck began to work a little bit better. I could crane my head up for a better look around.

As I did, R.J. came strolling in dressed in the casual garb of upper-class nobility. Black riding boots, plaid pants, gold vest with pocket watch, long red dress coat that went to the knee, wrap around black bow tie, and in keeping with his usual eccentricity, a tall black top hat that may have been crafted by the Mad Hatter himself. He came to the bedside, did a slight bow and removed his hat.

"You're forming a band?" I asked, trying not to laugh.

"Sense of humor undamaged, I see."

"Oh yeah, about that, what was that remark about my only body part that still might work?"

"In all fairness, it was."

"By the way, she never said I was ornery."

"It was implied. But, putting all important controversy aside, we should be celebrating your return to consciousness. That means now at least two parts of you are working."

"So, what happened at the collider?"

"You managed to switch off one circuit breaker before you were shot down like a dog. Elachia slapped the second one off just in time."

"And we died how many times?"

"We haven't heard yet. None of us seem ready to do the math. And anyway, don't make me think about that. It still makes me feel a little queasy."

"Look who you're complaining to. How's Elachia?"

"She handled it better than I. What's that Shakespearean quote we're always using? *Though she be but small, she is fierce*? Oh yeah, they've got this soothing gel bath here. I spent a week's days suspended in it after we arrived, sometimes with Elachia. It brought me back pretty good."

"What happened after the collider was shut down?"

"Oh man, where do I begin? At first, the only thing the people in the collider test area knew was that their test had failed. They had no idea that weeks had passed without them realizing it. There was this long sobering-up period they went through trying to assimilate reality. Elachia and I were immediately arrested. We had our hands tied behind us with twist ties and we were made to sit in a small closet area until the authorities arrived. By the way, the guy who did all the shooting was a SWAT guy from the local police working a side job, former military. In all those attempts we made, he never once missed a shot."

"Yeah I got that part. Just our luck."

"The bastards ordered the paramedics to twist-tie your hands behind you too, even though you were unconscious and seriously hurt. Bad way to treat a comatose man who just saved the world. I began trying to explain everything right from the start but there wasn't anyone smart enough to listen. I sounded crazy, even to me. When the real police arrived to discharge the security guys, we were taken up by elevator to a meeting room adjacent to the collider control room. Some big shots were waiting for us up there. They took a quick look at you and got worried looks and demanded you get loaded right up for a ride to the emergency room. First correct thing any of them did. After a few minutes of everyone arguing with everyone, they brought in an antigrav gurney and away you went. I didn't like that part. I didn't trust any of them."

"Elachia was okay at this point?"

"She was more exhausted emotionally than I've ever seen her. It worried me. I wanted her in the hospital too, but the collider managers and test conductors were livid. The Diamond Light particle stream had left the collider ring and gone out into space, lost forever."

"My God. The plan worked."

"Sure did. But try to explain to those people that they'd been trapped in a time loop for many weeks. I was trying to get them to take a look at a Mars station chronometer transmission, but that just sounded even crazier to them. They were so pissed off they were taking turns screaming in my face. Guess who was the worst?"

"I have a name in mind, but I can't bring myself to speak it out loud."

"You guessed it. Doctor Andrea DeSortes, our less-than-beloved benefactor from our trip to Saturn's A-Ring. She and her compatriot general were enraged. They began their questioning by telling us about the chemical shock treatment therapy that would be used to get the truth out of us. DeSortes wasn't very good at it either. At one point, Elachia, as tired as she was, broke out laughing at DeSortes' explanation of the horrid process that would be used. Finally, Elachia, more out of bored fatigue than of fear, told them that I was right. They should contact Mars Station before they continued making idiots of themselves. DeSortes and her associates stormed out of there. We requested medical care and at that point I guess they had to comply. We were taken to a different medical center than you. We were diagnosed with neuro-shock or something like that. We were admitted with guards on our hospital room doors. That was the point it really got weird."

"Oh, *that's* when it got weird."

"Yeah, you wouldn't think that was possible, would you? Let me rephrase that. That's when it got weirder, as unlikely as that seems. After the long browbeating we received, I kept expecting it to resume once I was in my hospital bed. And whatever it was they squirted into me to relieve the nervous system damage, I no longer had much of a care in the world. I would have told them anything they wanted to hear."

"Whoa, I just realized that's not so good. You and I do have a few pregnant secrets I would not want to get out."

"Yeah, afterward that scared the hell out of me." R.J. leaned closer and spoke in a low tone, "Like the crystal skull we have hidden aboard Griffin. Thank God that didn't come up." He straightened up and made the gesture of wiping his brow with one hand.

"Someday we've got to do something about that," I replied.

"Anyway, I waited for the interrogation torture to resume, but it never happened. It was like the last day of the Battle of Briton when the Nazi bombers suddenly did not show up anymore. Finally, I was allowed to have streaming on my room monitor. I was even allowed to have the news. People started being nice to me. But the news was pretty ugly. The best way to explain it; everything on the surface of the Earth and above was restored to the same state it had been in just before the first explosion occurred. But Earth was not in the same place it had been. Immediately after the restoration, the Earth's seasons returned to their natural state. It began to snow in some places that had been warm. Even the atomic clocks were way out of sync."

"The early reports are suggesting that the Diamond Light field did not extend all the way to Earth's core, as we suspected. That's why some people underground were less affected by it. But there have been several bad earthquakes from subsurface layers of the Earth that were out of sync with the surface geology. If you recall Elachia's guess about the Diamond Light field, she guessed that because the collider facility used earth for their grounding system, it became the ground plane for the Diamond Light field, just like an antenna uses its base as the ground plane, radiating around and above it. So, if you were far enough underground, the Diamond Light field did not affect you as much."

"So that idiot Dutch and his shopping cart full of gold were just far enough underground?"

"Yeah, I was just getting to that and man, it's ugly. He was far enough underground to avoid about fifty percent of the radiation, so he had only half the exposure of Diamond Light than everyone else. That's why he could still see us. The problem is, he was still onboard Griffin when we launched outside the moon's orbit to escape that next explosion. He missed getting reset by the collapsing Diamond Light field. Apparently after we dropped him off, because he was out of sync, he absorbed a ton more radiation from the repeated explosions. He wasn't getting reset by the collapsing fields. They found him right where we left him on the prison grounds, guarding his gold for six seconds after every restoration. But here's the ugly part; he took so much radiation that it saturated the soft tissue in his body. They say all that is visible of him is a semitransparent skeleton. A semitransparent skeleton gathering up transparent gold. They can't communicate with him because most of him is in a different dimension. He can't see or feel anything here. They're studying him in a laboratory somewhere, hoping the effects will eventually wear off."

"Maybe I should feel guilty, but I still believe he would have killed us all when he was done."

"He went after Elachia. He'll get no sympathy from me."

"Well, putting that little macabre gem aside, there must have been a lot screwed up Earth people."

"Earth's surface as a ground plane caused *some* good news and quite a bit of bad news. Some people were protected from the Diamond Light wave, but came up out of their underground positions to all the devastation and were then hit by the restoration and next explosion. Some people were trapped underground and died from lack of water and food. At some point there were no restorations at all deep underground. There were large crops that were restored in the final restoration only to be exposed to cold or other inhospitable climate change from the lost time that had passed. Ships had been to sea for weeks and made no progress. Businesses with heavy schedules were weeks behind. Hospitals had it the worst. An impossible backlog of surgeries. There were hundreds of other impacts, like climbers who began their ascents in warmer weather, suddenly caught in below freezing temperatures. Anything that had to do with time and date was royally screwed up."

"How's Danica and Griffin?"

"Danica is off somewhere with Elachia's neighbor. There may be no end to those two. That guy is a stiff-neck royalty type. He's got an English type accent. He's all very proper. I have to catch myself when I talk to him. I get this urge to mimic him, but that would be a mistake. He's well trained in combat. He's been in off-world wars. The Griffin is parked here in one of Fantasia's hangars. She's having the ten-year maintenance done on it. I'm not sure but maybe that's a ruse to keep you here once you're up and around."

"She doesn't need a ruse."

"Really? By the way, that damaged ship we found drifting outside lunar orbit? During early discussions with the bureaucrats, the question came up; shouldn't we have towed that thing back into Earth orbit so the restoration field would restore that crew to life?"

"We never thought of it."

"Yes, we were busy trying to save Earth. But anyway, the brains studying what happened looked at that. They say it would have been worse for the crew if we had done that. They say that crew was out of time sync with the Diamond Light. They had missed too many restorations. The collapsing field would not have restored them or if it had that would have been catastrophic."

"What did they do with them?"

"Taken back to Earth along with another crew that had the same fate. To be used for study of what happened. At least the people on the moon installations came out pretty good."

"What a freakin' disaster."

"Then there's the pirate ship that looted New York but got caught in the explosion and crashed into the sea. Those poor bastards kept finding themselves back in sub orbit and crashing over and over but when the final restoration happened they at last made orbit. Unfortunately, they were on Space Force Systems tracking radar almost immediately and our guys chased their asses down and they're in jail now too."

"It's the little things..."

"We contacted Admiral Lansing. He has no memory whatsoever of speaking with us. He has the report of what happened. He sends his thanks and wants to see you when you get time."

"And what of Dr. Andrea DeSortes?"

"Well, to begin with, her associate Doctor Brock Mullar, the man bold enough to remove that Diamond Light containment vessel, died from his exposure. At least they *think* he's dead. Creeps me out thinking about it. Doctor DeSortes is under house arrest while they figure out a long list of charges. Terrorism was originally among those, but has been put aside. The guess is she will be allowed to continue work in nonvolatile physics from a special reformatory for high IQ criminals. The military higher-ups who made Armageddon possible for DeSortes will not be so lucky. The jury is still out on them."

R.J. thought for second and continued, "There were two cool stories that came out of this too. You remember the Goth girl Elvi, full name Elvira Dorran, who helped us with the killer centipedes?"

"Sure."

"Elachia tracked her down to thank her. She has absolutely no memory of us, but of course every single person on Earth now knows what happened. Elachia told her everything she did to help us under very dangerous circumstances. Elachia has now sort of adopted the girl and her family. Those people now have a bright future. They'll be visiting here sometime soon."

"We made friends with a Goth. Holy cow!"

"Holy cow? I don't believe I've ever heard you use that euphemism before! The Sadhu folks from India, particularly Nepal, would agree with you I'm sure, but personally the cows I have met have shown no penchant for religion. The second interesting tale concerns the Mars Director's kid who suggested we think about an expanding-collapsing field effect. He's now a hero on Earth as well. Been offered admittance to a university in England. Taking a small bit of publicity heat off of us, I think."

"Bless him. I can raise my right knee slightly."

"Great! Two out of three legs working already."

"Very funny."

"So where was I, oh yeah, it took the authorities a week to figure out we had saved their butts. You still were in an intensive care unit not doing well. We wanted to take you back to Enuro for treatment. There were some fierce discussions and finally the doctors admitted there was nothing more they could do. But the bureaucrats still wouldn't release you to us. Late one night, Danica, Elachia, and I showed up at the medical center with a portable antigrav ICU module. We had no paperwork, no nothing, but every single person we ran into in that hospital helped us sneak you out including a rogue ambulance driver. We were beyond the Kuiper belt before the big shots found out you were gone. I believe they have issued some type of warrant for the three of us but the Enuro government is refusing to recognize Earth extradition requests."

"So, I cause big trouble even when I'm asleep?"

"I hadn't thought of it that way but now that you mention it, your reputation remains intact."

"And that means we can't go back to the planet we just saved without being arrested?"

"There's got to be another Shakespearian quote that applies here but I just can't come up with one at the moment."

"We're criminals not on the run."

"Holding up in a heavenly setting. Trapped in the briar patch. And, we're more popular than Robin Hood and his merry men... and women."

"They'll write fables about us."

"And sing ballads, no doubt."

"For a moment there I started feeling good about things. By the way, that woman I shoved behind me to take the disruptor shot will be okay I'm told."

"Oh, yeah. Lucky, lucky, lucky. The shooter tried to jerk his weapon up to miss her. Caught her just below the left shoulder. She needed some hospital and some rehab, but she's already almost fully recovered."

"Probably hates my ass."

"I wouldn't put it quite that way. I'll bet she has some form of a love-hate relationship with you. While she's hating you for shoving her into the line of fire, she has to face the fact she would have died had you not done so. You might see something about that on Earth news. You can get that now that you're awake. Enuro gets all the news media. It's sent here in packets. It's usually a week or two old, but at least you can see pretty much all of it if you choose to. You may get tired of seeing your name and photo a bit too much."

"Oh God...."

"Well, get used to it. At the same time, they are mulling charges for kidnapping you, the rest of the world is organizing a holiday in our names. And basically, Earth is waiting for us to return so parades, celebrations, and speeches can be broadcast to infinity."

"I think I'm having a relapse."

Chapter 27

Weeks of recovery helped avoid any parades on Earth. There was so much residual damage to Earth that the idea of a global party got lost in the recovery efforts. The side effects were monstrous. There were sky divers who had exited their planes on one day and touched down weeks later.

One late morning I awoke from one of many naps to find a life signs monitor band on my left arm. When I looked back, I was startled by someone sitting close on my right.

It was none other than Captain Aries.

It took me a minute to come to full consciousness. For some odd reason I wondered where he had obtained the ornamental red Victorian chair he was seated in. He was dressed in a futuristic-looking silver body suit. No seams, no apparent openings, high turtleneck collar. The suit seemed to have a glow to it. I looked at him. He returned my alarmed stare with a smirk.

"Nice suit, Aries," I finally said with slight, involuntary contempt.

"It makes it easier to be here. Couldn't wear it last time. They wanted me to look more familiar to you." He shifted in his seat but seemed unable to find a comfortable position. It was an odd sight. A futuristic man occupying ancient furniture. He gave up and leaned forward, "So, you did it after all! Congratulations!"

I had to cough to get my voice working again. "Lucky you didn't tell me what it would take."

"Consider it money in your heavenly bank, so to speak."

"Did I earn some answers?"

"Okay, but visiting you here is like putting on a mental diving mask where I have a narrow forward line of cosmic vision. So, when you ask metaphysical questions it's difficult because the scope of my mind's eye is limited, much like yours. But we can try, except often it's like trying to describe astrophysics to a five-year-old."

"Are we really that ignorant?"

"Not at all, but the universe is *that* complex."

"Are we good to go now? Did we really reset the Earth back to a previous point in time before the big screw-up?"

"No, you did not. Time had nothing to do with the restoration. The Earth and moon were reset to the state that the collective consciousness of the resurrected people thought it should be in. That's Diamond Light."

"Are you saying there will be differences from what it was?"

"Absolutely. Some thoughts and ideas that people were thinking about at the time of the explosion, may have become part of reality. Variations like that."

"This stuff is so far beyond our knowledge level. Where *do* you come from, really?"

"In Earthly terms, you would call it Heaven. More accurately I come from one of several higher dimensions."

"But you're dead?"

"I have graduated from the Earth life-death cycle. I no longer need to die and be reborn like most people here."

"So exactly what happens when you make it to this graduation-thing?"

"Well, depending on what part of Heaven your heart's desire takes you to, there's a long, very pleasant orientation period to help you remember things you already knew."

"Do I have any chance at getting there?"

"Hey, I'm not the Judge! Usually if you're ready for ascension, you will suddenly pass away here on Earth. So, we can assume you're not there yet. But that's not to say it won't happen soon. And, even if you *are* slated to return for another life, if you've done well in this life, chances are your next will be very enjoyable and rewarding. You know, I hate talking about this stuff. I'm a Captain not a Chaplain."

"Doesn't really matter anyway. I can guarantee you I'm not on the A-list."

"Hey, you want to know what life is *really* about? It's about mistakes you *need* to make."

I had to pause to apply that to myself, but decided the concept was going to take some time. "So, what happened with the Diamond Light containment vessel?"

"Already retrieved and on its way to a safe harbor. Earth's military is still frantically searching for it."

"Should I tell them?"

"No. Part of their penance."

"And the Earth?"

"Pretty messed up but they'll recover very quickly, fast as ants repairing a colony."

"Kind of a degrading comparison, isn't it?"

"The ants might say the same thing."

Before I could come up with an appropriate response, someone entered the far side of the room. It was Fantasia. She gave me a big smile and headed my way.

Aries did not seem to be aware of her approach. I decided to surprise him. Fantasia came up beside him and looked down at me with a warm expression. She paid no attention to Aries at all.

"You do see him, right?" I asked.

"See who?"

"The gentleman seated next to you?"

She looked and gave me an inquisitive stare. "There's not even a chair there. Are you feeling all right?" She placed gentle fingers on my neck to check my pulse. Aries smiled at me mischievously.

"Sorry, I was half awake. Still dreaming."

She stood upright and gave me a discerning look. "I'd better check the remote monitors. Be right back." She turned and headed for the door.

When she was out of ear's reach I said, "Nice trick."

"She is extremely beautiful, and I mean inside not out. An angel in your world *and* mine."

"I have one other question about the Diamond Light mess."

"I'll do my best."

"How did DeSortes know the Diamond Light was in that ship?"

"Artificial lucid dream implanted in her mind while she slept. She was manipulated by an individual from another dimension. Retrieving the light directly from the Daphne ship would have been too much exposure for those individuals but they believed once it was in a transport containment vessel, they could intercept it during your return trip to Earth. They would have eliminated all of you to cover their tracks. But, interfering with a human by an outsider is a high crime. The Daphne mission was already well underway by the time the offense was detected by Earth's Celestial Order. It took a while to backtrack it. Instead of them intercepting the Light, we intercepted them. The rest you know."

"Celestial Order? Where have I heard that name before?"

"Too much to explain. Please do not ever mention that name again, to anyone."

"Really?"

"So, this concludes our second and last visit concerning this affair. I will take my leave of you."

"Is there a way I could contact you if I needed to?"

"Not in this life, but I'll see you when you leave it."

"But I might be able to reach you through the Nasebiens, right?"

"Maybe, but I wouldn't count on it."

"Why not? Why can't there be contact with you?"

"Get on with your life, Adrian."

And he and his chair were gone.

Fantasia returned a moment later. She stared down at me with a kind, provocative smile. She placed one hand on my forehead and took a moment to assess the touch. "You're alright," she said. "We're on the far side of getting you up and around."

"Better get ready to run."

"Oh dear, I don't run that fast."

It took me a week using an external robotic skeleton to learn to walk again. It was more a reprogramming of muscle memory than exercise. There was a definite rush of joy at the freedom of finally free-walking. Long walks on the outdoor trails quickly brought jogging. The indoor pool provided swim exercise under the watchful eye of an attractive lifeguard, stationed there because of Fantasia's fear of seizure. A fencing instructor was brought in for an hour a day. I thought I would already be better than her. I was not. Once I proved my balance and coordination, Emperor was trotted over and stabled in Fantasia's horse guest house. I began long rides through the forests. I was allowed to go alone with a wrist communicator and life signs monitor. There were constant data packets and messenger-delivered spacegrams from Earth earnestly requesting our attendance at various functions for the four of us. We assigned a staff member who spoke eloquent English to beg off.

Fantasia was busy most days. Between diplomatic responsibilities, ambassadorships, and other Enuro affairs, I was not able to see her much during the day. Sometimes a quick kiss before leaving, other times only a wave. But, at night she was mine. Or, I was hers. Those nights became the most energetic of the recovery work outs.

I played golf one day with Elachia and R.J. even though I knew R.J. would be at his worst for comical comments. From the first tee, Elachia observed that my swing had the power of an Enuro gorilla. She asked R.J. how I putted to which he replied, "Same way." From there it was a running dialogue of how surprisingly well my putter was working.

When Fantasia's work schedule finally slacked off, we began early morning horseback rides through the estate. Fantasia had a partiality for jumping and knew where every possible natural jump was located. Emperor had an equal taste for it and seemed to have more fun than I did. Fortunately, my back muscles were finally in very good shape.

On a particularly golden sunny morning we took the horses out and rode side by side using a high-step trot in time with a piece of Enuro music that seemed to fit perfectly. It was a glorious ride. We ended up at the ravine.

Fantasia gave me a devious smile. "I've seen you make this jump before but I'm still not sure."

"I'm in much better shape now than I was then, my dear."

"Doesn't mean you and the horse will arrive on the other side at the same time."

"I could do it with my hands behind me."

"Oh, please don't"

"You are your delightfully angelic self this morning, but we're linked. I can tell something's bothering you and you're trying to hide it."

"My, my, that means you're paying close attention to me. I like that."

Emperor became impatient and began to prance in place.

"We shouldn't try that jump if one of us is distracted. What's going on with you?"

Okay, I guess now is as good a time as any. "I've brought you the antidote to our heart-link." Fantasia reached into her vest pocket and drew out a small vile of purple liquid. She reached it out to me. "You can take it when you're ready."

Emperor did a three-sixty in place. I leaned forward on the saddle. "Thanks, but you can take that vial and pour it out on the ground. I will never need it. But I'd understand if you plan to take one yourself."

Her horse reared slightly so that she had to collect the mare before she spoke. "I did not make one for myself. Are you sure about this?"

"I've never been so sure about anything in my life. I made the biggest mistake of my life last time and believe me, I've made some whoppers."

"Well, in a way this jump will prove you're fully recovered. That would mean I could stop going easy on you. Can you take it, Tarn?"

"Careful what you wish for."

"It's possible all my wishes have already come true." And with that, she charged off toward the ravine. I held Emperor back, just for the pleasure of watching her jump. The mare bolted off the edge, hindquarters fully rippled with muscle. The horse stretched out, front feet together reaching for the other side. Fantasia was standing in her stirrups, up over the horse's withers, leading the jump as any pro jumper would. They came down together on the opposite side with far more grace than could be expected. She swung the mare around to face us and laughed out loud at me. "The future's over here, Tarn. Can you make it?"

I had no doubt.